Vendetta

Rebecca Deel

Copyright © 2017 Rebecca Deel

All rights reserved.

ISBN: 1979819238
ISBN-13: 978-1979819237

DEDICATION

To my amazing husband.

ACKNOWLEDGMENTS

Cover design by Melody Simmons.

CHAPTER ONE

Paige Jensen's fingers hovered over the keyboard of her laptop. Heart slamming against her ribcage, she listened for the strange noise again. The building should have been empty.

Total silence.

She sighed. Maybe her imagination was running wild. In recent weeks, she had lost count of the times she whipped around to confront the person following her, but saw no one except friends and neighbors giving her puzzled looks.

The hallway outside her office at the Otter Creek Community Center was wreathed in shadows, as it should be at ten o'clock at night. The knowledge didn't slow her racing heartbeat.

Although Otter Creek wasn't a crime-riddled metropolis, having her cell phone handy might be wise. She walked to the closet where she stored her purse and outerwear. Thrusting her hand inside the bag, she felt around for her phone, then frowned. Where was her phone?

She mentally retraced her steps through the day and came up with zilch. She blew out a breath. Great. Now she had to search the rooms where she'd been during the day. In other words, a tour of the entire building.

Another uneasy glance toward the hall which led to the center's hub. For the first time, Paige questioned the wisdom of working so late by herself. She hadn't planned to stay, but realized she needed to finish the report on the center's activities for the town council meeting before she left tonight. Her plan to work on it throughout the day had been a bust. A broken pipe, spilled paint, multiple fights, skinned knees, and strained muscles had derailed her plan. She doubted tomorrow would be better.

The day had been crazy, starting with old man Lawrence complaining some of her teens had unlatched the gate so Bonnie and Clyde, his granddaughter's camels, were free to roam around town. Those camels were notorious escape artists, especially Bonnie. Paige wasn't convinced her teens were to blame for the prank. According to the grizzled farmer, though, the teens were to blame for all the mischief in town.

Another glance at the dark hall. Even if she went home to her grandmother, Paige still needed her phone. If one of the kids found it before she did, they would capitalize on the opportunity to post goofy pictures or a smart aleck quip on her social media links meant to promote the community center. She had been battling Mayor Parks for almost a year to increase the center's budget. She couldn't afford negativity associated with the center.

Despite the creepy feel of the empty community center, Paige walked to the door, paused to listen again. Still nothing. Must have been her imagination. So why didn't she feel safe?

She flipped the switch and light flooded the hallway, dispelling the shadows. Empty. Paige rolled her eyes. Nice. She'd scared herself. Confident all was as it should be in her building, she walked the length of the hallway and stepped into the gym, the last place she remembered having her phone in her hand before dealing with a seven-year-old girl's skinned knee.

She turned on the gymnasium lights and was halfway across the floor to the stage when she heard the noise again. Paige hesitated, her head whipping in the direction of the boys' locker room.

Not her imagination. Someone other than her was in the center. She should check. On the other hand, Paige didn't want to be the too-stupid-to-live heroine of a book or movie, one who went to investigate a mysterious noise and ended up dead. Her grandmother hadn't raised a fool.

She should call the police. Yeah, they would probably laugh at her for calling about a funny noise. Still, she would feel better having a burly policeman to go in the locker room first.

Paige hurried to the stage. Relief flooded her when she spotted her phone partially hidden by the curtain. Scooping up the instrument, she tapped the screen.

Before she could dial the number for the Otter Creek police, the locker room door opened and one of her teens skidded to a sudden stop when he noticed the lights were on. The tall, skinny boy with a head full of blond curls shifted his backpack off his shoulder and glanced around. His eyebrows soared when he saw Paige.

"What are you doing here, Ms. Jensen? Shouldn't you be asleep or something?"

Thankful she wasn't about to meet an ignominious death, her lips curved into a smile for Dalton Reagan. "Asleep? It's just after ten. I'm rarely asleep before midnight." Not with her schedule and the mountain of paperwork associated with her job. Who knew community centers generated enough work for three people when the budget only allowed for one and a half people? "What are you doing here this time of night?"

Dalton patted the backpack at his feet. "Forgot to grab this when I left this afternoon. I have homework to do before first hour tomorrow."

Paige's eyebrow rose. "And you're just now noticing your bag was missing?"

The teen lifted one shoulder. "Been busy."

He must have been helping his younger brothers with their schoolwork and showers. The fourteen-year-old was doing his best to hold his family together while his mother worked two jobs to put food on the table and pay the bills. "You're lucky I was still here. Otherwise, you would have been out of luck until tomorrow morning. And, no, I don't want to hear you planned to pick the lock again." The gangly teen was quite skilled at handling locks. He'd learned when he kept forgetting his house key, and he and his brothers were locked out of the house while Mrs. Reagan worked her second job, a job without an understanding boss.

Another shoulder shrug. "I haven't forgotten your last lecture. Besides, I didn't have that much work left. I finished most of it this afternoon. Could have completed the rest before class started."

"For once, I'm glad I was here this late. Can't have you rushing through an assignment. You need a good grade in English."

The teen rolled his eyes. "Don't remind me. I better go. Mom will be worried if I'm not back soon. See ya." And he was gone.

Paige grinned. This same boy six months before couldn't be bothered about school. Now he returned to the center to retrieve his backpack for schoolwork. She couldn't wait to share the news with Marcus Lang, pastor of Cornerstone Church. The handsome dark-haired minister volunteered at the center and was as invested as Paige was in the lives of Otter Creek's kids. He'd been instrumental in helping Dalton see the value of school.

She'd asked Marcus how he got through to Dalton. He had smiled and said his success was a secret between him and Dalton. As long as the teen was on the right track, Paige didn't care how Marcus succeeded, just that he had.

Retracing her steps to the office, she dropped onto the squeaky desk chair. Time to shut down for the night. She was too tired to wrestle with the numbers and personnel problems. Guess that meant coming in early tomorrow morning and finishing the report. The council meeting was tomorrow night at 7:00. That should give her enough time to complete everything.

Paige shoved her computer into her bag. After turning off her desk lamp, she grabbed her purse and computer, and walked from the office three hours past the center's official closing time. Passing each area, she turned off the lights she'd switched on earlier, once again giving the center she loved a creepy feel as the shadows created deep pools of darkness.

Perfect setting for a horror movie. She shoved that thought to the back of her mind. No need to spook herself again.

Her footsteps echoed in the gym. She glanced inside the girls' locker room to make sure the light was off, then approached the door for the boys'. As she reached to push open the door, lights in the gymnasium went out.

Paige froze. No way. Those hideously expensive lights in the gym couldn't all go out at one time. She'd just replaced most of them two months ago. Had a breaker tripped?

A brush of fabric against a wall made her pivot to face the foyer doors which led to the street. "Dalton, did you forget something else?"

No response.

Cold chills surged up her spine. "Come on, Dalton. This isn't funny." As she spoke, Paige heard the nervousness in her voice. Whoever was messing with her was sure to hear it as well. Maybe that would be enough. No doubt the prankster would make fun of her.

A heavy footstep sounded close. Too close for her peace of mind. "Who's there?" When no one responded, she shrugged her purse and computer off her shoulder and placed them against the wall. If she had to run, she didn't want the extra weight slowing her down.

"Last chance," she said, forcing strength into her voice despite the terror boiling in her gut. "My phone is in my hand and I'm calling the police."

Paige tapped her screen and realized she had made a serious mistake. The screen shined like a beacon and showed the intruder exactly where she was standing. She spun and ran toward the other side of the gym where the corridor exited beside the library. She could hide or run across the square to the police station where a cop was always on duty at the desk.

Before she sprinted more than ten feet, the intruder hit Paige from behind. Her phone flew out of her hand and skidded across the gym floor out of reach.

She fought against the heavy weight holding her pinned to the floor. "No!" Harsh laughter sent panic cascading through her. Paige redoubled her efforts, dislodged the man, and scrambled away.

The intruder caught her again as she reached the corridor. He grabbed her arm in an unbreakable grip, spun her around, and shoved Paige against the wall.

"What do you want? Money? You're out of luck. The center doesn't have money on site."

The man's hands wrapped around her throat and squeezed.

Paige fought hard to break his hold to no avail. His fingers were like a vise, his arms roped with muscle. She desperately needed air. Unless some miracle happened in the next two minutes, she was going to die.

CHAPTER TWO

Marcus Lang climbed into his truck, slammed the door, and tipped his head back against the seat. His heart ached for the sweet family that just lost the patriarch of their clan. Jeb Kirkland had lived a long and full life, his death expected after a long illness. Small comfort for his family, though. At times like this, Marcus felt inadequate, unequal to the task.

After another silent prayer for the Kirklands, he drove from the parking lot of Memorial Hospital. He should go home and eat. The frantic call from Kirkland's wife had come before Marcus heated one of the meals left in his freezer by Serena Blackhawk, owner of Home Runs, a personal chef service.

As a diabetic, he couldn't afford to skip meals. Unfortunately, his job was 24/7 and that meant he missed meals when a person or family experienced a crisis.

He cruised slowly down Main Street, glancing at the community center as he drove into the Otter Creek town square.

Marcus frowned. Paige's car was still parked in front of the center, but the lights were off. Had she gone to dinner with friends and left her car to pick up later? He almost continued toward home, but couldn't shake the urge to check on her.

He circled the square and parked his vehicle in the space beside hers. If the doors were locked, he'd know she was fine and could take himself home to eat and fall into bed. The next few days would be a challenge for him and the Kirklands.

Marcus walked to the double doors and tried the knob. Unlocked. His stomach knotted. Had Paige forgotten to lock the door? He'd never known her to do that. In his experience with the center's director, she was careful to protect the facilities.

He twisted the knob and stepped inside the darkened interior of the gymnasium. "Paige?" he called. A curse and running feet sounded in the darkness.

His skin prickled seconds before someone shoved him to the side and raced from the building. Marcus slammed into the gym wall, fought to regain his balance.

He started to go after the guy, but he was more worried about Paige than the intruder. "Paige?" No response. More concerned now, he felt along the wall for the light switch. A second later, light flooded the large cavernous area where he'd spent a number of hours playing basketball with kids and adults alike.

Marcus quartered the gym. A quick glance around told him she wasn't here or on the stage. Office? He started that direction when he spotted a pair of tennis shoes at the mouth of the corridor on the other side of the gym.

Ice water poured through his veins as he sprinted to the corridor and the person crumpled on the floor. "Paige!" He dropped to his knees, brushing long, dark hair away from her face. He prayed she was still alive. A world without Paige Jensen's bright light in it didn't bear thinking about.

Marcus checked for a pulse, breathed a sigh of relief when he found a steady beat. He turned on the hall light, then grabbed his phone. He called for emergency help, afraid to move Paige.

Two minutes later, Nick Santana, a friend who was also an Otter Creek police detective, walked into the gym. "Marcus?"

"Here, Nick." He waved the cop over.

"Ambulance will be here in two. What happened?"

"I'm not sure. On the way home from the hospital, I noticed Paige's car parked out front but all the lights were off in the center. Looked odd, so I checked the doors. They weren't locked. I came inside, called Paige's name. A man cursed, ran toward the front doors. He shoved me into the wall and took off. I found Paige on the floor, unconscious."

At that moment, Paige moaned, stirred.

Marcus gripped her hand. "Don't move. Help is coming."

"Marcus?" she croaked, winced.

"You're safe now." He frowned. She hadn't sounded hoarse earlier when he'd dropped by for a game of pickup basketball with the elementary kids. That's when he noticed the red streaks on her throat. Fury erupted in his gut. That creep had choked Paige. "Nick." He motioned to her throat.

The detective crouched beside the fallen community center director, scowled. "Paige, it's Nick Santana. Who did this to you?"

She shook her head slightly.

Marcus and Nick exchanged grim glances. Was she protecting someone or did she not recognize her attacker?

"Talk to me," Nick encouraged. "I need all the information you can give me to find this guy."

"I heard a noise, went to the stage to retrieve my phone. Dalton Reagan was in the boys' locker room to get his backpack. He left and I returned to my office to shut down for the night. When I was going to my car, the lights went out. I thought it might be Dalton, playing a joke. It wasn't. A man laughed. I turned, ran. He tackled me. I fought him off and escaped. He caught me again, shoved me against the wall, and choked me. I thought he would kill me."

"You're lucky Marcus stopped to check on you."

"Please find my phone. Gram will be calling soon. I don't want to scare her if I don't answer."

"I'll find it. Did you see the man who attacked you?"

"Too dark. He was heavy, though."

"Heavy?"

"Muscular. I tried to break his hold around my throat, but couldn't."

"Is it possible you scratched him?"

Paige blinked. "Maybe."

"I'll come to the hospital later to talk to you again, see if you remember more. I need my crime scene kit. If we're lucky, we'll find evidence of your attacker under your nails." He squeezed her shoulder briefly. "Marcus will stay with you, and I'll only be a minute."

No one would slip by Marcus to hurt Paige a second time. After Nick jogged from the gym, Marcus swiveled, scanning the gym floor. "I see your phone, Paige. I'll be right back."

He hurried to the center of the gym, picked up the phone, and glanced at the screen. His cheeks burned. She had keyed in the first numbers for the police. Marcus returned to Paige's side and laced his fingers with hers. "Got it."

Relief flooded her face. "Thanks."

The swirling lights of the ambulance created a kaleidoscope of color on the gym wall. Marcus tightened his grip on Paige's hand. Who wanted to hurt her?

A moment later, the door opened again and Rio Kincaid, a medic with Fortress Security, strode into the room leading a collapsible gurney followed quickly by a young EMT. The detective also walked into the gym, carrying a black case. "Marcus, Nick," Rio said. "What happened?"

"Someone attacked Paige, choked her out. Give me a second to scrape under her nails, then I'll get out of your way." Nick quickly took the nail scrapings, then stood and moved back so Rio could take his place.

"How you doing, sugar?" Rio knelt beside Paige and pulled out a penlight to check her pupils.

"Been better."

He smiled. "I bet. Pupils look good. What hurts?"

"Throat. Head."

Rio checked her skull, paused when she hissed. "Got a good-sized knot back here."

"He shoved me against the wall."

Marcus's jaw flexed, furious at what she had been through. He was so glad he'd listened to his gut and stopped to check on her.

"Might have a concussion. We'll take you to the hospital and let the docs check you out."

"It'll scare Gram."

"She'll worry more if you don't go," Marcus said. "This town has a grapevine that works faster than the Internet. Jo will know before tomorrow morning what happened whether you tell her or not. At least you can ease her mind about your injuries."

"Listen to Marcus," Rio said. "If you're lucky, you'll be out of there in a couple hours."

Scrutinizing his friend's expression, Marcus had a feeling Paige would be admitted to the hospital until tomorrow sometime.

The medic gently checked Paige's neck. "You will have some serious bruises. Use an ice pack a few times a day, twenty minutes at a time. Anything else hurt?"

"I don't think so. Why are you working with the EMTs?"

"Volunteering with the county tonight. They're shorthanded."

"Lucky for me." She gave him a weak smile.

Rio motioned the EMT forward. "Let's get her to the hospital."

Marcus reluctantly released Paige's hand and moved out of the way. As soon as he stood, he realized he was weak. Great. He'd grab something to eat at the hospital. He wasn't letting her go alone, especially since they didn't have an ID on the creep who hurt Paige. The hospital had many entrances and exits. The guy who hurt her could walk right in and no one would recognize the danger.

Rio's eyes narrowed as he took in Marcus bracing himself against the wall. "You okay?"

"I'll be fine."

"Marcus."

"It's nothing serious." Not yet, anyway. "I haven't had dinner yet."

"You going with her to the hospital?"

He nodded.

"Hey, I'm right here, you know. You don't have to go with me, Marcus. Please, go eat." Paige protested.

"I'll be all right."

She didn't look convinced.

"Wasting your time arguing with the preacher, Paige. Let's go." Rio motioned for the other EMT to proceed.

Marcus followed the two men, scooped up Paige's purse and laptop case as the other two men maneuvered the gurney through the gym and into the back of the ambulance. He climbed in after Rio. After slamming shut the doors, Rio's partner for the night slid behind the wheel and cranked the engine.

"Is this really necessary, Rio?" Paige asked.

"Yep. Suck it up, cupcake." The medic reached into a large black bag, pulled out a protein bar, and handed it to Marcus.

His cheeks burned, but he wasn't stupid enough to pass up the bar. "Thanks. You always carry your mike bag when you volunteer?"

"I never go anywhere without it. Never know when I might have a cranky pastor to deal with."

Marcus sighed as he ripped the wrapper from the bar. "Sorry, man. It's been a long day."

"Anything you can talk about?"

"Jeb Kirkland passed away not long ago. I spent a couple hours with his family."

"Aww, man. Sorry to hear about Jeb. I enjoyed talking to him. He loved to come to PSI and watch Durango put the trainees through their paces."

That news didn't surprise Marcus. Jeb had been fascinated with all things military despite the fact he never served. No better place to indulge the fascination than to hang out with Rio's Delta team or Trent St. Claire's team at Personal Security International, the bodyguard training arm of Fortress Security. "I'm sure he enjoyed that."

Rio snorted. "Not sure what he enjoyed more, seeing the trainees go through training or eating the food Nate prepared. We always fed him when he was on our campus."

"Probably enjoyed both." Nate Armstrong, Durango's EOD man, was also a trained chef.

The ambulance made the turn into Memorial Hospital as Marcus finished the last of the protein bar. At the emergency room entrance, he hopped down and moved out of the way, trailing behind the gurney into the hospital.

With Paige's bags in his hands, he followed the entourage into the examination room. Rio flashed him an amused glance. Again, his cheeks burned. Too bad. He wasn't leaving her in this room alone until the doctor arrived and he was positive his friend was safe.

CHAPTER THREE

Paige scowled at the doctor. "Tell me you're kidding."

"Sorry, my dear." John Anderson's blue eyes twinkled at her. "You need to stay overnight for observation."

"I don't want to leave Gram by herself. She has guests at the bed and breakfast tonight."

"I'm sure she'll understand. Jo Jensen strikes me as a sensible woman. She'd want you to have the care you need. Look at this this way. If you go home, your grandmother would be forced to wake you every two hours to check on you. If you stay here, a nurse will check you."

"You used to be my favorite doctor," she groused. "All right. I'll stay. But I want your word you'll be here first thing tomorrow morning to spring me from this prison. I have a report to finish for the town council meeting tomorrow night. I also need to help Gram turn the rooms because we have more guests arriving in the afternoon."

"I'll do my best to arrive early for my rounds." Anderson patted her hand. "Rest as much as you can tonight."

A minute after the doctor left, a light tap sounded on the door to the exam room. Marcus Lang poked his head around the door frame. "All right if I come in?"

"Sure."

He walked inside, carrying her purse and computer bag. "I thought you might want these."

"Thank you, Marcus."

"What did the doc say?"

She wrinkled her nose. "I need to stay overnight for observation."

"I was afraid of that. Want me to call Jo?"

For a minute, she was tempted. "I'd better do it. She'll worry more if she doesn't hear my voice."

"I'll step into the hall while you talk to her."

"Don't leave." Didn't make sense, but she didn't want him to go.

With a nod, he handed Paige her phone.

At the first ring, Jo Jensen snatched up the phone. "Don't tell me you're still at the center, honey."

"I'm not, Gram. I'm at the hospital."

"Why? What happened?"

"Someone broke into the center."

"Were you hurt?"

She hesitated, not wanting to alarm her grandmother more than she already was. She also didn't want to lie to her. "I have a concussion."

"Paige."

Oh, man. That tone of voice. Her grandmother knew she was holding back. "A man broke into the center and choked me, Gram. But I'm okay. I have to stay in the hospital for observation because of the concussion."

"Oh, honey. I'll get someone to stay at the house in case our guests need something, then stay at the hospital with you."

"You don't need to do that. Marcus is with me."

A pause. "You called him before you called me?"

"He drove by, noticed something wasn't right at the center, and stopped to check it out. Marcus chased the guy off."

15

"Thank God for that. Are you sure you don't need me to come?"

"I'm be fine, I promise. Dr. Anderson promised to spring me tomorrow morning. Get some rest, Gram. I'll see you in a few hours."

"Nicely done." Marcus's eyes twinkled. "You realize Jo thinks I'm staying here with you, right?"

Her cheeks burned. Yeah, she'd sort of given her grandmother that impression. "I didn't want her to come. She'd feel obligated to stay up all night and watch over me. Gram has to cook breakfast tomorrow morning for a family of eight." She hoped Dr. Anderson did arrive early for his rounds. She had promised to help Gram in the kitchen.

"Is there someone else you want to call?"

She squashed the disappointment spiraling through her. Stupid. Of course, Marcus wouldn't want to stay. It's not like they were dating. Wishing he would ask her on a date didn't change the fact that he hadn't. Of course, every single woman in town seemed determined to rid Marcus Lang of his pesky bachelorhood. To her knowledge, he hadn't been on a date since he arrived in town. "No. Thanks for staying this long. I'll see you tomorrow."

Before he could respond, an orderly arrived pushing a wheelchair.

"Ms. Jensen, I'll take you to your room now."

Marcus walked with her to the elevator and up to the third floor. Once she was settled, Marcus came into the room, shifted the chair to her bedside, and sat.

"Marcus, aren't you going home?"

He shook his head. "I'm not leaving you, Paige. You need someone with you right now."

She stared. "Do you always stay overnight in hospital rooms with church members?"

"When they need me to, sure. But I'm not here as the pastor. I'm here as your friend."

So, what exactly did that mean? Paige was too tired to untangle her thoughts and emotions. "Thank you for what you did."

"I didn't do anything except let the guy who hurt you get away." His voice reflected the disgust he felt at that.

"You followed your instinct to check on me. If you hadn't stopped, he might have finished what he started and we wouldn't be having this conversation."

"I wish I could have caught the guy so you wouldn't worry about him anymore. Did you recognize anything about him? His voice, a smell, anything?"

She couldn't think with her head hurting so much. "Not that I remember, but I'll keep trying tomorrow. Can you turn off the overhead light? The glare is making this headache worse."

He crossed the room and turned off light.

Paige sighed, relieved the intensity of the headache eased without the overhead lights burning.

"Better?"

"Much."

"Rest while you can. The nurse will be in soon to check on you. I'll be here."

Paige held out her hand. Marcus took it in his, squeezed. She expected him to let go. Instead, he scooted his chair closer, retaining her hand in his.

His touch sent warmth through her. Shouldn't have been possible, but his touch chased the lingering chill from her body. For the first time in hours, Paige felt safe. "Thank you for staying with me."

"Shh. Rest."

Paige closed her eyes and drifted. Later, the nurse came and asked her questions, checked her vitals, and continued on her rounds. She glanced at Marcus, found him watching her.

"How do you feel?" he asked.

"Headache is still bad. Throat hurts." She realized with surprise he was still holding her hand.

"Need anything?"

"I would kill for a glass of ice."

He chuckled as he stood. "I'll see if I can scrounge up ice. Can't have a friend commit a felony."

Friend. Not church member. Did that mean anything? She sighed. At two in the morning, why was she torturing herself with a question she couldn't answer?

When Marcus returned, he carried a large Styrofoam cup and a plastic spoon in one hand, an ice pack in the other. He positioned the rolling table by the side of the bed and handed her the ice.

She scooped a spoonful of ice. Heaven. Once she'd consumed a quarter of the glass, she set the rest on the table. "Thanks, Marcus."

"Get comfortable and I'll lay the ice pack on your throat."

Paige settled against the pillow. Seconds later, Marcus placed the ice pack against her throat, then draped a blanket over her. That done, he returned to his seat. This time, he was the one who offered his hand. That had to mean something, right?

She shouldn't read too much into simple human contact. She and Marcus were friends. She squeezed his fingers and closed her eyes. Better not to ask questions right now.

At four, the nurse returned. Marcus took Paige's glass to find more ice while the nurse asked her the same questions about her name, the date, the president. By the time she finished checking Paige's vitals, Marcus returned with more ice and another ice pack.

"Marcus, you should go home and rest."

"I'm fine, Paige."

Her eyes narrowed. "I know better. Every time I woke, you were awake."

"I catnapped. Besides, my truck is at the community center and I'd rather not call someone to come get me this early in the morning. If you want me to leave, I'll go to the waiting room."

Paige covered his hand with hers. "I was thinking of you, not myself. I'm glad you're with me."

"Think you can sleep?"

"Doubt it. I usually get up around this time anyway. When we have guests, I help Gram prepare breakfast before I leave for the center."

"Do you have a lot of traffic through the B & B?"

"It's fairly steady year-round. We have more reservations during the summer and early fall when people are interested in visiting the mountains and the Cherokee reservation."

"How long have you lived in Otter Creek, Paige?"

"Since I was five. My parents died in a car wreck. Gram took me in and raised me." She smiled. "She says I keep her young."

"Jo is a special lady. If I was old enough, I'd make a play for her myself."

Paige laughed. "I'll tell her you said that when I need a pass from the dog house. She's impressed with you." She eyed Marcus a moment. "Would you answer a question for me?"

"If I can. Ask."

"Why haven't you dated anyone since you arrived in Otter Creek?"

His eyebrows rose. "Noticed that, did you?"

"Hard not to. Several women are disappointed you haven't shown them any interest."

He flinched. "They're still talking about that? The parade of casseroles left at my doorstep finally stopped when I hired Serena Blackhawk to cook my meals. I hoped the speculation had stopped at the same time."

"Sorry to disappoint you. You didn't answer my question." She squeezed his hand. "Chicken?"

"Maybe the right woman hasn't shown interest yet."

Did that mean there was a woman who interested him? Disappointment spiraled through her. "Maybe she doesn't know you're interested."

"Think I should tell her?"

She frowned, hearing his uncertainty. That wasn't characteristic of Marcus. "Why not?"

"Dating a pastor is a challenge for any woman. Doing it in a small town presents unique difficulties. Any romance is going to be fodder for the Otter Creek gossip mill. If the relationship doesn't work out, she might feel the need to leave the church because she's uncomfortable seeing my face three times a week."

He was interested in someone at Cornerstone? Paige's heart sank. Bad enough to know he was interested in a woman. It was worse to know his interest focused on someone she attended church with.

A light tap sounded and Rio pushed open the door, smiled when he saw Paige was awake. "Hi, Paige. How do you feel?"

"Like some mad elf is pounding on my head with a sledge hammer. Other than that, I'm peachy."

The medic chuckled as he walked further into the room. "How's the throat?"

"Marcus has been getting ice and ice packs for me all night." She frowned. "I hope my throat doesn't look too bad. I don't want to upset Gram more than I already have."

"Your grandmother is a tough lady. She can handle a few bruises." Rio turned to Marcus. "Need coffee?"

"That would be great."

"Hey, what about me?" Paige asked. "I could use a cup."

"Wait until your stomach settles down. I'll bring you a soft drink. If you think you can handle coffee later, I'll buy you a cup."

"Sounds fair. You finished playing EMT?"

"I finished my shift at midnight."

She blinked. "What are you doing here this early?"

"I'm always up this early. PSI classes start at six and Darcy has to be at the deli about this time." He patted her hand, then turned toward the door. "Back in a minute."

No sooner had he left, then the door opened again. Paige's eyes widened. "Nick, what are you doing here?"

"We need to talk."

At this time of morning? Couldn't be good. "This can't wait?"

"Afraid not. I found a body in the boys' locker room at the center."

CHAPTER FOUR

A ball of ice formed in Marcus's stomach. A body? He threaded his fingers through Paige's and squeezed gently. "Can you tell us the identity?"

Nick sighed, his expression grim. "Word will leak soon anyway. It's Van Wilder. I just notified his father."

Sorrow and shock wrapped twin ribbons around his heart. This news must have devastated Van's father. The single dad doted on the teen as he was the only member of his family to survive a devastating house fire soon after Marcus arrived in town. "That must have been difficult for you, Nick."

"Death notification is the worst part of the job. Paige, if you're up to it, I need to ask you questions about what happened. Time is critical."

Paige brushed tears from her face with her free hand. "I understand. I'll do my best, but I don't know what else I can tell you."

"Take me through what happened at the center from the beginning." The detective moved a chair to the foot of her bed and sat. He pulled out a small notebook and pen.

"I worked late again. I have to give a report to the town council on the community center. They don't want to approve the funds for me to hire another staff member."

A snort. "Mayor Parks pinches pennies so hard they squeal."

A fact Marcus knew all too well. Parks was on the trustee board at the church. Board meetings were never fun, but adding Parks to the board had made the meetings even more trying. The mayor always seemed to have a personal agenda in mind above the church's business.

When Paige uttered a watery laugh, Marcus passed her a box of tissues.

"Thanks." She pulled one free and dried the tears from her face. "Anyway, I heard a strange noise about 10:30, which spooked me pretty good since I was supposed to be alone in the building. I love working at the community center, but that place is creepy at night."

"What kind of noise did you hear?" Nick asked.

She frowned. "I'm not sure exactly. Metal on metal, I guess."

"What did you do next?"

"I was going to call the police to come investigate so I wouldn't be the too-stupid-to-live heroine in a bad movie. I figured if the noise was the HVAC system or something, the officer who responded would have a good laugh at my expense. If the noise was trouble, I wanted a cop at my side."

"Smart," Marcus said.

"Would have been a smarter idea if my phone was in my pocket. Unfortunately, I left it on the stage in the gym when I dealt with a skinned knee yesterday afternoon. Anyway, I found my phone on the stage and was going back to my office to call the police when the door to the boys' locker room opened. Dalton Reagan came out."

"What was he doing there that late at night?" Nick's pen hovered above his pad. "Curfew is at 11:00 for teens under 18."

"He forgot his backpack and needed to finish some homework before class this morning."

"Waited kind of late to do schoolwork."

"His mother is working two jobs. Dalton helps his brothers with their schoolwork and baths until his mother comes home. He also cooks their dinner if his mother forgets to put something in the slow cooker for them. He was too busy to notice the missing backpack."

A smile curved Marcus's lips. That's what he wanted to hear, that Dalton actually cared about his schoolwork. Made all the hours he'd spent with the teen well worth the effort. Dalton was a good kid who was having to grow up too fast since his father walked out on the family three years earlier.

"Go on," Nick said.

"Dalton talked to me for a minute, then left. I went to my office and decided I was too tired to finish the report. I shut down my computer, stuffed it in my bag, and grabbed my purse. Following my normal routine, I checked the girls' locker room to make sure the light was off, then went to the boys' locker room."

"Did you open the door?"

"No. Before I could, the lights went off in the gym." Her words choked off.

"What did you do?"

She started to talk, but couldn't.

"Paige," Marcus said, voice soft. "Do you need a break? Nick will give you a couple minutes if you need them."

Rio walked into the room with coffee and a soft drink. "Nick, you're awake early."

"Never made it to bed."

Vendetta

The medic handed the coffee to Marcus. "It's black." He opened the soft drink bottle and gave it to Paige. "Slow sips. Your stomach won't tolerate much for a few more hours."

Since Paige didn't seem interested in letting go of his hand, Marcus left his hand wrapped around hers. Had to admit he liked holding her hand a lot more than he should considering they were friends.

As she drank a few sips, Marcus noticed her hand trembling. He slid a pointed look at Nick.

The detective stood. "I need to call Madison. I'll be back in a few minutes." He patted her foot and walked to the hallway.

"I could have continued." Paige scowled at the closed door. "I don't want this interview hanging over my head."

"Don't worry." Rio propped one shoulder against the wall. "This won't be the last time Nick asks you questions about what happened. Take your time. When did the doc say you could leave?"

"Dr. Anderson promised to come in early to do his rounds. If he's happy with my progress, he'll release me then."

"Excellent. I'll stick around until he springs you and take you home and drop Marcus at the center to get his truck."

"My car is there, too."

"Sorry, Paige. You'll have to be cleared by Doc Anderson before you drive. If he says it's okay, I'll drop you off as well."

She frowned. "I thought you had to be at PSI by six. What if Dr. Anderson doesn't arrive early?"

"I called Josh. He asked St. Claire's medic to cover for me if I'm late."

Nick returned, phone in his hand. "Sorry. I didn't want Madison to worry when she woke and realized I never

25

made it home last night." He sat again. "Are you ready to continue?"

Paige's hand tightened around Marcus's. "Yes."

He opened his notebook again. "You told me you found your phone and planned to go back to your office to call the police and the lights went out. What did you do?"

"I thought it might be Dalton, playing a trick on me. The kids love to do that and they haven't pranked me for a while."

"But it wasn't Dalton."

She shuddered. "I called Dalton's name, told him the joke wasn't funny, but of course he didn't answer. Someone came into the gym. I asked who was there, and instead of answering, he laughed. I told him I was calling the police." Paige closed her eyes for a few seconds. "I started to tap in the numbers when I realized the light from my phone pinpointed my location. I ran for the hall where Marcus found me. There's an exit to the alley there. I planned to run across the square to the police station for help. I couldn't go out the front because the man was blocking the front door." She dragged in a wheezing breath.

"Paige." Marcus waited until her gaze locked with his. "Slow and easy breaths. You're safe."

She gave a slight nod and reached for the soft drink. She drank a few more sips before continuing. "I made it to the center of the gym before the man tackled me. When I fell, my phone flew out of my hand and skidded out of reach. I got free, ran again for the hall. He caught me a second time, spun me around and shoved me against the wall. I told him if he wanted money he was out of luck, that we didn't have cash in the center."

"Is that what he wanted? Did he say that?" Nick asked, pen hovering over the pad.

"He didn't say anything. He wrapped his hands around my throat and started to squeeze. The last thing I remember was thinking I was going to die unless a miracle happened. I woke up on the floor and Marcus was with me."

Just hearing what she went through had fury surging through Marcus. Why would someone want to hurt Paige? As far as he knew, she had no enemies. If he'd arrived even a minute later, the attacker might have finished the job and Marcus would be planning her funeral as well as Mr. Kirkland's instead of hoping for a date with this beautiful woman.

"You didn't see his face, Paige?" Nick asked.

"The gym was too dark."

"Did you recognize his voice?"

A head shake.

"Was it low-pitched, medium, high?"

"Low. Not as deep as Ethan's voice but more than yours or Marcus."

"Good. What about his size? Tall, average, short?"

"Tall. Maybe the height of Rio. He was muscular, too. He was strong and had a broad chest. No matter how I struggled, I couldn't break his grip on my throat."

"I'll give you some pointers," Rio said. "There are some easy things you can do that will work, techniques I've taught Darcy."

"I might take you up on that."

"Paige," Nick said. "I want you to close your eyes and think about any scents or textures you might have noticed. What kind of clothes was he wearing?"

Her brow furrowed as she closed her eyes. She was silent a moment, then said, "His pants were denim. He wore a short-sleeved shirt with smooth material. Soft cotton. Maybe a t-shirt."

"Good. What about his hair? Did you touch his hair?"

She gasped. "Yes. It was wavy."

"Not curly?"

Paige shook her head. "Wavy."

"Excellent. Now think about the scents. Was he wearing cologne?"

"No, not like...."

"Not like who?" the detective prompted.

Cheeks pink, she said, "Not like Marcus." Paige kept her gaze averted from his.

Marcus's lips curved. So, she'd noticed his aftershave lotion. Nice to know. Maybe she was more aware of him than he thought. That was indeed good news. He hoped his interest was reciprocated.

"So, he doesn't smell like Marcus. Guess that takes our pastor off my suspect list," Nick said.

Her eyelids flew up and the color in Paige's cheeks deepened. "This guy carried a scent of soap, sweat, and some kind of sharp, metallic odor. I didn't recognize the metallic one."

"Did he have gloves on his hands?"

"No. The back of his hands was hairy, too."

"Did you scratch him?"

Finally, a smile curved her lips. "You bet."

A nod from Nick. "Then we have his DNA."

Rio glanced at the detective. "I have my Go bag in the SUV. I carry gun oil."

"Gun oil?" Marcus straightened in his chair. "You think that's what Paige smelled on her attacker?" The implications made his blood run cold. If Paige had smelled gun oil, that would mean the man had a weapon on him.

"It's worth a shot to let her sniff the oil. My wife is sensitive to smell and that's how she describes it when I clean my weapons."

Nick motioned for the medic to go ahead. After Rio left, the detective smiled at Paige. "You're doing great. Let's go back to Van Wilder for a minute. Was he in the center today?"

"He came in to play basketball." She turned to Marcus. "You saw him, didn't you?"

"He was leaving as I came in to play with the younger kids."

"Did you notice when he came back?" Nick asked Paige.

"I had no idea he returned."

"Has Van had problems with anyone?"

Paige bit her lip and glanced at Marcus.

He squeezed her hand again. "Tell him. He needs to know."

"Paige?" Nick tilted his head. "Talk to me. Everything matters now. In a murder investigation, there are no secrets."

"He and Dalton have been doing a little pushey-shovey on the basketball court and off. I had to ban Van from the center for three days last week."

"Do you know what the problem was?"

"I asked. They wouldn't tell me, but I saw enough to know that Van was the aggressor."

Rio walked into the room with a small bottle in his hand. He twisted off the top. "Is this what you smelled on the man who attacked you?"

CHAPTER FIVE

Paige sniffed at the open bottle and jerked back, nausea building fast in her stomach. She clamped a hand over her mouth. Oh, no. Not with an audience in the room, especially Marcus.

Rio reacted fast. He put the bottle of gun oil on the roll away table, grabbed the small plastic tub nearby, and rolled her onto her side away from Marcus. He said something to Nick that Paige couldn't catch over the sound of her retching.

Instead of leaving like she hoped, Marcus wrapped a strong arm around her to hold her steady and with his other hand kept her hair away from her face. If the bed turned into a black hole and swallowed her, life would be perfect.

A minute later, something cold covered the back of her neck. When her stomach spasms finally subsided, Paige was as weak as a newborn kitten and too lethargic to bury her hot face in the pillow.

"I'm going to roll you to your back," Rio said. "We'll go nice and slow. If you feel sick again, sing out. Ready?"

She gave a short nod.

"Marcus, keep the ice pack in place." The medic gently eased Paige to her back.

Instead of moving away from her as she expected, Marcus stayed in the same position. She ended up in the circle of his arms with her face pressed against his chest.

She really should move back, but was too tired to bother and too humiliated to look at the face of the man she was interested in dating. Looked like that idea was shot now. Kind of hard to date a man when you couldn't look at him without knowing he'd witnessed the worst moment of your life.

Rio took the plastic tub away as Marcus positioned a second ice pack on Paige's forehead. The nausea receded to merely annoying. Wow. Who knew ice packs worked like magic on an upset stomach?

The medic returned with a cleaned plastic tub. "Better now?"

"Yes. Sorry."

"Normal reaction to a concussion. So, did you recognize the scent of gun oil or was this a reaction to any strong smell?"

"That's the scent on the man's hands." She peered at Nick through her lashes. "Does that mean what I think it does?"

His expression was grim. "I think it's safe to assume he had a weapon on him. If he had chosen to use the weapon, Marcus would have discovered your body in that hallway instead of arriving in time to scare him off."

When Paige shuddered, Marcus eased her closer. "Not what I wanted to hear," she muttered.

"Are you able to answer more questions?"

"Can't it wait, Nick?" Marcus protested.

"I'm sorry, my friend. Every minute counts. The longer I wait, the more details Paige will forget."

"It's okay, Marcus." Paige laid her hand over his heart. She blinked when it skipped a beat before continuing in a faster rhythm. Huh. Interesting. "Ask your questions, Nick."

"How did Dalton seem when you saw him come out of the boys' locker room? Was he nervous?"

"He was fine. Not nervous, scared, or uptight. He acted like everything was normal. He was in a hurry because of the curfew and didn't want to worry his mother. If you're asking if he looked as though he'd seen a body or killed someone and was anxious to leave, the answer is no."

Nick made a few notations, then glanced up. "What about you?"

She frowned. "What about me?"

The detective slanted a hard look at Marcus before returning his gaze to her. "Did you see Van's body?"

"No, of course not. I would have called the police immediately if I had."

"Did you kill him, Paige?"

Did he seriously think she was a murderer? "I never laid a hand on that boy. For all his troublemaking tendencies, I liked Van."

"You said yourself you banned him from the center last week for three days. Maybe he came in last night and you two fought. Things spiraled out of control. You lost your temper and killed him."

"I didn't kill him, Nick. I never touched him."

"Can anyone corroborate your story?"

Mocking laughter escaped. "Sure. Find the guy who choked me. Other than him, I only saw Dalton after seven last night. The rest of the time, I was holed up in my office wresting with numbers that won't support hiring help without another cash infusion which the mayor will refuse to consider."

"Did anyone call you?"

She started to say no, paused. "Wait. I talked to Nicole Copeland. She's planning a surprise birthday party for Mason." The dog groomer was crazy about Rio's cousin and their romance was the talk of Otter Creek.

"What time did she call?"

"I don't know."

"Guess," Nick snapped.

She thought back through the events of the night before. "Maybe fifteen minutes before I talked to Dalton. So that would make it about 10:15. I didn't look at the clock."

"What phone did you use?"

"Cell phone. The center doesn't have a landline. The council is too cheap to put one in."

"I'll need your phone."

Her phone? Oh, dear. She didn't want to give up her phone. It was her lifeline to her grandmother. Gram wouldn't be able to reach her in an emergency if Nick took her phone. "Isn't there another way to get what you need? Gram won't be able to reach me if I don't have my cell phone." Her grandmother had been receiving odd phone calls lately and Paige didn't want to be out of touch in case she was needed.

"Do I have permission to access your phone records?"

"Absolutely." She didn't have anything to hide.

Nick turned to Rio. "Would Fortress be willing to access the records for me?" A small smile curved his lips. "Your techs are faster than ours."

"No problem." The medic pulled out his phone. "Paige, what's your cell number?" Seconds later, Rio tapped in a number and put the call on speaker.

"Murphy. What do you need, Rio?"

"You're on speaker with Nick Santana, Marcus Lang, and Paige Jensen. I need a favor."

"Name it."

He gave the man Paige's phone number. "Access her records and send the result to my email. I'll forward it to Detective Santana."

"Ms. Jensen, are you okay with this?"

"Access the records, please. The detective needs proof that I was on the phone when I said I was."

"Copy that. I'm Zane Murphy, by the way. I'm a computer and communications tech at Fortress Security."

"He also saved Durango's hide more times than we can count," Rio added.

Paige smiled. "So, you're the amazing Z they talk about all the time."

"They're good friends."

"Aww." Rio grinned. "I knew you had a soft spot for us."

A snort. "Don't let it go to your head." Computer keys clicked in the background. "How are you, Marcus?"

"Great, thanks for asking. You planning to come back up this way soon?"

"Hope to. Claire wants to take pictures in the area." A pause, then, "Rio, the records are in your email. Anything else I can do for you?"

"Not right now, buddy. Give Claire a hug from me."

"Will do." And he was gone.

Nick chuckled. "What Zane just did in two minutes would have taken at least two days to accomplish with our own people. Forward the information to me." He turned to Paige. "Have any enemies?"

"None that want to kill me."

"What does that mean?" Marcus asked.

"Not everyone is happy with the way I run the center. In fact, a couple people believe I should be replaced."

"Why?" Nick flipped to a new page.

"Some think I cater too much to the teens and kids at the center. Others want the senior citizens shuffled to another facility. Still others are positive I'm wasting the center's money by padding my own pocket."

Marcus scowled. "That's ridiculous. I've seen the budget and what you do with it is amazing."

She smiled. "Thanks."

"You sure you don't have enemies, maybe someone in your past who is exacting revenge now?" Nick asked.

"I'm the most boring suspect you will ever have. I don't have an enemy past or present. I might irritate a few people, but nothing that would inspire the attack at the center."

"I will have more questions for you. Be available." The detective stood, laid his hand on her foot again. "I have to do my job, Paige. I'll follow the leads wherever they take me."

"Do you really think I'm guilty of murder?"

He squeezed her foot gently. "No, I don't. But I have to ask questions that will seem as though I do believe you're guilty. I hope you understand."

She didn't like it, but she did understand. Hopefully, the detective would find the information necessary to prove her innocence. "Have fun trolling through my phone records."

They were boring. Calls from friends and her grandmother, occasionally from Marcus. Texts from the same people. Her cheeks burned. The only text conversations she saved had been with Marcus. And yes, that was seriously embarrassing because the conversations hadn't been anything personal, simply passing information between them about the center, church, and her grandmother. What would Nick make of that? She hoped the detective was discreet.

"I'll talk to you later, Paige." Nick nodded at the other two men and left.

Rio waggled his phone. "I'm going to call Darcy, make sure she's okay. She was pretty tired last night when I left for the EMT shift. I'll be back in a few minutes. Marcus, keep those ice packs in place for another two minutes, then you can remove them."

Silence filled the room once the medic walked into the hallway. So how did you handle facing the man you wanted to impress after you had barfed with him holding your hair out of the line of fire?

"Feeling better?" Marcus asked.

Apparently, you faced it head on. Paige sighed. "Yes. I'm sorry, Marcus. That episode was an unpleasant surprise."

"Wouldn't be the first time I've rendered aid to a sick friend."

She risked a quick peek at his face. "Didn't realize that was part of your pastoral duties."

Shadows clouded his eyes for a moment. "It's not although I've sat at the bedside of many ailing church members."

"I'm a captive audience for at least another two minutes. Want to talk about it?"

"Another time. I'd like to ask you something."

"Go ahead."

"You asked me why I haven't dated anyone since I arrived in Otter Creek."

"I remember." Where was he going with this?

"You were right about the campaign to rid me of my bachelorhood. I've had plenty of offers, but I'm only interested in dating one woman."

Oh, man. This better not be a question about how to capture another woman's interest. That might break her heart. Secretly pining for the pastor of your church wasn't easy. Watching him romance someone else in their congregation would be painful.

Marcus removed the ice packs and set them aside, then wrapped his hand around hers. "We've been friends for years, but I hope you'll give me a chance to be more than a friend."

Her heart skipped a beat, then surged ahead. "That's not a question, Marcus."

"Here's my question. Would you be interested in going to dinner with me?"

She wanted to say yes, but what did this mean? A one-time deal or the start of something new? "Is this a one-time offer?"

"I hope not. I want dinner to be the beginning of many dates to come."

"You want to date me?"

"If you aren't interested in that kind of relationship with me, I'll back off. We'll stay friends."

She smiled. "Marcus, I've been hoping you would ask me out for a long time."

His hand tightened around hers. "You have?"

"Didn't you notice I haven't dated anyone since the first year after you arrived in Otter Creek? Once you caught my interest, no one else would do. I would love to date you and see where this goes."

"And if it doesn't work?"

"I'll hold you to your promise that we'll still be friends. My grandmother loves you and Cornerstone Church. I won't pull her away from there because I'm uncomfortable. That means if our dating relationship doesn't work out, you have to live with the fallout, too."

"Thank God," he murmured. "You don't know how long I agonized over broaching this subject. I don't want to lose your friendship."

"This will change how we interact if things don't work out between us."

"I can live with that. Are you sure, Paige?" A smile curved his lips. "We'll be dating in a glass fishbowl. Everybody in town will be watching."

She laughed. "I enjoy a good challenge."

He kissed the back of her hand. "Thank you for taking the chance."

Was he kidding? Paige had waited more than six years for this chance. No way was she holding back because of a little attention from the gossip mongers in town.

Dr. Anderson walked into the room. He smiled at them both. "You appear to be much better this morning, Paige. Let's have a look at you."

"I'll wait in the hall," Marcus said, squeezing her hand before leaving the room.

Minutes later, Doc Anderson was back on the top of her list of favorite doctors. "Thanks for giving me early parole."

He chuckled. "You're welcome, my dear."

"What about driving?"

"Let's wait for 48 hours to be safe, then I think it will be fine for you to resume driving. If your vision blurs again, I expect to hear from you immediately."

"Yes, sir."

Anderson patted her shoulder. "I'll inform the gentlemen waiting for you that you'll be ready to leave as soon as you dress. The nurse will be along shortly with your discharge papers."

As she changed clothes, Paige thought through the logistics of getting where she needed to go for the next two days, and smiled. Maybe Marcus wouldn't mind playing chauffeur occasionally. Nicole would taxi her around as well if Gram was busy. Only two days. She could handle it. The danger to her was in the past. She'd be fine now.

She swallowed another sip of the soft drink, grimaced at the reminder of how she'd gotten the sore throat. Nick would find the culprit soon. She hoped.

CHAPTER SIX

Paige opened the door, release papers in hand. "I'm ready," she told Marcus and Rio.

"Excellent timing." The medic smiled. "I'll have just enough time to take you home, drop off Marcus, and still make my class."

"That's not necessary," Marcus said. "I'll take Paige home."

Rio's lips curved slightly. "Suits me. That will leave me time to steal a kiss or three from my gorgeous wife before I run PSI trainees into the ground."

"I think you enjoy showing up the bodyguard trainees." Marcus's hand rested against Paige's lower back as they walked to the elevator.

"How could I not? Most of the trainees are ten to fifteen years younger than we are, and think they're ready for any situation thrown at them. Our job is to show them they're wrong, then teach them how to protect themselves, their teammates, and principals. Do we get a kick out of showing up a bunch of hotheads who think they're invincible? You bet. We demonstrate how a cohesive team operates, then train them hard to create a unit we trust to have our backs on a mission."

Since they were alone on the elevator, Paige asked, "How do your wives handle your job?"

"They're strong. We couldn't do our jobs without their support. They encourage each other when our team is out. If there comes a time when one of the wives can't handle our deployments, Durango will ask Maddox to assign us permanently to PSI as trainers without deployments. Our wives mean more to us than the job."

"You and your teammates are so blessed, Rio," Marcus said. "Your wives are your greatest treasure."

The medic nodded. "We never forget that, either."

Paige's heart squeezed. She hoped someone special would feel the same way about her one day. Maybe Marcus? She pushed that thought aside for now. Too soon. They hadn't been on one date yet.

They exited the hospital and climbed into Rio's black SUV. The sun was peeking over the horizon and the day promised to be a beautiful one, perfect for Gram's guests to visit the mountains and Cherokee reservation.

The sunlight also aggravated her headache. Paige found her sunglasses and plopped them on her nose. The relief was immediate.

Rio glanced in the rearview mirror. "If the headache worsens, let me know or contact Anderson, Paige."

"I will, I promise."

He parked beside Marcus's truck. When they all exited the vehicle, he said, "If you need help, call me."

"Thanks, Rio." Paige stood on her tiptoes and gave him a quick hug. "I appreciate what you did for me."

"Glad I was available. If Durango can help, we will. All you have to do is ask."

Tears stung her eyes. "Thanks."

He turned to Marcus. "Same goes for you, too, buddy. If you need us, pick up the phone."

"Appreciate it."

With a wave of his hand, the medic crossed the square to That's A Wrap, the deli his wife owned.

"Let's get you home, Paige." Marcus unlocked his truck and helped her into the passenger seat, then handed her the seatbelt. He circled the hood of the truck and climbed behind the wheel. Minutes later, he parked in the circular driveway of the bed and breakfast.

Home had never looked so good. She loved the Victorian house on the outskirts of Otter Creek. While not as massive as Darcy and Rio's place, the B & B was large enough to be spacious for guests yet small enough that she and Gram didn't feel lost in the place when it was just them in the house. The white house with black shutters and wraparound porch spoke of comfort and love to Paige. Truthfully, any place Gram lived would do that for her.

Marcus walked with her to the porch, waited while she unlocked the door, and followed her inside.

"Gram's probably in the kitchen. She might need help fixing breakfast for our guests."

"Lead the way."

She walked through the large living room and dining room, and hung a left into the spacious kitchen. Sure enough, her grandmother was standing in front of the double oven. Blueberry muffins, from the scent wafting through the room.

"Need help, Gram?"

Brown eyes peered at her over a slender shoulder. "I could use an extra pair of hands. How do you feel, honey?"

"Like a mad miner is whaling on my head with a mallet."

"Let me take these muffins from the oven, then I want to take a look at you."

"I'll take care of that, Jo," Marcus said. He held out his hand for the pot holders.

Jo Jensen clasped Paige's hand and led her to a barstool at the breakfast bar. She turned Paige's head first one way, then the other, examined the bruises on her neck, and scowled. "Do the police have the man in custody?"

"Not yet, Gram. Nick's working on it."

"I'll have a word with him after breakfast."

"He's been working all night. I hope he's going to sleep soon."

"Nick will work as fast as possible." Marcus deposited the muffins from the pans on the cooling racks and turned them right side up. "He's a top-notch investigator."

She kissed Paige's cheek and circled the bar. "I know you're right. But this is my granddaughter we're talking about, not some stranger who is the unfortunate victim of a senseless crime. No one has any reason to hurt my girl."

"What else can I do to help?" he asked.

"You any good at manning a toaster?"

"I think I can manage that."

"Good. When breakfast is ready, you'll sit down and eat with us. It's the least I can do because you stayed with my Paige at the hospital."

"I was happy to spend time with her. What am I toasting?"

"Bagels. They're already pre-sliced." A sly look from her grandmother. "I learned the hard way to buy them already cut. Saves visits to the ER for a certain young lady."

Paige sighed. "Gram, I was twelve. I'm more careful with a knife these days."

"And our bank account thanks you." She handed a package of sliced plain bagels to Marcus. "Here you go. Toaster is beside the canisters."

Paige cracked eggs and mixed in milk, salt, and pepper for scrambled eggs. The normal act settled her as nothing else could besides a hug from the favorite woman in her life.

Gram waved her off when she volunteered to make the eggs. "I can handle this. Why don't you set the table for our guests in the dining room? They're a family unit and don't need help carrying on conversations. We'll eat in here with Marcus."

Sounded good to her. She wasn't up to entertaining visitors. She hopped down, winced at the stab of pain in her head, and crossed to the cabinets containing plates and glassware.

"You okay?" Marcus murmured as he dropped two toasted bagels into a waiting bread basket.

"Headache."

"Take some over-the-counter pain reliever." Her grandmother pressed a bottle of the medicine into her hand. "That with a chaser of green tea might help."

"Sounds good." She shook out a couple tablets and swallowed them with water. After setting the table in the dining room, Paige filled the tea kettle with water and waited not so patiently for it to heat. She dumped a couple heaping teaspoons of her favorite green tea with chamomile mix into the special container and screwed on the filter.

Her grandmother and Marcus carried a platter with eggs and the two bread baskets filled with muffins and bagels to the dining room. Another trip for the butter and cream cheese, and the pitchers of orange juice and apple juice plus a carafe of coffee.

Finally, the guests arrived for breakfast. Once Gram got them started on the meal, she returned to the kitchen and sat at the breakfast bar with Marcus and Paige.

"Do you want some eggs, honey?" Jo's spoon hovered over the second smaller platter of eggs she'd reserved for them to share.

Paige's stomach immediately twisted. "No, thanks, Gram. I think I'll try a plain bagel this morning." She sipped the tea, grateful the mix was doing its job in settling her stomach. She definitely didn't want a repeat of the earlier episode. One embarrassment today was enough, thank you very much.

"Coffee, Marcus?"

"I'll get it, Jo. Thank you for inviting me for breakfast." He slid off the stool and circled the bar. He filled his mug. "You want coffee?"

"Please. I don't know where Paige got her taste for green tea." She inclined her head toward the clear tea carrier with green tea, chamomile, and assorted other leaves floating free. "Looks and tastes like grass clippings from the yard to me."

Marcus chuckled as he slid onto the stool beside Paige. "I have to admit it doesn't have the same appeal as a good cup of Serena's coffee."

"She's the one who got me started on green tea." Paige nibbled on her bagel, grimaced and set it aside. Nope, not going to stay down if she tried to force herself to eat. Looked like she was drinking her breakfast today.

After Marcus finished his meal, he scrubbed his face with his hands.

Paige laid her hand on his arm. "You need to go sleep, Marcus. You were awake all night."

His lips curved. "I look that bad?"

"Of course not." Her cheeks burned. "But I know you have a tough couple of days ahead of you."

"Why?" Jo asked, her gaze shifting from Paige to Marcus. "What else happened?"

"Jeb Kirkland passed away last night."

"Oh, no. I'll call Nancy later, offer my condolences and our guest rooms for the family members coming to town." Jo pushed her plate aside and leaned her folded arms on the bar. "What else should I know?"

"Ma'am?"

"Don't 'ma'am' me, Marcus Lang. I know when someone is holding out on me. Let's hear it. What else is going on?"

"You're right, Gram." Paige wrapped her hands around the warmth of her tea cup, the heat doing little to alleviate the chill sinking deep into her bones. "Something else happened at the center that I didn't know about when I called you from the hospital. Van Wilder was found dead in the boys' locker room."

Jo set her coffee mug down with a thud. "Oh, dear. His father will be devastated. How did the boy die?"

Paige frowned, exchanged glances with Marcus. "We don't know. Nick didn't say." A deliberate omission on the detective's part.

"Did the man who attacked you kill Van?"

"We don't know that either, Jo." Marcus carried his dishes to the sink and rinsed them before placing them in the dishwasher. "Nick Santana is excellent at asking questions, not so good at disseminating information."

"If he was good at the latter, Chief Blackhawk would have fired him despite the fact Nick is his brother-in-law." Jo crossed to the coffee pot. "Would you like to take some coffee with you, Marcus?"

"Please. I'm afraid the days of me being awake for more than 24 hours without drawbacks are long gone."

She poured the steaming liquid into a to-go cup and handed it to him. Jo kissed his cheek. "I have to check on our guests. I'll see you later, dear."

"I'll walk you out." Paige slid from the stool and walked with him to his truck. He set the cup in his holder and turned.

"Take it easy today, Paige." He wrapped his warm hand around hers. "Would it be too soon to ask you to dinner tonight?"

She smiled. "I would love that. What time should I be ready?"

"Seven o'clock okay?"

Paige started to say yes, then winced. "Oh, man. I have to go to the council meeting at seven. Can I take a raincheck?"

"What if I pick you up for the meeting, then take you to dinner afterward?"

"Are you sure you want to do that? The meeting may run long." Although she seriously hoped it didn't. She'd rather spend her time with Marcus than Mayor Parks and his cronies.

Marcus lifted his hand and ran the backs of his fingers gently down her cheek. "I'm sure. I'll pick you up at 6:30. Will you be here or at the center?"

"Center. My part-timer doesn't arrive on site until four today. He has an afternoon class at the community college."

"Be alert. I hope the attack was a random thing, but I'm not comfortable assuming it was." He squeezed her hand. "If you need me, call."

"I'll be fine. Go rest, Marcus." As she watched him drive away, she prayed it wouldn't be necessary to call him for help. She wasn't sure she would survive a second attack by the same man.

CHAPTER SEVEN

Marcus sat bolt upright, threw the blanket aside, and swung his legs over the side of the couch. He glanced at the clock as he crossed to the front door. Not quite noon. To be honest, he was surprised his sleep wasn't interrupted before now.

He opened the door, stared at the construction worker standing on his porch with a tool box in one hand. "Mason, what are you doing here?"

The other man pulled off his sunglasses, his gaze puzzled. "You wanted me to check the leak in your master bathroom."

"Right. I forgot." Marcus stepped back. "Come in. How have you been?"

"Better than you from the looks of it. You just getting up?"

He glanced at the rumpled blanket on the couch. "I was up all night at the hospital with Paige Jensen. Some clown roughed her up at the community center last night and I didn't want to leave her alone."

"I heard about the attack. Nicole would have stayed with her if Jo couldn't."

"Although Jo had guests at the B & B, I wanted to be with Paige and would have stayed at the hospital regardless of who else was there."

Mason's eyebrow soared. "As the pastor or something else?"

"Not as the pastor."

"You're interested in Paige."

"Very much."

A nod from the other man. "This will be fun to watch."

Marcus chuckled. He imagined a lot of people would find the new relationship entertaining. Like he'd told Paige, they would be dating in a fishbowl. The whole town would keep tabs on their progress or lack thereof.

Now that Mason knew, he would be sure to tell Nicole, his girlfriend. From there, word would spread around town that he and Paige were involved. Marcus wanted that information to spread as fast as possible. Maybe whoever attacked Paige would think twice before going after her again if he realized her boyfriend was watching out for her.

And that term sounded strange after all these years. It had been a long time since he'd referred to himself that way. Pain squeezed his heart. Grateful the hurt wasn't as severe any longer, he closed the door and led Mason to the master bedroom.

Marcus opened the vanity doors to reveal the mop bucket under a pipe currently dripping water like it was Niagara Falls.

Mason whistled softly. "Not good."

"Tell me about it. I especially don't like getting up twice a night to empty the bucket. Gets old, let me tell you." Unfortunately, when he returned home after leaving the B & B, he'd been faced with cleaning up a flooded bathroom before he could go to sleep.

"I can imagine. If you have things to do right now, I'll take a look, then hunt you down to let you know what I find."

"I'll take a shower in the guest bathroom and be back in a few minutes."

"No problem." Mason set down his tool box and knelt on the tile. "Take your time."

Marcus grabbed a change of clothes and headed for the guest room. While he showered, he considered the day ahead of him. The only bright spot was his promised dinner with Paige. He'd waited a long time to approach her. He had valid reasons for that beyond the ones he'd given her.

Shoving his woolgathering aside, Marcus mentally listed the things he needed to do before picking up Paige for her town council meeting. First on his list was a stop by the Wilder place to offer his condolences to Van's father. Afterward, he'd circle around to see Nancy Kirkland to confirm the details for Jeb's service. Now, instead of one midweek message, he needed to also prepare a short message for Jeb's family and friends.

When he emerged from the bathroom refreshed and dressed, he sought out Rio's cousin. "Tell me you can fix the leak with plumber's putty or even duct tape."

Mason glanced up, grinned. "According to Rio and his teammates, duct tape is a necessary part of their equipment bags. As for your pipes, I can temporarily patch the leak."

"Uh oh. That doesn't sound good." He leaned against the doorjamb. In fact, Mason's careful choice of words made his muscles tense. "Let's hear it."

"Your house was built in the seventies, Marcus. At that time, it was common practice to use iron pipes for the plumbing in houses. After a while, those pipes corrode. Eventually they break and have to be replaced."

Oh, boy. He could feel the bite in the church coffers already. "And the solution to my problem?"

"Replacing all your pipes."

Yep, definitely not what he wanted to hear. The board, namely, Mayor Parks, would be unhappy with this news. "What will this run the church?"

"I'll have to work up an estimate for you. I'm sorry, Marcus, but it won't be cheap. A lot of man hours involved."

"Patch the pipe for now. After I look at the estimate and present it to the board, we'll talk about doing something more permanent." A wry laugh escaped. "I don't suppose you offer discounts to clergy."

"Not to clergy specifically, but I'm sure Brian would allow me to apply my employee discount to your bill."

"Excellent. I would appreciate any help Elliott Construction sees fit to offer and so would the church's bank account. Have you had lunch yet?"

Mason shook his head.

"I'm not sure what Serena left in my refrigerator and freezer yesterday, but I'd love company for lunch if you can spare the time before your next job."

"I'd like that. Thanks. I'll patch your pipe and be out in about ten minutes."

Marcus went to the kitchen and rummaged in the refrigerator. Serena Blackhawk had outdone herself yesterday. His refrigerator and freezer were full of food and drinks appropriate for his diet. Somehow, Serena always made his meals and snacks look appealing even if they were healthy. The best thing he'd done for himself since he was diagnosed with diabetes was sign a contract with Home Runs, Inc. The personal chef was worth her weight in gold. Dr. Anderson also heartily approved of Marcus's glucose numbers since Serena had taken over preparing his meals.

He pulled lunchmeat, cheese, whole-grain wraps, and lettuce from the refrigerator. Another trip netted him fresh cut fruit and cherry tomatoes, a weakness of his, plus a couple bottles of unsweetened sparkling water. He hoped Mason didn't mind having a wrap instead of a regular sandwich. Processed foods, including bread, messed with his glucose level and he'd rather not have to resort to taking insulin unless it was absolutely necessary.

By the time he had the wraps assembled and fruit and tomatoes on their plates, Mason walked into the kitchen and set down his tool box near the back door. Once he'd washed his hands and sat at the dining table, Marcus prayed over their meal, then slid one of the loaded plates to the construction worker. "Eat what you want, Mase. The sparkling water is unsweetened. Serena also made tea for me if you prefer to drink that. I have a natural sweetener you can add to the tea."

"The sparkling water is fine. Nicole drinks it all the time."

"Things seem to be working out well for you two." A fact which delighted Marcus. His friend had been through a rough time and so had his girlfriend. They both deserved happiness.

Mason's face lit up. "I don't know why she gave me a chance, but I'm so glad she did."

"Nicole sees the real man, not the label."

"I wish others in town would do the same. I still have problems doing my job in some homes. I can't tell you how many people have refused to let me inside the house without a co-worker from Elliott Construction along to keep an eye on me and make sure I don't steal anything. I didn't do time for stealing."

No, his friend had spent 13 years in prison for manslaughter. He'd driven his vehicle while drunk and ended up killing a mother and her child. Mason Kincaid paid a steep price for a lapse in judgment. Since his release, Mason had lived in Otter Creek and worked hard to rebuild his life and earn the trust of those around him.

"Do what you've been doing, Mason. People are noticing your work and integrity. You have many staunch supporters, including me."

"I won't win over everyone."

"You're right. Your boss and co-workers trust you. The woman who looks at you like you hung the moon certainly trusts you. You have good friends and family who believe in you. You've turned your life around and you're gifted in construction. You contribute much to this community, Mason. I'd say you're doing everything right. What do you think?"

Mason's haunted gaze locked with his. "I wish everyone else would see who I am now, not the stupid 22-year-old who made a terrible choice. I'm not the same man. I haven't touched a drop of alcohol since I was released last year. But no one will let me forget the past."

Marcus thought about the tone of his voice, the demeanor. "Mase, has the family of the mother and daughter been harassing you again?"

"Today would have been the little girl's sixteenth birthday. Her family sent another age-progressed picture of her in the mail."

"I'm sorry, buddy. Her family is still grieving and important dates like this one bring the loss back."

"I know, Marcus. I understand that. But what good does it do to send me the pictures? I can't bring them back. Why won't they drop the reminders? It's been fifteen years."

His heart hurt for his friend. "If the family stops sending the reminders, it's like they have moved on and forgotten their loved ones. The family doesn't want to let go of them."

Mason dragged a hand down his face. "I don't want Nicole hurt by this. Maybe I should talk to the family, tell them how I've turned my life around, and ask them to lay off."

"Won't do any good, my friend. They have to forgive you and heal enough themselves to stop sending the pictures voluntarily." He reached over and laid his hand on the other man's shoulder, squeezed. "You don't have to keep the reminders, but when you receive them, pray for the family's healing and for your own. No matter how much pain they cause, you can't give in to bitterness and anger. If those emotions take root, they will affect everything in your life. You can't change them, Mason, or control what they do. The only control you have is over your own reaction. The rest is out of your hands. Don't let them derail what you've accomplished and the progress you've made, the new life you have."

"How did you become so wise?"

A snort. "Hard experience. Why don't we talk about more pleasant things? Are you taking Nicole to dinner tonight?"

"I was afraid to make plans. Haven't been in the best mood since yesterday."

"Call her. Do something special for her and yourself."

A smile curved Mason's lips. "Didn't know you offered advice for the lovelorn as well as words of wisdom."

Marcus grinned. "Pastors are multipurpose counselors. This advice, though, is coming from a man who considers you one of his best friends."

"I think I'll follow your prescription tonight and ask Nicole to dinner. Thanks for letting me vent about the other stuff."

"That's what friends are for, Mase."

"I'll think about your advice." Mason stood, carried his plate to the dishwasher. "I need to go. I'll send you the estimate later tonight." He grinned. "After my date with Nicole. If board approves changing out the pipes, the parsonage won't have water for a couple days. You can stay with me if you want."

"Appreciate the offer, Mase. I'll let you know if I need to take you up on it." As he watched the construction worker drive away from the parsonage, Marcus's cell phone rang.

53

He glanced at the screen, eyebrows raising. "Lang."

"How are you, Marcus?"

Hearing Brent Maddox's voice was a surprise. If anything, he'd expected a call from Zane Murphy, but not from Fortress Security's CEO. "A little tired. Had an interesting night."

"So I hear from Zane. Glad you were on hand to help. Did you get a piece of the creep who roughed up your friend?"

"Unfortunately, not. He shoved me against the wall and ran out the front door. I could have chased him down, but I was more worried about Paige than I was catching him."

"Understandable."

"What do you need, Brent?"

"A favor."

"Ask."

"Would you be willing to serve as a counselor for my operatives and PSI trainees in Otter Creek?"

"Absolutely. It's a small favor to ask considering what you did for me."

"You'll be compensated, of course."

"Don't care about that."

"Figured that would be the case. You're still getting paid." He named a retainer fee that surpassed his monthly income from his pastor's salary.

Marcus blinked. "Are you serious?"

"Business is booming."

Must be. Good grief. "It's not necessary to pay me, Brent. I'm glad to help."

"You're a Fortress consultant. You will be paid for your services."

Knowing he would lose an argument with the stubborn SEAL, he changed the subject. "How is your family?"

"Fantastic. Rowan is keeping busy with the coffee shop. Alexa is doing great in school, and taking ballet and karate. She knocked me off balance and took me to the ground the other day."

Marcus chuckled even as a longing for a family of his own welled up in his heart. "You must be proud of her."

"Being a father is the best thing that's ever happened to me besides being a SEAL and marrying Rowan. So, tell me about Paige Jensen."

"She runs the community center in Otter Creek."

"Rio tells me you're interested in this woman."

"He's correct. I've been interested in dating her for a while."

"You should have called me to run a background check on her."

Marcus flinched at the stark reminder of the past he'd rather forget. "I know. Our first date is tonight."

"How long have you known her?"

"Since I moved to Otter Creek. Paige and her grandmother are members of Cornerstone Church, and they've lived in Otter Creek their whole lives."

"It's probably not going to be a problem, but you can't take chances."

"I understand." Hated that it was necessary. "If things become serious, I'll have to tell Paige the truth."

"Only if you know beyond a doubt that she can be trusted with your life, Marcus."

CHAPTER EIGHT

Paige's phone chimed. She opened her eyes, blinked at the glaring afternoon sunshine pouring through the blinds. Grabbing her phone, she read her message, and smiled. Marcus checking on her.

Instead of replying by text, she called. "I'm okay, Marcus. Did you sleep?"

"About four hours. How's the head?"

"Still hurts some," she admitted. "At least my vision isn't blurry now. Would you mind picking me up at the B & B? Nick called and said the center will have to remain closed at least until tomorrow, maybe the day after."

"No problem."

"Do you know what's going on with Mason?"

A pause. "Why do you ask?"

"Nicole is worried about him. He's been moody the last two days. She's afraid she did something to make him angry."

"She didn't do anything wrong. If you talk to Nicole, tell her to ask Mason about it."

The knots in her stomach loosened. "He talked to you."

"He did."

"I'm glad. So, what have you been doing since you left here?"

"You didn't ask for details." He sounded surprised.

"You're a pastor and counselor. People trust you with confidences. If you can tell me details, you will."

"Thank you for understanding."

"Back to my question. What have you been doing since you left the B & B?"

"I mopped a flooded bathroom, ate lunch with Mason, stopped by the Wilder house, and visited with Nancy Kirkland. I'm on the way to the hospital to visit some ailing church members. After that, Nick asked me to stop by the police station."

"The detective is supposed to come by here in a few minutes for follow up questions."

"Do you want me to swing by the B & B first, then go to the hospital?"

"You don't have to do that, Marcus. I'm not afraid to talk to Nick by myself."

"Is your grandmother with you?"

A smile curved her lips. "No, she and her friends went to a movie and then they're going to dinner." Her grandmother and her friends planned to watch an action film. No one would guess Gram was a closet commando.

"Do your guests need an innkeeper in residence?"

"They checked out right after lunch. We don't have anyone booked for a few days. The group that was coming in canceled on us."

"I'll come to the B & B. We'll talk to Nick together, then I'll take you with me on the hospital visits. We'll go to the council meeting from there. If you get tired at the hospital, you can wait for me in one of the lounges. How does that sound?"

"Like a good plan. I'll see you in a few minutes."

Otter Creek wasn't that large. She needed to hurry if she was going to freshen up. By the time Marcus arrived at the front door, Paige had raced through a shower, applied light makeup, and changed clothes since she wouldn't be returning to the B & B until after her dinner date. The thought of that long hoped-for date sent a zing of excitement through her blood.

Paige opened the door, smiled at the man she'd dreamed about during her nap.

"Hi." Marcus leaned down, kissed her cheek. "You look beautiful."

Oh, boy. Dating this man was going to be fun. "Thank you. Would you like a soft drink or more coffee to go?"

"I wouldn't turn down a bottle of water."

"Follow me. Do you want the water cold or room temperature?"

"Cold, please." Marcus trailed her to the kitchen. "Do you have any preference on restaurants for dinner?"

"I've been wanting to try the new steakhouse. What do you think?"

"Sounds perfect unless you prefer me to take you to a restaurant out of town."

Paige grabbed two bottles of water and an apple in case Marcus needed a snack before dinner. "The minute we step out of this house together, rumors will start flying around town. People will talk no matter where we have dinner."

"It doesn't bother you?"

"I do mind that people will also be talking about me in connection to the attack and Van's murder at the center. But going on a date with you? No, it doesn't bother me at all if they talk. Being with you makes me happy, Marcus."

His gaze softened. "I didn't want to add pressure at the early stages of this relationship."

"Can't be helped. I'll handle the extra scrutiny."

Marcus cupped her cheek with his palm. "We'll handle it, Paige. If the pressure bothers you, tell me. I'll do what I can to alleviate the problem."

Vendetta

"Ha. Not going to happen. I hoped for a chance with you for more than six years. I'm not backing off because of a little notoriety."

"Good." He bent his head, brushed his lips gently over hers. "Come on. I think I heard a car door slam. That might be Nick."

Whew! The preacher packed a punch without any effort. She drew in a careful breath as she trailed him to the front of the house.

A moment later, the doorbell rang and she opened the door to admit Nick Santana.

His smile widened when he saw Marcus. "Well, this is a surprise. I'd planned to talk to you in a couple hours, Marcus."

"Decided to save myself a trip."

The detective's eyes twinkled. "Not sure I believe your presence here is a matter of convenience."

"Come in, Nick." Paige waved him inside. "Would you like some water or a soft drink? We also have iced tea if you prefer that."

"Water, please."

"Here." She handed him the bottle in her hand. "Living room okay for your questions?"

"Will we be interrupted by guests?"

She shook her head. "The family we've been hosting checked out today, the other guests due to arrive this afternoon canceled, and Gram is with her friends at the movies."

"Living room is fine, then." He waggled the manila folder in his hand. "Good thing I brought both of your statements with me."

"Now who's capitalizing on convenience?" Marcus broke the seal on his water.

Nick shrugged. "I see you several times a day. Otter Creek isn't the size of Nashville or Knoxville. I figured there was a good chance I might run into you." He chose the recliner.

Marcus sat beside Paige on the loveseat. "There are a couple things I need to tell you before you begin the questions."

A shuttered look settled on the detective's face. "Go ahead."

"I stopped by the Wilder home and spoke to Van's father. I wanted to offer my condolences. While I was there, he asked me to officiate the service for his son."

"Oh, Marcus." Paige's heart hurt for the man at her side. She laid her hand over his, squeezed. "That's two funerals in one week."

He raised their clasped hands and kissed the back of hers. "Can't be helped."

"I'm glad you can offer help and comfort during this time." Nick pulled out his notebook. "What's the second thing you wanted to tell me?" His lips curved slightly. "Although I can probably guess." His gaze dropped to their clasped hands.

"Paige and I are dating."

"I'm happy for both of you, but why tell me that news?"

"Feel free to mention that Paige and I are involved in casual conversations around town."

Paige's brows knitted. What was up with that?

A snort from the detective. "Have you ever known me to be a gossip?"

"Nope, but I'm hoping you'll make an exception in this case."

Nick was silent a moment, then, "You want word to spread so Paige's attacker knows he'll have to tangle with you when he comes after her again."

Wait. When her attacker came after her again? "Hold up. Are you telling me I'm still in danger?"

"I'm afraid so."

"But why? I can't think of anyone who wants to hurt me. I was in the wrong place at the wrong time." Wasn't she? From the expression on Nick's face, he wasn't convinced. Oh, man. Definitely not what she wanted to hear. And what about Gram? Was she in danger?

"Did you hear anything that stood out last night at the center besides the metal on metal sound?"

"Like?"

"Anything." His gaze was intense.

Paige glanced at Marcus, not sure if she should say what she was thinking.

"No matter how odd or strange you think it is, tell him," he murmured.

She turned to Nick. "This is going to sound stupid, but I thought I heard a cough. When I saw Dalton, I assumed he coughed while he was retrieving his backpack."

Beside her, Marcus stiffened.

"A cough." Nick frowned. "You heard the cough when you were in your office?"

"That's right."

"You're sure?"

"Sound carries in that gym. The builders didn't bother insulating the walls. Guess they figured the gym would be noisy anyway and no one would notice." Either that or the builders were best buddies with Mayor Parks and followed in his cheapskate footsteps. "When it's quiet, I can hear conversations in the locker rooms from my office."

"How did Van die?" Marcus asked.

"Shot once through the heart."

Shock rolled through Paige. "How is that possible? I would have heard the shot."

"Silencer." Marcus's voice was grim.

Nick's eyebrows shot up. "That's my guess. Keeping secrets, Marcus?"

"Plenty."

Hmm. Something there. Paige wasn't sure what she was hearing, but she had a feeling the man who had caught her interest wasn't talking about confidences from a counseling session.

"Any you can share?"

A sigh from the man beside her. "I'm familiar with weapons."

"Yeah, I figured that much from the short conversation you had with Rio when you were shot at the church. Can you tell me more?"

"No."

"If I decide it's relevant to my case, I'll have to insist."

Marcus inclined his head, but remained silent.

Acknowledgment but no agreement. Nick wouldn't be happy about that. Hopefully, Marcus would be able to tell her these personal secrets at some point. "Any more questions, Nick?"

"Did you think of anything you want to add to your statement?"

She shook her head. "What happens now?"

"I find Van's killer and the man who attacked you."

Paige stilled. "It's the same person, right?"

"Maybe."

Goosebumps surged over her body.

CHAPTER NINE

Marcus laced his fingers with Paige's and walked with her into the hospital. As they crossed the lobby to the elevator, he felt eyes on them, followed by the excited whispers.

Good. Let them talk. The sooner word got around he was involved with Paige, the better he'd feel. He didn't want to alarm her, but he was certain her attacker would try again. The question was, when and where? A question that bothered him more was why Paige was a target. Marcus wanted to believe she was in the wrong place at the wrong time, much like he had been seven years ago, but he couldn't quite convince himself that was the case.

He couldn't keep Paige with him all the time. Both of them had jobs and he wouldn't cage her. He had to trust she would take precautions.

His jaw tightened. Didn't mean he wouldn't give her tips to minimize the risk. He'd probably make her angry with him if he offered suggestions. Too bad. Sharing tips based on experience would make him feel better.

As the elevator rose to the fifth floor for his first stop, he glanced at Paige. "You aren't going to ask me questions?"

"You'll tell me what I need to know when you're ready. Have to admit, though, the curiosity is about to get the better of me."

"I have a good reason for the secrecy." Man, the last thing he wanted was to scare her off. Marcus never thought this conversation would be necessary. The attacker had forced his hand. He couldn't wait for the perfect timing to take the next step in their relationship. There never would be a perfect time. He also hated the real possibility his past could endanger the woman who had fascinated him for long months.

"When you're ready, Marcus."

In a perfect world, he'd never be ready and wouldn't have to tell Paige the truth. This wasn't a perfect world.

The elevator stopped and the gleaming doors slid open. He steered her to the left toward Ruth Rollins' room. He knocked, smiled when the querulous voice told him to enter.

"Hello, Ruth. How are you today?" He walked further into the room to see the white-haired aunt of Otter Creek's police chief covered with the white sheet and blanket to her waist. A metal frame surrounded her arm and held pins in place. Shew! He hurt just looking at her arm.

"Ready to get out of this bed." Her scowl morphed into a surprised smile when she saw Paige. "Hello, my dear. What a pleasant surprise."

"I hope it's all right that I tagged along with Marcus to visit you."

"Of course. Please, sit down." She waved to the chairs at her bedside. "Ethan just went to the cafeteria for me. I had a craving for ice cream." She sneered. "The menu options are lacking in this place."

"How is the arm?" Marcus sat beside Paige.

"It's fine. I don't know why Dr. Anderson won't spring me. It's not like I don't have experience with broken bones, you know."

"I remember. Has Ethan forbidden you from riding another skateboard?"

A scowl from the best-selling mystery writer. "Of course. He never lets me do anything fun these days."

"I heard that." The police chief's voice rumbled from the doorway. Ethan Blackhawk, a six foot four Native American, crossed to her bedside in a few strides, a container of chocolate ice cream in his hand. "Keep it up, Aunt Ruth, and I'll be eating the ice cream myself." He nodded to Marcus and Paige. "Thanks for stopping by to visit my favorite troublemaker."

"Hand over the chocolate." Ruth held out her hand.

He opened the container and handed it to her along with a spoon. Ethan turned to Paige. "How are you feeling, Paige?"

"Better. Slight headache. Throat is still sore. Grateful to be alive to complain about a few aches and pains."

"Wait a minute." Ruth's spoon hovered over the treat. "I've been out of circulation for a couple days. What happened?"

"Paige was attacked at the community center last night." Marcus tightened his grip on her hand. "The guy choked her."

"What did he want?"

"I don't know." She grimaced. "He wasn't interested in talking."

Ruth frowned at Ethan. "You didn't tell me about this."

A snort from the chief. "I don't tell you a lot of things. Somehow you find out anyway."

"How are Serena and Lucas?" Paige asked.

"Perfect," he said, pride and love evident in his expression and his voice.

"Since Ethan won't tell me about what's happening at the community center," another frown at her nephew before she returned her gaze to Paige, "Why don't you tell me about you and Marcus." Her eager gaze fell on their entwined hands. "That is bound to be a good story."

Marcus chuckled. Good grief. The woman was determined to get a story of some kind. Might as well be one he wanted to spread around town anyway.

Would the story end up in Ruth's next Olivia Tutweiler mystery? He was a big fan of her mysteries, but wasn't sure he wanted his personal life included in a best-selling novel, even with the names changed. Too much risk. "This is new, Ruth. In fact, I'm taking her on a date for the first time after the council meeting tonight."

Ethan growled. "Don't remind me about that meeting. In my opinion, the council meets entirely too many times a year."

"Can't argue with that. I hate those meetings. Seems like it's just a platform to tout Mayor Parks' latest agenda," Paige said. "Ruth, there's nothing much to tell yet so there isn't a story to share."

The woman scooped up a spoonful of ice cream. "I don't believe that for a minute. I'm an old woman. Indulge me. I want details."

Paige glanced at Marcus, an exasperated look in her eyes. He winked at her and turned to Ruth. "Like Paige said, there isn't much of a story yet. I've been interested in her for a while, but held off asking her out." With good reason. "When I walked into the center last night and saw the attacker with his hands around Paige's throat, I realized I'd been foolish to delay asking her to go on a date with me. If I had been a minute or two later, I wouldn't have had the chance. We're friends, Ruth. Have been for six years. I didn't want to mess that up."

"I can understand that. What about you, Paige? Anything to add?" Her sharp gaze narrowed. "Wait. You haven't dated anyone since I moved to Otter Creek. Is Marcus the reason for that?"

A soft laugh from the woman at Marcus's side. "You are one smart lady, Ruth. I'm beginning to think no secrets are safe from you."

Triumph shone in her eyes. "I wish other people would keep that in mind." She slid that gaze to her nephew who rolled his eyes.

"Is there anything we can do for you before we leave?" Marcus asked. "More ice cream maybe?"

"No, thanks. I plan to have Ethan run all my errands while I'm laid up with this broken arm. After all, I can't have Serena running everywhere with my great-nephew in tow."

"Good plan. What will you do about your writing? I assume your keyboarding will be limited for a while."

"Ethan bought me a digital recorder and Gladys agreed to type my dictation into my computer. We'll see if I can create that way. If not, I'll have to investigate computer programs that will transcribe for me." She scowled at her arm. "I'd rather not have to use the second option. It's bound to be an exercise in frustration teaching the thing to recognize my speech patterns. I have a book deadline looming in four weeks. I don't have time to fiddle with a computer program."

"If Gladys can't type for you, let me know." Paige gently squeezed Ruth's fingers. "I'll be happy to help out. Besides, that would give me a sneak peek at your next book."

Ruth's eyes narrowed. "You would be sworn to secrecy."

"I'm a vault when it comes to keeping secrets."

Marcus hoped that was the absolute truth because when he told Paige his secrets, she would hold his life in the palm of her hands. He turned, caught Ethan's somber gaze on him.

His heart skipped a beat, then thudded madly against his ribcage. No. Ethan couldn't know the truth. Could he?

Something in the police chief's gaze told Marcus that Ethan knew more than he should. Was there a leak in his security or was Ethan just that good?

He should touch base with Zane to make sure there wasn't a problem. Before he and Paige left, Marcus prayed with Ruth and Ethan, then escorted Paige from the room.

The police chief followed them into the hallway. He handed Marcus and Paige a business card each. His cell phone number was written on the back. "If you need me, call." His gaze lingered on Marcus.

How was it possible? He'd been so careful. Brent had given him a list of rules and he'd followed them exactly. Had he slipped? "Thank you. I hope it won't be necessary."

"As do I." He turned to Paige. "You notice anything odd or feel uneasy for any reason, call me. If I'm not close, I'll know who is. I don't care if you're just seeing shadows when nothing is wrong. Trust your instincts, Paige. Keep your phone on you at all times, even in the house or car. Do not make the same mistake you made last night and leave your phone somewhere else. Always lock your vehicle. Check under it and through the windows before you get in. Don't work late again by yourself. Until we catch this clown, you can't take chances with your safety."

"Yes, sir."

The corners of his mouth tugged upward. "Sorry if I sound overbearing. I'm concerned about you. How is Jo handling this?"

"She's taking it in stride. Gram is a rock. You might want to warn Nick that if he doesn't make some progress soon, she'll be hunting him down to find out why not."

Amusement lit his eyes. "I'll pass the word along. Has Jo been having more problems?"

Paige wrinkled her nose. "More pressure from the developer. They're not giving up easily."

"A lot of money is at stake. Tell her to call me or drop by the station if things don't improve soon."

"I'll do that. Thanks, Ethan."

With a nod, the policeman returned to his aunt's room.

As they walked to the opposite end of the hall to visit his next congregation member, Marcus asked, "What's going on with Jo?"

"A land developer is pressuring Gram to sell out so they can build the shopping center the whole town is buzzing about. Gram is refusing. Her father built the B & B so it's not only a business to her, but a family legacy, one she's giving to me when she dies."

"Are they threatening her?"

"Oh, no. Nothing like that. They keep upping the amount of money they're willing to pay for the house and land. Apparently, Gram is the lone holdout and since she owns so many acres, without her property, the project is dead in the water."

Marcus whistled softly. "I had no idea that was going on. The scuttlebutt I heard had the project all but approved."

"That's Mayor Parks talking. He wants the project passed because of the potential tax revenue to fill the town coffers." A wry smile curved her lips. "I don't have proof, but I think the mayor will profit from the deal."

Parks always had his own best interests at heart first before considering Otter Creek's benefit. "The nearest shopping mall is only thirty minutes away," Marcus pointed out. "No one I've heard discussing it has complained about the drive."

"True, but the revenue is going to another town and county."

The next four visits went without difficulty. On the way to his truck, Marcus's phone vibrated with an incoming text. This one was from Brent. *She's clear. Best of luck.*

He hadn't expected otherwise although Marcus was pleased his gut instinct was on target. Once he was back at the parsonage, he would call Zane and see if his bots had flagged trouble. Marcus had more than himself to be worried about now.

CHAPTER TEN

A few minutes before seven, Paige and Marcus found seats near the front of the meeting room reserved for the town council. Paige was surprised at how many people were packed into the room. Usually these meetings were attended by the council and anyone with business to present. She estimated more than a hundred people were crammed into this space. The usual number was closer to twenty.

As she scanned the audience, she spotted many of her friends and neighbors, including those who had property of interest to the developer. An air of excitement filled the room as evidenced by the loud conversations and laughter, and the animated body language. Paige, Marcus, and Ethan were the only somber people in the place. Even the council members appeared to be chipper.

Marcus turned and surveyed the audience. "They act like the project approval is all but assured."

"I know. And that worries me. I'm afraid the pressure on Gram will increase." From the expressions of the people with the most to gain, they might join in trying to persuade Gram to sign over her property.

Mayor Parks pounded the gavel twice and called the meeting to order. For the first thirty minutes, mundane business matters were addressed and resolutions passed.

"The next item on the agenda is funding for the community center." Mayor Parks glanced up to scan the room. His gaze widened when Paige stood with her copies of the budget and her explanation for the requested increase. "Ms. Jensen, I'm surprised to see you here this evening. I was prepared to postpone the center's funding discussion until the next session. I understand you were injured last night."

"I'm ready to proceed Mr. Mayor." Without giving him a chance to put her off for the third month in a row, Paige launched into her explanation for the proposed budget for the center. At the end of her presentation, she said, "The community center needs another full-time employee. We're open thirteen hours a day, six days a week, and five hours on Sunday. As the only full-time employee, if my part-time help can't work his shift, I have to cover those hours. If I don't, the center is closed."

Parks sighed. "There isn't money in the budget to add to your bottom line, Ms. Jensen. That's why this shopping center is the perfect solution to all our money woes. However, from your explanation, this problem appears to be more of a time management issue than a money issue. Perhaps your education should have included classes in management. If you're unhappy with your job, you're welcome to seek employment with better hours."

Her fists clenched. "I have a bachelor's degree in business administration as well as a Master's degree in the same field. Mr. Mayor, I love my job. The center is the heart of the Otter Creek community. We have classes and activities all throughout the day, activities you and your grandchildren have participated in. We serve as the town's gym since there isn't a privately-owned facility in the county, a fact which you know since you arrive at seven o'clock five days a week. We also have senior activities during the day to keep our older citizens healthy in body and mind. But the fact is it's unreasonable to expect me to work over eighty hours a week. I daresay the only people in this room who work those kinds of hours are Marcus Lang and Ethan Blackhawk. You don't work those hours and you've had three vacations this year. I haven't had a vacation in five years because there was no one to cover at the center."

The mayor's cheeks flushed. "Ms. Jensen, this discussion isn't about me."

"I was making a point of comparison, Mr. Mayor. The children and teens at the center need another full-time adult, preferably a male."

"You have many men who volunteer, including the police chief and Pastor Lang," he pointed out.

"Yes, sir, we do. I'm thankful for every one of the men who volunteer their time. But they have responsibilities elsewhere. They can't be available all the time when the center's doors are open. The kids know I love them, Mr. Mayor. However, they need a male role model who is consistently on site. Sometimes they just need a father figure to talk to. I can't be that for them."

"A fact well documented since one of the punk teenagers attacked you last night." Parks' eyes glittered.

Gasps were heard around the room.

Paige leaned closer to the microphone. "I can assure you my attacker was a full-grown male. It was not one of my teenagers."

"That's not the way I heard it," said one of the female council members.

"Whoever told you that was wrong." She smiled. "I ought to know. I was there, after all."

A wave of laughter swept through the room, alleviating some of the tension.

"We'll discuss your proposal, Ms. Jensen. Unless new funding comes through, the most you can hope for is another part-time helper. If you really want to help the center, talk to your grandmother. She holds the key piece of property for the shopping center. The developer is promising a fair price for the land. She will be well compensated and I'm sure a real estate agent will find her a beautiful site to build a new bed and breakfast."

The applause breaking out in the room had Paige's jaw clenching. Once the noise died down, she said clearly, "That is my grandmother's decision. I will support her, whatever her choice. Mr. Mayor, council members, thank you for seriously looking at the community center's budget and my request for hiring more help at the community's heartbeat. The citizens of Otter Creek will be benefited by having their community center better staffed."

By the time she returned to her seat beside Marcus, Paige was shaking and her headache was back in spades.

Marcus clasped her hand and squeezed gently. "Great job," he murmured as the council moved on to other business.

She felt as though she had wasted her time. Mayor Parks wasn't interested in increasing the center's funding. His only agenda was pushing the land sale to the developer and practically blackmailing her to persuade Gram to give up her family home in favor of progress.

When the time came for questions from the floor, a handful of people jumped up and approached the microphone to ask clarifying questions about the possible shopping center. The mayor seemed to have a great deal of information to share. So where was the developer? Why wasn't he attending this meeting to answer questions?

All Paige wanted to do was go to dinner with Marcus. Didn't know if she could eat after all this because of the knot in her stomach, but she wanted a glass of cold tea and time with the handsome man at her side anyway.

Finally, the meeting ended. As friends and neighbors filed from the room, several stopped to talk to Paige and Marcus. No one asked about the B & B or encouraged her to consider selling out, thankfully. Many were curious about the attack and how Paige was feeling. Some wanted to know when the center would reopen, a question she would love to have answered herself. If she wasn't out too late, she might call Nick and ask when she could go back to work.

Fifteen minutes after the meeting adjourned, Marcus unlocked his truck and helped Paige into the passenger seat. "Are you still interested in dinner tonight? If you're too tired, we can pick up something from Delaney's and go back to the B & B."

She shook her head. "I've been looking forward to dinner with you for a long time."

He looked skeptical, but nodded. "All right. If you start to feel worse, tell me. I want to spend time with you, but not at the expense of your health."

"How did you know I'm not feeling the best?"

"Your eyes." He circled the hood and climbed behind the wheel. "You did a great job tonight, Paige. I didn't know you were working so many hours a week, and I don't think anyone else in that room did either."

"I'm not the only one who works long hours." She slid a glance his direction. "You do the same thing without any help. At least I have Caleb to give me some assistance."

"I knew when I accepted the pastorate at Cornerstone what I was in for. I'm just thankful that not all weeks are like this one is turning out to be."

"How is Mrs. Kirkland?"

"Missing her mate, but happy that Jeb is no longer in pain."

"How long were they married?"

"Sixty years, a record I would love to match one day."

"Me, too." She laid her hand on his arm. "Thank you for going with me tonight, Marcus. Knowing you were there helped."

At the steakhouse, he spoke to the hostess a moment. She nodded and pulled out the menus. "Follow me, please."

What was that about? Paige glanced at Marcus. Instead of an explanation, she got a wink. Huh. Guess she'd find out soon enough. The hostess took them to the back-corner table.

Nice. They were in public, but the corner table was in a dimly lit portion of the restaurant and gave them a semblance of privacy. Marcus seated her, then sat with his back to the wall, catty-cornered to her.

Perfect. With this seating arrangements, they would be able to talk without having trouble hearing each other. Paige glanced around the restaurant, noticed that several of the patrons were watching them with avid interest. "We're attracting attention."

"Does it bother you?"

"Ha! Not a chance. The sooner the single women in town know you're off the market, the better."

He burst into laughter, his eyes twinkling. "You think so, huh?"

"Absolutely. Female hearts will be breaking before midnight."

"I needed that laugh. Thanks."

"Anytime. Now, what looks good?"

"Besides you? Everything."

Her cheeks burned. Oh, boy. This was indeed going to be fun. "You are turning out to be a charmer."

"I have my moments. Order whatever you want. I bet your appetite isn't quite up to par yet."

"Hmm. Charming and smart, a hard combination to beat." She skimmed through the menu and chose something light. Once they gave their orders to the waitress, a string of busybodies stopped by their table to greet them. Paige wanted to laugh, but restrained herself. The interest was more than obvious though no one dared to ask the question burning in their eyes.

After their orders were brought to the table, Marcus covered her hand with his and asked the blessing over the food.

At her first bite, Paige sighed, delighted with the taste of the perfectly seasoned grilled chicken breast. "No wonder this restaurant is so popular."

"I'm glad you suggested this place. This steak is practically melting in my mouth."

The interested patrons of the restaurant kept their distance long enough for Paige and Marcus to finish their meal. When the waitress brought out refills of their iced tea, the parade started again as more people arrived and others who hadn't spoken to them earlier stopped by on their way out of the restaurant.

By the time Paige finished her tea, she was more than ready to leave. Good grief. If she'd known the town residents would be so nosy, she would have suggested eating someplace out of town.

When Marcus cranked the truck, he glanced at her. "I'm sorry. I didn't realize we would generate so much interest. I guess I should have insisted we go over to Cherry Hill for dinner. At least there, you would have been able to take more than two bites before having to answer questions."

"Next time we'll do that. Actually, it was probably good that I ate slowly. My stomach was in a knot after the council meeting. At least this way, I was able to eat a whole meal and enjoy it. We'll have to go back to Tennessee Steakhouse when we're not such a hot gossip commodity in town."

By the time Marcus turned onto her street, Paige was ready to drop. She didn't think she'd ever been this tired in her life, but she didn't want the evening to end. Maybe

Marcus would like to sit on the porch swing for a while. Gram wouldn't be home for at least another hour, maybe more. She and her buddies loved to go to Delaney's after a movie and drink coffee together.

As she thought about how to propose an extended evening with her date, she noticed a strange orange glow lighting the night sky. "What is that?"

Marcus glanced where she pointed. The truck surged forward. "Fire."

CHAPTER ELEVEN

Marcus's hands tightened on the steering wheel as he raced to the B & B. "Call the fire department." He slowed for the turn into the driveway and parked on the grass, leaving room for the fire trucks.

Paige pulled her phone from her pocket and threw open the door. She sprinted toward the inn.

"Paige, no!" Marcus raced after her. What if this was a trap? She could walk into an ambush.

"I have to make sure Gram isn't here." She didn't slow her stride as she skirted the corner and ran toward the detached garage.

Marcus caught her and stopped the frenzied race to the structure. "The inn isn't on fire. Look." He pointed toward the grove of trees at the back of B & B.

"Oh, man. The apple orchard." She called 911 to report the fire, then said, "If Gram's car is in the garage, I need to check on her. She would have been out here if she was able."

"Agreed. Let me check for her car."

She frowned. "Why?"

"In case this is more than a fire." He cupped her cheek. Her skin was so soft. "I want you safe." He led her to the garage and positioned her against the wall. "Stay here."

Wishing he was armed, Marcus covered the twenty yards separating him from the window. He peered inside, breathed a sigh of relief. Empty. He returned to Paige. "She's not here."

She sagged against the wall. "Thank goodness."

"Come here." When she straightened, he wrapped his arms around her and held Paige until her trembling subsided. "Let's sit on the porch and wait for the fire department. We'll call Jo from there."

He sat on the wooden swing with her and draped his arm around her shoulders. Warmth wrapped around his heart when she leaned into his side as she talked to her grandmother. He was so blessed to gain the interest of such a beautiful, kind woman.

At the end of her call, the fire department's pumper truck turned into the driveway and raced to the orchard's access road. From the size of the blaze, Marcus wasn't sure Otter Creek's fire department could handle the flames alone. He wouldn't be surprised if they called in another engine from a neighboring town.

Ten minutes later, Jo parked in front of the house. "Gram!" Paige met her grandmother at the foot of the stairs and the women embraced.

Marcus stood by the stair post, wanting to be close if either woman needed him. He scanned the area. No obvious signs of someone lurking in the darkness. Two incidents involving Paige within a 24-hour period wasn't a coincidence. He prayed his past hadn't caused trouble for the Jensens. Yeah, calling Zane at the first opportunity was a definite priority.

"You're not hurt?" Jo set Paige away from her to see for herself if Paige had injuries.

"I'm fine. When Marcus and I returned from dinner, we saw the orange glow. I'm afraid to find out how many trees we lost."

"We'll plant more. I'll start looking online tomorrow for nurseries with the right apple trees."

"But it won't be the trees your grandfather planted."

Jo patted her arm. "Those trees are growing on the left side of the orchard. The burning trees are the ones your father and grandfather planted when we expanded the orchard. As long as you're safe, the rest will take care of itself, Paige." She turned to Marcus. "So, you and my granddaughter went to dinner together."

He stilled. "Yes, ma'am. Should I have talked to you first?"

"Don't be ridiculous. You're both adults and I trust you. I think it's past time for this to happen. You and Paige have been circling each other for too long. You deserve to be happy, Marcus, and so does Paige."

A police SUV parked behind Jo's car. Nick Santana climbed out and jogged toward them. "I heard about the fire on the police radio. You okay?"

"We're fine, Nick." Jo sighed. "I'm afraid my apple orchard isn't."

"Do you know how the fire started?"

"We've only been here a few minutes," Marcus said. "Paige and I saw the orange glow in the sky when we arrived. We called the fire department and Jo."

"There hasn't been a storm or lightning strikes tonight. Is there equipment in the orchard that might spark a blaze?"

Jo shook her head. "The highest tech thing we own is the trucks we use to collect apples."

The fabulous dinner Marcus had enjoyed at the steakhouse now felt like a rock in the pit of his stomach. From his friend's body language and questions, Nick suspected arson.

He moved to Paige's side and threaded his fingers through hers. "How soon will you know if this is arson?"

"The investigator will inspect the damage in the morning. If I'm not available, either Rod or Stella will be here."

Marcus squeezed Paige's hand. Both of the detectives were the best in the business according to his friends from Personal Security International and Fortress. "Thanks for coming, Nick."

A nod. "Did you notice anything out of the ordinary when you arrived?"

Paige frowned. "I was too worried about Gram to look around. We checked the garage for Gram's car, then waited on the porch for the fire department."

"Would you mind if I looked through the house to be sure everything is secure?"

Jo extended her hand with her key. "Go ahead."

"When I'm finished, you and Paige can go through with me to see if anything has been disturbed." Nick turned to Marcus. "You'll stay here with them?"

"Of course." No way was he leaving them out here alone. None of the firefighters were close enough to help if someone tried to hurt them. After Nick walked into the house with his weapon drawn, Marcus turned to Jo. "How was the movie?"

"Fun. I love movies based on superheroes. The good guys always win in the end."

"Where did you go for dinner?" Paige asked.

Marcus shrugged out of his jacket and draped it over her shoulders, hoping the extra cover would quiet the continuous shudders wracking her body. She smiled at him and turned back to her grandmother.

"Delaney's. We thought about going to the steakhouse, but figured the place would be full of people. We didn't want to wait a long time to be seated."

Her granddaughter grinned. "Marcus took me to the steakhouse. You and your friends need to go next time. The food is amazing."

"And the company?" Jo's eyes twinkled.

"Better than the food."

Nick returned, his expression grim. "Paige, come with me. I have something to show you."

The blood in Marcus's veins ran cold.

"We'll all go," Jo said. "I assume we shouldn't touch anything."

"Yes, ma'am."

"How many rooms are involved?"

"Only Paige's room."

That rock in the pit of his stomach grew into the size of a boulder. Based on Nick's face when he returned for Paige, this wasn't going to be good.

On the second floor, Nick turned left and led them to the end of the hall. "Remember not to touch anything. I'll need to search for prints and anything else the perp left behind."

At the doorway, Paige hesitated, glanced around. "I don't see anything wrong."

"In the bathroom."

She walked inside the room and headed for the door to the left with Marcus a step behind. Whatever she would see, he didn't want her facing it alone.

Paige crossed the threshold and pulled up short. All color drained from her cheeks as one hand drifted to her throat.

Careful to angle away from the door frame, Marcus stepped into the bathroom. He laid his hands on her shoulders and read the threat written on the mirror. *Next time, you die.*

CHAPTER TWELVE

"Are you okay?" Marcus asked Paige, his voice soft. She sat at the breakfast bar and her skin seemed almost translucent. Although he longed to end her problem, he couldn't, he didn't know who was targeting Paige. His inability to do anything but offer comfort frustrated him.

She glanced up from her mug of tea, a ghost of a smile curving her lips. "Not really. You should go home, Marcus. You must be exhausted."

Really? She was worried about him after the blows she kept taking from this unknown threat? He cupped the side of her neck, feathered his thumb over her jaw. "I'm not leaving you." Something inside him rebelled at Paige and Jo staying here alone overnight. What if this guy came back? Two defenseless women against a man who already showed his willingness to hurt an innocent woman? Not good odds for two of his favorite people surviving the next encounter. He couldn't let that happen.

"Are you serious?"

"Very."

"I appreciate the offer but you can't stay. This is a small town. People will talk, especially since we're a hot item on the gossip circuit. We have to guard your reputation, Marcus. Your ministry matters and I don't want to compromise that."

"I have the logistics worked out and Nick's permission as long as no one enters your room until he finishes processing the scene."

Curiosity replaced fear in her eyes. "You are a man of secrets."

More than she knew. "This is a good one and won't remain a secret for long." At that moment, the doorbell rang. "Stay here."

"The man who attacked me won't ring the bell for admittance," she pointed out.

"I'd rather be sure you're safe. Indulge me."

She grasped her mug. "I'll wait here. This time."

He grinned. Oh, yeah. Paige was sweet, but not a pushover. Marcus checked the peephole. Perfect timing.

He opened the door to admit Nicole Copeland and Mason Kincaid. "Thank you for coming at such short notice."

"Where's Paige?" Nicole set her purse beside the sofa and shrugged out of her jacket.

"Kitchen. She doesn't know about the arrangements. I thought this would be a good surprise for her."

"I'll bring our bags inside." Mason turned toward the door.

"I'll help." He trailed his friend outside, closing the door behind him.

The construction worker glanced at Marcus as they headed toward the driveway. "How bad is it?"

"Bad enough. Early reports from the fire chief says Jo lost at least twenty trees. They were able to keep the fire from spreading to the adjoining property. Inside the house, the only obvious place touched by the intruder was Paige's room. No actual damage, just a threat written with lipstick on her mirror."

Knowing the man who attacked Paige had been in her personal space sickened Marcus. If she had been in her room asleep when he broke in, Paige would be dead and Marcus would be planning yet another funeral this week, maybe two if Jo tried to save her granddaughter.

Mason unlocked his truck and opened the back door. "What did the threat say?"

"Next time, you die."

A scowl from his friend. "She okay?"

"Shaken up. I didn't want to leave her and Jo alone tonight in case he comes back after the fire is out." He held out a hand for one of the bags.

"Any idea what caused the blaze?"

"Not in so many words, but I think Nick suspects arson. Jo said there wasn't equipment in the orchard that could catch fire. No storms tonight. I'm afraid Nick is right. Someone deliberately set Jo's orchard on fire."

A soft whistle from the contractor.

Inside the inn, Marcus led Mason to the two rooms Jo assigned to the couple. "Paige is staying in the corner room until hers is processed by Nick. I thought Nicole might like the room next door so they could spend time together easily."

"Sounds perfect. The bag you're carrying belongs to Nicole as well as this one." He hefted the suitcase onto the bed.

"Have you talked to Nicole yet?"

Mason smiled, his cheeks turning red. "I did. After she scolded me for scaring her into thinking I wasn't interested in her anymore, she kissed me senseless."

He clapped the construction worker's shoulder. "Told you."

"How are things going with you and Paige?"

Marcus led the way to Mason's room across the hall. "Asking her out was the best decision I ever made, a step I should have taken months ago."

"I agree." Jo's amused voice had both men twisting around to face Paige's grandmother.

"How are you, Jo?" Mason wrapped one arm around her.

She patted his black t-shirt covered chest. "I'm fine. Trees can be replanted. I'm more worried about Paige than I am myself. Who would want to hurt an old woman like me? My granddaughter, on the other hand, seems to have attracted a boatload of trouble."

"Now that Mason and Nicole are here, I'll go home and pack a bag. Do you need anything while I'm out?" Marcus pulled his keys from his pocket.

"I'm in the mood for apple pie. What about stopping at Delaney's for one of their pies? I have vanilla ice cream in the freezer. While you're gone, I'll start brewing a pot of coffee. I can't think of anything better for a late-night snack."

"I'll be happy to get one for you." He wouldn't be able to indulge in a slice of pie. Delaney's menu didn't include sugar-free desserts. He was thankful Serena had experimented with baked goods using stevia for him. He didn't indulge often, but enjoyed the treats when he did. "I'll stop by the kitchen and tell Paige where I'm going. I won't be gone long."

Jo patted his arm. "We'll be fine until you return."

Marcus returned to the kitchen, relieved to see the bloom of health in Paige's cheeks. When Paige smiled at him, his heart skipped a beat. "I'll be out for a few minutes. Jo has a craving for apple pie."

"That's her comfort food when she's stressed. Want company?"

"Visit with Nicole. I'll be back soon." He leaned down and kissed the top of her head. Later, he hoped to win a real kiss from the lady.

As soon as he turned onto the street, Marcus hit his speed dial.

"Everything okay, Marcus?" was Zane Murphy's greeting.

"There's been another incident in Otter Creek."

"Talk to me."

He explained about the fire and the ugly message left on Paige's mirror.

"How is she?"

"Scared, but trying not to let it show. Jo is furious. If this guy thinks Jo Jensen will wilt, he's in for a surprise."

"Do you want Fortress to relocate you?"

"I'm staying, no matter what happens. You've been monitoring the Internet for any mention of my name?"

"No hits on the bots. I would have called if there had been any searches for you. I'll dig deeper into the communications, see if something pops that even hints of a hit."

"Keep me posted. Paige and Jo's lives are on the line as well as mine. If what's happening to them is because of me, I need to know." He would do what was necessary to keep them safe, even if it meant calling in favors with the Delta team assigned to PSI. Josh Cahill and his teammates were the best in the business and Marcus counted them all as friends.

"Copy that. I'll update Maddox and Cahill."

"You have more than enough to do. I'll call Josh although I suspect Nick and Ethan will get to him before I do." In addition to working for Fortress and training bodyguards at PSI, Josh was also a local cop, an excellent one from what he'd seen and heard.

"Watch your back, Marcus."

His next phone call was to Delaney's to request two apple pies to go. By the time he finished that conversation, he'd parked in his driveway.

After a quick check to be sure his home was undisturbed and secure, Marcus packed a bag. Ten minutes later, he drove to the 24-hour diner.

When he walked into the B & B, laughter and the scent of coffee greeted Marcus. He scaled the stairs two at a time and dropped his bag in his room, then headed for the kitchen.

"You're just in time," Jo said when he walked in with the two pies. "The coffee is ready. Nicole, we need plates and cutlery. Paige, you're in charge of pouring coffee. Mason, the ice cream is in the freezer, dear."

Jo and the others bustled around the room, filling bowls and mugs. Marcus waved off the offered dessert. "Just coffee for me."

Paige handed him a mug filled with the steaming brew. "Would you like a different snack, Marcus? Another apple or a banana?"

He lifted the mug. "This is fine." Thanks to the steakhouse meal, he wasn't hungry.

"I apologize, Marcus." Jo sat across from him at the dining table. "I forgot about your diet restrictions."

"Paige offered an alternative, but I'm more interested in the coffee than anything else." Except for the kiss he wanted from Paige. With a house full of guests and her obvious fatigue, that kiss would have to wait for a better time. He just hoped it was soon.

By unspoken consent, the conversation around the table remained light. Nicole kept them in stitches with the antics of her grooming clients and Mason contributed funny stories from his childhood, several that included mishaps with his cousin Rio.

When the food and coffee were gone, they carried the dishes to the dishwasher. When Mason followed Nicole upstairs, Jo turned to Marcus. "Ed told me he would check for hotspots in the orchard throughout the night. He promised to stop by before the fire truck left the premises." She yawned. "I thought he would have been here before now."

"If you want to go on to bed, I'll wait for him and come get you if Ed needs to talk to you."

"Thank you, Marcus. I'll take you up on the offer." She hugged Paige. "Don't stay up too late, dear. You're still recovering and should take it easy for another day or two at least. Wake me if you need me."

"I will. Good night, Gram."

As Jo walked upstairs, Marcus clasped Paige's hand. "I enjoyed dinner with you. After the parade of interruptions, do I have any hope for another date?"

She grinned. "As long as the next one is out of town. I'd like you to myself for a couple hours."

Thank goodness. "I know a quiet restaurant in Cherry Hill you might like. Is Friday night too soon?" He wanted more time with her before then, but his responsibilities made the chances of an evening out with Paige before Friday slim. When the community center reopened, he could bring lunch to her office. They could spend time together without attracting unwanted attention.

"Sounds great."

"Six o'clock?"

She nodded. "Caleb works Friday evenings so the center will be covered."

"Nicole's waiting for you," he murmured. "I'll be close if you need me."

"Thank you for asking Nicole and Mason to stay. That was a great surprise."

"The arrangement was the best way for me to stay as well. I wasn't comfortable leaving you and Jo here alone."

Paige hugged him. "You're a thoughtful man, Marcus."

He tightened his hold and just held her for a few minutes. To have this chance with her was a miracle, one he'd never take for granted. He knew how easily life could flip you on your head and change everything. "The typical end to a date includes a good night kiss."

"I'm out of practice."

"Are you?"

"I've been waiting for a certain man to notice me and I'm afraid my skills are rusty."

Marcus cupped the back of her neck. "Let's find out." He leaned down and brushed her lips with his own once, twice, then captured her mouth for a longer, deeper kiss. Minutes later, he eased back, pleased to see her eyes filled with heat instead fear. He brushed her swollen bottom lip with his thumb and turned her toward the stairs. "Go visit with Nicole."

She flashed a smile over her shoulder. "Good night, Marcus."

He held himself still as she climbed the stairs when his instinct was to go after her and demand more kisses. He couldn't do that to her or himself. She needed to rest and he needed to cool off.

To keep his mind occupied, Marcus checked his emails and text messages. Nothing from Fortress, an excellent sign. Knowing his life was on the line, Zane would have made the deep search a priority if Fortress didn't have a crisis pulling his attention elsewhere. Marcus also added reminders to his electronic calendar and replied to two messages requiring a response.

Heavy footsteps crossed the porch, followed by a knock on the door.

After checking the peephole, he stepped out on the porch. "Hello, Ed."

The fire chief's eyebrows shot up. "Pastor Lang. Surprised to see you here."

"What's happening in the orchard?"

"Fire's out. Damage wasn't as bad as I feared. Jo lost fifteen trees. Could have lost them all if the wind had shifted on us. We'll check for flare ups through the night."

"If there's a problem or another flare up, call me. Mason, Nicole, and I are staying at the B & B tonight with Jo and Paige."

Understanding filled his expression. "No problem. Be glad to call you. The ladies all right?"

"They're shaken, but holding strong. Your people are uninjured?"

"Howard tripped over a tree root and sprained his ankle. Other than that, we're good."

"Thanks for your quick response and stopping by with the update."

"You bet. Here's hoping for an uneventful night."

Amen to that. Marcus closed and locked the door after the fire chief drove away. He turned the table lamp to its lowest setting and, after checking the back door, went upstairs to his own room.

Three hours after his head hit the pillow, his cell phone rang. "Lang."

"Preacher, help me!"

CHAPTER THIRTEEN

Marcus swung his legs over the side of the bed. "Dalton, what's wrong?"

"I'm in trouble. Please, you gotta help me."

"Where are you?" He placed the call on speaker and started lacing his tennis shoes. Afraid he might face Paige's attacker before the night was over, Marcus had slept in his clothes. Now he was doubly glad he'd taken that precaution. From the sound of the teenager's voice, every minute counted.

"At the old Croft place. I'm in the trees, hiding. Hurry before he finds me." With that last urgent plea, Dalton ended the call.

Marcus debated calling him back to demand further information but feared he might endanger the teenager. He grabbed his keys and wallet, and headed for the hallway.

He tapped on Mason's door, poked his head inside. "Hey, sorry to wake you," he murmured. "I have to leave. I'll be back as soon as I can."

"Leave my door open. I'll keep an eye on things."

"Thanks, Mase."

As he reached the front door, a loose board squeaked behind him. Marcus swiveled, his eyes widening when he saw Paige. "Did I wake you?"

She shook her head. "Couldn't sleep. What's going on?"

"I have to go. Got a teen who called me for help."

Paige moved closer. "Who?"

"Dalton."

"Wait for me. I'm going with you."

Before he could protest about the possible danger, she dashed upstairs. In under a minute, she returned dressed in jeans and a sweatshirt. She was carrying her shoes. "Let's go."

"Paige, he sounded scared. This could be dangerous. I don't want to take you into the middle of an unknown situation."

She unlocked the door. "We're wasting time, Marcus."

He followed her outside to his truck. "Only if you agree to follow my orders if there's trouble."

"I promise."

Still afraid this was a major mistake, he cranked the truck's engine. At the road, Marcus turned left. Thankfully, the Croft property bordered Jo's. Wouldn't take them long to reach Dalton.

He activated his Bluetooth and called Ethan Blackhawk.

"Blackhawk."

"It's Marcus. Paige and I are headed for the Croft place. Dalton Reagan called three minutes ago, begging for help. He's hiding in the woods, says someone is after him."

"Turn around and go back to the inn. I'm leaving now. Josh is on duty tonight. He'll be there soon."

"Can't wait, Ethan. Dalton sounded terrified and we're only four minutes away." A growl from the police chief made Marcus flinch. Yeah, his friend was going to tear a strip from Marcus's hide when this was over.

"Don't do anything stupid. You have more than just yourself to worry about."

Marcus glanced at Paige who was tying her tennis shoes. "I'm very aware of the risk involved. Paige's safety is my first priority."

"Watch your back, Marcus. I'll be there as soon as I can."

A quarter mile from the property, Marcus turned off his lights. At the entrance to the long driveway, he pulled off the road and backed his truck into the tree line. With the dark paint, hopefully the vehicle would be overlooked if someone was after Dalton.

He unlatched his seatbelt. "Are you sure you want to do this?"

"We're wasting time. Let's go."

Marcus turned off his dome light and opened his door. He met Paige at the front of the truck and held out his hand. "Walk as quietly as you can. Since the driveway is gravel, we'll walk on the grass. If I give you an order, do it without question."

When she nodded her agreement, he set a fast pace for the Croft house. The woods skirted the right side of the estate.

Why was the boy out here at this time of night? He should have been at home hours ago. His mother would be worried if she found he was gone.

Cloud cover drifted away from the moon, illuminating the area. If the man after Dalton was still searching for him, the extra light made it easy for him to see. If Marcus wasn't careful, he and Paige would be visible to anyone looking their direction.

His gut tightened into a knot at the thought of his girl in danger again. He should have insisted Paige stay in the truck. Knowing her, though, she would have followed him on her own. Dalton was one of her kids, and she would do anything to protect him.

The driveway curved to the right, leading to the ramshackle antebellum house. Once a beautiful mansion, the place had fallen into neglect as old man Croft aged and became ill.

Marcus led Paige closer to the woods that bordered Jo's orchard. The wind shifted, carrying with it ash and the scent of burned wood. He didn't think Dalton had anything to do with the fire in the orchard. The police, though, may not be as trusting as Marcus.

At the clearing, he stopped, nudged Paige behind him, and listened. The woods were eerily quiet. Not good. There should have been some signs of life. He'd visited old man Croft several times in the months before he died. Not once was it this silent. The urgency to find Dalton increased.

"Stay behind me," he whispered.

Paige squeezed his hand in answer.

He took them into the wooded area, carefully placing his feet to cushion his progress. Nice to know he hadn't forgotten his skills. He glanced at Paige over his shoulder, amused to see she was trying to walk in his footsteps.

The further they traveled, the denser the tree cover became, and shadows from the pines, maples, and elms deepened. Marcus didn't dare turn on his flashlight app for fear of alerting Dalton's pursuer to their presence. What he wouldn't give for a good pair of NVGs. Never thought he'd say that again. Maybe he should ask Josh to hook him up with a pair of the night-vision glasses.

Something or someone running through the trees made Marcus adjust his course. He moved further to the left, nearer the tree line. With someone chasing him, the teen couldn't turn on a light to see where he was going. More than likely, he wouldn't have moved too far into the woods. Since Marcus wasn't positive of the soundness of his logic, he'd stay out of sight until he was sure the runner was Dalton.

A soft curse drifted on the early morning breeze, followed by a quickly muffled shout. Marcus hustled Paige to the largest tree he could find and pressed her back against the trunk. "Stay here."

"Be careful."

With a nod, he followed the sounds of the scuffle. He broke into a small clearing to see Dalton struggling to escape the clutches of a large, muscled man dressed in black.

Fury exploded in his gut. "Hey! Let him go."

The thug swung around, shoved Dalton away from him, and grabbed a weapon from behind his back. He pointed the barrel at Marcus who dived behind the closest tree.

"Give it up, man. I called the cops. They'll be here any minute."

Another vile curse from the stranger's mouth.

The sound of crashing through the underbrush reached his ears. Marcus peered around the tree trunk he'd sheltered behind. The guy was gone. Dalton, however, still lay on the ground where he'd fallen.

Marcus raced to the teenager and crouched beside him. When he laid his hand on Dalton's shoulder, the teen tried to scramble away. Marcus tightened his hold. "It's Marcus. You're safe. The guy's gone, buddy."

Dalton's frantic movements ceased and he shifted toward Marcus. "You came."

"Of course, I did. We're friends, and friends have each other's backs."

"Yeah, they do."

"Are you hurt?"

"Nothing an ice pack won't cure." A small smile curved the teen's lips.

Some of the tension eased from Marcus's muscles. "Good. I brought someone with me who's very anxious to see you."

He led Dalton back to Paige. Relief flooded her face when she saw the teenager.

"Dalton." She threw her arms around his neck and hugged him. "Are you okay?"

"A little banged up. I'll live, thanks to Marcus."

She set him away from her and looked him over for herself. "What happened? Why were you out here at this time of night?"

"That's what I want to know." Ethan Blackhawk strode toward them, his weapon held by his side. "You okay, Dalton?"

"Yes, sir."

"Marcus, Paige?"

"We're fine." He circled Paige's waist with his arm, tightened his grip when he felt her trembling. "Thanks for coming so fast."

The police chief moved into a patch of light, his gaze assessing the three of them, then scanning the area. "Who should I be looking for?"

"Big guy, dressed in black to his shoes. Six feet two, curly black hair, couldn't see the color of his eyes. Armed with what looked like a 9 mil. I couldn't see the weapon clearly from where I was standing because he stayed in the shadows. When I confronted him, he shoved Dalton away and shot at me."

Had to be the same man who attacked Paige. Why was he out here and what did he want with a teenage boy? He glanced at the woman by his side, noted her puzzled expression.

Marcus mentally reviewed his statement to Ethan. Oh, man. A "normal" pastor probably wouldn't have noticed all those details, certainly not the information about the weapon. Yeah, those secrets were becoming a problem.

Ethan pulled a flashlight from his pocket. "Show me. I'll see if I can track him."

Not wanting to leave Paige alone again in case Dalton's attacker circled back, he retraced his steps with Paige at his side. Dalton walked with Ethan. When he came to the small clearing where the scuffle had taken place, he showed Ethan where the man had been standing when he fired the shots.

Ethan crouched, turned on his flashlight, and studied the ground. "I'll take it from here. Josh will be on scene soon. Go back to the Croft driveway and wait for him." With that, he walked deeper into the trees following the trail of the shooter, his steps silent.

"Let's go," Dalton muttered. "This place is creepy at night."

Marcus agreed with him. Near the driveway, he located the stone bench Mr. Croft had loved to sit on, and nudged Paige that direction. "Come on. We might as well be comfortable while we wait for Josh."

"Good idea. My legs feel like rubber right now. Come sit with me, Dalton."

"I'm okay."

Marcus looked at the teenager, whistled. "You'll have a shiner in a few hours, buddy."

"Oh, man. My mom will have a fit when she sees my face."

"From what I saw, you're lucky that's the worst of your injuries."

"Yeah, I know." Dalton swallowed hard. "He came out of nowhere and chased me down. I thought I got away, but obviously I didn't."

"What were you doing out here, Dalton?" Paige wrapped her arms around herself and shivered.

Probably nerves and the chilly temperatures. Marcus sat beside her and slipped his arm around her shoulders to share his body heat. The teenager stared, his eyebrows raised. Amused at the teen's reaction, he winked at his basketball buddy. Wouldn't hurt to have another pair of eyes watching over Paige.

He dropped his gaze. "I was looking around. Nothing bad, honest. The gossip around town says this place will be the first one bulldozed when the developer starts working on the shopping center. I wanted to see inside the house before it's gone." The teenager shrugged. "I like old buildings. They're cool."

Marcus frowned. Dalton was lying about something, but what?

"Have you been looking at the websites I recommended?" Paige asked.

"I looked up several that weren't on your list, too. The school librarian helped me find more."

Puzzled, Marcus glanced from one to the other. "What websites?"

"Historical homes and architectural sites. Dalton is interested in designing homes and buildings. He's also looking into rehabbing old houses like this one."

"Elliott Construction rehabs houses. If you're interested in that side of the business, you should talk to Mason Kincaid. He helped rehab the Victorian mansion Rio and Darcy live in."

The teenager raised his head, eyes wide. "Do you think Rio or Darcy would give me a tour of the house?"

"I'll be glad to talk to them about it."

"Thanks, Marcus."

"I'll do it on one condition."

"What's that?"

"Tell me why you lied a minute ago."

CHAPTER FOURTEEN

Paige stared at Marcus, then Dalton. "Dalton?"

Before he answered, twin headlights swept over them as an Otter Creek police cruiser drove into sight and stopped. A tall, broad-shouldered officer climbed from the vehicle. "Everybody okay?" Josh Cahill asked.

"Paige and I are fine," Marcus said. "Dalton needs an ice pack. You wouldn't happen to have anything like that in your cruiser, would you?"

A quick smile from the Delta soldier. "I have one in the med kit Rio makes every member of Durango carry." He returned to the vehicle and opened the trunk. A moment later, he handed Dalton a chemically-activated ice pack. "Some battle scar."

"Thanks," the teen muttered, avoiding direct eye contact with Josh.

What was wrong with him? He hadn't acted like this in several weeks. Was he worried about punishment for being out past curfew or concerned about something more serious?

"What's the story?" Josh's lips curved. "It's bound to be an interesting one to bring the three of you out at this time of night."

When it became apparent Dalton wasn't going to answer, Marcus explained about the phone call. "Mason, Nicole, and I are staying at the B & B with Paige and Jo. Paige heard me going to the door after Dalton's call and volunteered to come with me."

A snort from Josh. "I have a strong-willed wife, mother, and triplet sisters. What you said is a nice way of saying she insisted on coming along despite the possible danger."

Paige grinned. She had been afraid to let Marcus come by himself. She wasn't a cop, but she could handle a cell phone like a pro and scream with the best late-night thriller actress.

"It's well past curfew, Dalton. Why were you out here this late?" Josh folded his arms across his chest.

The teen refused to answer.

"Ethan will question you. Unless you want to cause yourself and your mother a heap of trouble, level with him. Do you know about the fire at the Jensen orchard?"

Dalton swallowed visibly, nodded.

"Doesn't look good for you to be in the vicinity of a possible arson and refusing to talk. People will assume you're the firebug."

"No way! It wasn't me."

"Then start talking. Why were you out here?"

More silence.

"Dalton, please." Paige touched his hand. "We want to help."

"I can't say. I'd be violating the bro code."

Marcus frowned. "You need to tell Josh and Ethan everything. That's the only way they can help you and the person you're protecting."

Before Marcus finished, the teenager was shaking his head. "Nobody knows who the other person is."

"You sure about that? You didn't think anyone knew you were out here either, but the guy who tried to kill Paige came after you tonight. Your friend is in just as much danger as you and Paige are. Who else has been with you? We're trying to keep him alive, Dalton. So, I'll ask you again. Who are you protecting?"

Dalton slid a glance to Josh.

"He doesn't have to know you gave up his name," Josh said. "How will you protect your friend? You can't be at his side 24/7 and you couldn't save yourself a few minutes ago. There's no shame in asking for help when you need it, Dalton. I've called on my teammates over and over for years. I know they have my back. If you don't tell us this kid's name, we may not be able to save him like Marcus did you."

A deep sigh and Dalton dropped his gaze. "It's Seth Parks."

"The mayor's grandson?"

He nodded.

Josh rubbed his neck. "Ethan's not going to like this news. What's the story, Dalton? Why were you out here?"

"I told Paige and Marcus the truth. I wanted to see the old house before the developer tore it down."

"You broke into the place?"

"No, I swear. The back door was unlocked. I walked right in."

"Still against the law, buddy. What about Seth? Did he explore with you?"

Paige had a feeling Josh and Ethan might overlook his foray into the house if he wasn't guilty of anything more serious than poking around in the old house. And listen to her. She felt guilty even thinking the teenager might have been involved in something more sinister than being nosy.

"We split up. He didn't want to walk around in the Croft place. Said it was weird to be in there when the owner was dead."

"What were you doing out here in the first place?" Paige asked.

"Walking around."

And there went that gaze again. He'd looked away. Why was Dalton lying? "After midnight?"

"Mom worked until 11:30. I was supposed to meet Seth earlier, but I was watching my brothers and working on homework."

"And you couldn't wait to talk to Seth until tomorrow at school?" Paige frowned. This didn't make sense. The boys could have talked on the phone, a safer alternative to wandering around at night. "Why didn't you call him?"

Dalton adjusted the ice pack. "I've been tutoring him in geometry. It's not a subject I can help him with over the phone. Besides, he's embarrassed about needing help with his math, especially since I'm an eighth grader. His math class is first period and he has a test. I couldn't put off tutoring him. If Seth doesn't do well on this test, Coach Russell will bench him. And his dad? Man, I wouldn't want to be in Seth's shoes if his dad finds out he's been benched. Mr. Parks is pressuring him to step up his game in the quarterback position. He's banking on Seth earning a full-ride scholarship to one of the SEC schools."

Paige scooted closer to Marcus as her shivering grew stronger. The temperature had dropped and the breeze picked up.

"Cold?" Marcus murmured.

She nodded.

"Josh, you have a blanket Paige can use while we wait for Ethan?"

"Sure." A moment later, policeman draped a blanket over the shoulders of Paige and Marcus. He handed a second blanket to Dalton. "Wrap up in this while I take a look at your eye." He gave a soft whistle after examining the injury. "That's going to be a beauty, Dalton. No way to hide that one from your mom."

The teen looked morose. "I know. I'll be lucky if she lets me leave the house for anything except school and church for a month."

"I'll talk to her," Paige said. "How about next time you need to do some tutoring you do it at your house or his? If it's early enough in the evening, you can use one of the classrooms at the community center. I'll make sure no one bothers you if you choose that option."

"The center would be perfect. It's halfway between my house and his. I don't think we can use Seth's house. His dad doesn't know he's being tutored. Seth's afraid to tell him."

"If the center isn't open, call me," Marcus said. "My dining table is a great place to do school work and the parsonage is close to the center."

"That sounds like the perfect solution." Josh took the ice pack, gave the teen a stern look. "You have safer options, Dalton. Choose one of them next time. If you have another run-in with the clown who hurt Paige, you might not be so lucky."

"Yes, sir."

Josh shifted position to stand in front of the three of them, his gun up and aimed at the entrance to the driveway.

What did he hear? Paige listened carefully, but heard nothing except the wind.

"Coming in soft," Ethan called out.

She expected Josh to relax and put away his weapon. He didn't. He remained in position until Ethan moved into a bright patch moonlight. He was alone.

"Find anything?" Josh asked as he returned his gun to his holster.

"Several good footprints and tire tracks where the perp left in a hurry." Ethan turned to Marcus. "Did you see a vehicle parked off to the side of the road?"

He shook his head. "Sorry. I was more concerned with finding Dalton."

"I did," Paige said. "A black SUV. I can't tell you what kind. I just got a glimpse of it. It was parked back in the tree line, maybe one hundred feet from where Marcus parked the truck."

Ethan dragged a hand down his face. "There are too many black SUVs in town to count, several of them belonging to PSI. Josh has access to those himself."

"I was on the other side of town answering a prowler call. You can ask Mrs. Hendrix to verify." Josh grinned at his brother-in-law.

"Great. That only leaves nineteen other black SUVs in PSI's stable of vehicles to check out plus the other unknown number owned by the citizens of Dunlap County." He turned to the teenage boy. "What are you doing out here, Dalton?"

After a glance at Josh who gave him a slight nod, silently encouraging Dalton to tell Ethan the truth, the teen went through his explanation. The police chief listened to the details to the end without comments or questions. "When I find Seth, and ask him for an explanation, he'll confirm what you just told me?"

"Yes, sir. At least I hope he will. If you contact him tonight, he might deny everything in front of his dad. Same deal tomorrow at school. He's embarrassed about the tutoring."

"No shame in having a tutor. I had one for five years in high school."

Dalton's mouth dropped. "You did?"

"Sure. My cantankerous aunt. My dad wasn't too worried about me attending classes regularly so my education was lacking when I went to live with her. Ruth is a book nerd and a whiz at everything. If she didn't know something, she found someone who did, and the two of us learned how to do my assignment. She might look like a sweet old lady, but Ruth Rollins is a taskmaster. She made my drill sergeant look like a pushover compared to her."

"Wow."

"Officer Cahill will take you home. You stay there until you go to school. Do you ride the bus?"

"Can't. I have to make sure my brothers get on their bus on time. I ride my bike."

"Can your mom take you this time?"

Dalton shook his head. "She has to be at Delaney's by six for her shift. I think she's working a double today plus the office cleaning job tonight. I probably won't see her more than thirty minutes until late tonight."

"I can swing by and take him to school," Josh said. "I'm off shift and my first class at PSI doesn't start until 9:00."

"I can't go to school in the cruiser," Dalton said, his expression conveying his horror at the idea of being seen in a police vehicle. "Everybody will think I got busted for something."

Both policemen chuckled.

"I'll take him," Marcus said. "I'm meeting Van Wilder's father for coffee at 8:30 to plan his son's funeral. I'll go early and wait for him in the coffee shop."

Paige's heart sank. Another day of little to no sleep for Marcus. How did he keep up with this kind of schedule? Although she knew he kept long hours, she had no idea the pace was so hectic. How he continued to stay in good health and top physical shape was a mystery to her.

Dalton turned his face away from all of them, but not before Paige saw sadness fill his expression. The boys had been at each other's throats off and on. That didn't negate the fact they were friends.

"That arrangement work for you, Dalton?" Ethan asked.

"Sure," came the choked response.

"Come on." Josh laid a hand on the teenager's shoulder. "Let's get you home. You'll have a few hours to sleep. We'll make arrangements for an undercover car to pick you up after school and bring you to the station. We still need your statement on record."

He shook his head. "I have to watch my brothers and help them with homework and stuff."

"No problem. We'll drive you home and take your statement there." The two of them walked away and were soon leaving the Croft property.

Ethan scanned the area. "Marcus, did you get a look at the perp's face?"

Plastered against his side, Paige felt him tense at the question.

"I did."

"You willing to work with a sketch artist?"

A sigh. "I'll do it, but I might not be able to testify if this comes down to a trial."

CHAPTER FIFTEEN

Ethan's eyebrows raised at Marcus's warning, and Paige stared at him. Yeah, this wasn't how he wanted to spill the news of his hidden past to the woman who meant so much to him. Would the truth scare her out of his life? Man, he hoped not. Paige Jensen was burrowing into his heart, fast. Losing her would hurt far worse than losing Chelsea, a truth that surprised him. Maybe that indicated how much he'd changed in seven years. He wasn't the same man, and Chelsea was gone.

"Care to explain?" the police chief asked.

"I owe Paige an explanation first."

"Do it fast, Marcus. I'm assuming from your description the man who attacked Dalton is the same one who hurt Paige. For now, I will give the sketch to Nick and have him build a case aside from the picture. If we can't make the case without your identification, we won't have a choice. Letting this man skate away free is too dangerous for Paige."

That rock in the pit of his stomach grew to the size of a boulder. Again. "I understand." Although he had told Zane he planned to stay in Otter Creek, he didn't want to endanger Paige. That's what would happen if he didn't identify the man who choked her. Coming out of hiding put Marcus in the crosshairs again, but nothing mattered more than protecting her. If O'Reilly came for him again, he would handle it, perhaps with the help of PSI.

This town crawled with Special Forces soldiers. They wouldn't mind watching over Paige. In fact, most of them were friends with her and Jo. He could look after himself if the black ops groups were spread too thin. His main concern was the woman shivering in his arms. "Paige is cold. Are we free to leave?"

Ethan gave a curt nod. "You and Paige need to stop by the station tomorrow to give a statement. We'll go through your story again in detail." His eyes held a warning.

The story he'd hoped to avoid telling Paige couldn't be delayed any longer. "Jeb Kirkland's funeral is tomorrow at two. We'll come to the station tomorrow morning after I talk to Mr. Wilder, but I have to leave by noon whether your interrogation is finished or not." He turned to Paige. "All right with you?"

"It's fine. Nick hasn't cleared the community center so I don't work for at least another day. I'll go to the coffee shop with you and visit with Sasha while you talk to Mr. Wilder. That will save you a little time."

"I'll walk with you to the truck." Ethan positioned himself on the other side of Paige. "How's the head?"

"Better. Nausea is gone and the headache is low grade. The only residual effect is bruises around my throat."

"You're lucky." Another pointed glance. "Very lucky."

Marcus gathered Paige against his side, the feel of her breathing and body heat a comfort. His blood still ran cold at how close he came to losing Paige before he had the chance to really know her. He couldn't allow that to happen again, no matter the cost to himself.

"I know. I'm grateful to be alive."

When they reached the truck, Ethan held up his fist. Marcus stopped in his tracks, keeping Paige at his side. Mentally, he berated himself for not considering a tracker or an explosive device attached to the undercarriage. Been too long since he'd had to be so vigilant. Time to awaken those old habits.

The police chief pulled out his flashlight and began a careful sweep of the truck. When he was satisfied, Ethan dropped to the ground and checked the undercarriage. Finally, he stood. "You're clear. I'll see you later this morning."

Marcus opened the door for Paige and tucked Josh's blanket around her. He turned, shook Ethan's hand. "Thanks for not pushing for information."

"Yet. I will when I take your statement."

He blew out a breath, nodded. Not much time to tell Paige his story and perhaps see his greatest gift walk away from him for good. As he drove toward the B & B, a final glance in the mirror showed Ethan standing at the side of the road. Guess his friend wouldn't return home anytime soon. Ethan was in a class of his own. Otter Creek was lucky to have him leading their police department. He knew Ethan had been offered jobs in various cities across the country, jobs he'd turned down to remain here with his aunt and his wife's family.

Marcus turned on the seat heater for Paige and considered the best place to tell her his story. She shouldn't be outside although he would love to sit on the swing for this discussion. Despite longing to be in the open, Paige's safety was still paramount. Next best option was the first-floor library with the gas fireplace to banish the last of the chills for her. The warmth would help him as well. Talking about the past always froze him to the bone.

"The heat feels great." Paige snuggled deeper into the seat and wrapped the blanket tighter around herself.

He cranked up the heat another notch. "We need to talk before we pick up Dalton. Can we use the library?"

"Of course." Paige twisted toward him. "Is this the discussion you didn't want to have, Marcus?"

"I wanted more time to cement our relationship."

"It's that serious?"

"More than you could ever guess." More than he would have dreamed in his worst nightmares until the nightmares became reality and Marcus lost everything and everyone he held dear.

"But you would have told me at some point?"

"Before things grew too serious between us. I want a rock-solid relationship with you which means sharing the secrets I must keep from others."

Paige's soft hand curled around his own. "A man of mystery. Good thing I enjoy solving mysteries. I'm honored you trust me."

He parked away from the access road in case the fire department needed to douse a rekindled blaze. He prayed their presence wouldn't be necessary. Although Jo had acted as though replacing trees wasn't a big deal, he'd seen the hurt in her eyes. The trees were part of the Jensen heritage, a heritage she longed to leave her granddaughter. Losing the trees was like losing members of the family.

When Paige reached for the door handle, Marcus caught her arm. "Wait," he murmured. Although Marcus turned off his headlights, he waited to see if anything changed or a dark shadow separated from the others.

"Why are we waiting?"

"Safety precaution." Five minutes later, he was satisfied that they weren't being observed or targeted by her attacker. How long before the man took another run at her?

Marcus tucked Paige against his side again and, scanning the area, walked into the B & B. The house remained silent and undisturbed. "Start a fire in the library while I check in with Mason." He climbed the stairs and tapped on the door frame to Mason's room.

"You're back." His friend sat up. "No trouble while you were gone."

"Good. Paige and I will be in the library. We need to talk and she got chilled while we waited for Ethan at the crime scene."

"The kid okay?"

"Yeah. He was lucky. You can go back to sleep."

"I wish. It's time for me to get moving. I have to be at the job site by six."

"Sorry for the short night, but I appreciate you watching over Jo and the house, Mase."

"Yep. I'll start coffee after I shower." His lips curved. "Nicole isn't a fan of mornings."

Paige sat on the loveseat facing the fireplace, Josh's blanket folded and draped across the back. He made a mental note to take the cover to the police station. Ethan could return it to Josh's cruiser.

Paige smiled and patted the floral-patterned cushion. "Sit with me. Anything happen while we were gone?"

"Everything was fine." Marcus sat and faced the fire. How did he explain his past without terrifying her?

"Start at the beginning."

A lifetime ago. "Seven years ago, I was a chaplain in the Navy but had signed the papers to muster out, my separation date two weeks away. I was at a restaurant with a woman. She worked the second shift at a local hospital so it must have been close to midnight by the time we finished dinner."

"What's her name?"

"Chelsea Daniels."

Paige looked thoughtful. "The name sound familiar?"

"You probably saw her name mentioned in the national news."

She reached for his hand. "What happened?"

"As we walked from the restaurant to the parking lot, I heard a gunshot. I told Chelsea to stay put while I went to see if I could help. When I moved away from the building, I saw two men fighting. One had been shot. I recognized him as a commander from one of our SEAL teams. I didn't recognize the other man. I told Chels to call 911 and ran to help the SEAL. By the time I reached the men, the SEAL had his attacker subdued and unconscious. The commander didn't realize the attacker had a partner waiting in the shadows with a gun drawn, ready to shoot. As he squeezed off the shot, I shoved the commander out of the way and ended up with a bullet in the gut. The SEAL hadn't moved from where he fell, and I wasn't sure he would. He'd lost a lot of blood."

Paige tightened her grip. "What about the man who shot you?"

"He fired several rounds as I fell. When I hit the ground, I saw a weapon near my hand. I shot the gunman before he killed the SEAL or me. The police were close. With the gun battle was over, I expected Chels to come running since she was a nurse. She couldn't. One of the gunman's rounds struck her in the heart. According to the ER physician, Chels died instantly."

"Oh, Marcus. I'm so sorry. Were you close to Chelsea?"

He laced their fingers together. "We were engaged."

Paige drew in a sharp breath. "I can't imagine the pain you went through losing the woman you loved on top of your own injury. What about the Navy SEAL? Did he survive?"

Finally, something to smile about. "He recovered and started Fortress Security. He's Zane's boss."

"You saved Brent Maddox's life?"

"You know Brent?"

"Only by the stories from Josh and the others. Grace St. Claire can't say enough good things about her husband's boss. I understand wanting to protect his secrecy, but why were you reluctant to tell me your role?"

"I was in the wrong place at the right time to aid a good man. Brent had separated from the Navy the month before, and was in the process of starting Fortress. Helping a SEAL wasn't the issue. The problem was the identity of the man I killed to protect Brent."

"What was his name?"

"Mick O'Reilly."

She frowned. "I don't recognize his name."

"If he did his job right, you wouldn't. Mick was connected to the Irish mob based in New York City. He was the oldest son of Sean O'Reilly, the head of the mob. He was also his father's hit man. When I woke from surgery, Brent and two of his teammates were sitting in my room, armed to the teeth. I was Fortress Security's first client. Brent and his buddies were there to protect me because Sean O'Reilly had placed a price on my head for killing his son even though the police declared the shooting self-defense. Sean didn't care that the shooting was justified."

He turned to Paige, surprised to see tears trickling down her cheeks. "Sweetheart?"

"I hate what happened to you and the loss of Chelsea. Do you still love her, Marcus?"

"A part of me always will, but I'm a different man now. My memories of her are sweet, the loss an ache, not the agonizing pain I experienced when I woke in the hospital."

She was silent a moment. "What else do you need to tell me?"

How could she know? "You're sure there's more?"

She pressed a soft kiss to his mouth, a balm to the renewed ache of the memories from his former life.

"If you look up Chelsea Daniels' name, you'll see she was engaged to a man named Matt Watson who disappeared from the hospital and is presumed dead."

Paige blinked. "You're living under an assumed name."

"Matt Watson doesn't exist anymore. He died in that hospital. I'm also Fortress's first client for private witness protection and relocation. I haven't seen my family in seven years. I could probably have Brent arrange a meeting. I just haven't."

"Because you're afraid the Irish mob will target them. Does your family know you're alive?"

"Brent contacts them once a month to tell them I'm safe."

"Will you ever be able to go home again, Marcus?"

"When the price on my head is lifted or Sean O'Reilly is dead." In other words, probably never. The Irish mob had a long memory.

"Is there anything Brent can do? According to his people, he's a miracle worker."

"In the beginning, I spent my time healing. When I was well enough to be released from a doctor's care, I tried not to dwell on what I'd lost, and concentrated on creating a new life for myself. That's part of the reason I didn't pursue a relationship with you sooner. I was a work in progress."

"And now?"

He raised their entwined hands and kissed the back of hers. "Now you see all there is. If you remain a part of my life, you'll be under the same restrictions I am. You can't tell anyone my real name until it's safe, if it's ever safe. Even with O'Reilly gone, his cronies have long memories. Now that you know my secrets, are you still willing to take a chance on me?"

Paige released his hand. Marcus clenched his jaw to stop himself from begging. Rather than walking away for good, Paige wrapped her arms around his neck and drew his head to hers to indulge in long minutes of deep, heated kisses.

When their mouths finally separated, Marcus reeled from the emotions rushing through him. He couldn't believe he'd been blessed to find a woman who would stay with him despite the danger she would face. "Thank you for taking the risk. I promise to protect you with my life."

"You're worth the risk, Marcus."

He prayed she never regretted that statement.

CHAPTER SIXTEEN

Paige climbed onto one of the red-cushioned stools at Perk's counter. A woman with dark brown hair pulled back into a ponytail turned and smiled.

"Hi, Paige. It's so good to see you. What can I get for you this morning?"

"Do you have to be so perky, Sasha?" Fatigue from the interrupted night's sleep had hit Paige like a ton of bricks on the drive into town. How could her friend be that energetic when the woman arrived at the coffee shop by four o'clock every morning?

The shop proprietor laughed, her brown eyes sparkling. "I sample my shop wares, especially the espresso."

"A vanilla latte with two pumps of espresso sounds perfect this morning. If you have anything infused with great heaps of energy, I'll take that, too."

Shaking her head, Sasha began assembling Paige's drink. "I planned to call you later today to see how you were. You look great considering your ordeal."

"A scary situation, one I never thought I would face in Otter Creek. Marcus scared the guy off just in time."

"You didn't recognize the man who attacked you?"

"The community center was too dark to see his face. Nick and Ethan will capture him before he hurts someone else." At least she hoped they would. She worried over her grandmother's safety. Despite Jo Jensen's gritty attitude, she was growing older, her body frailer than Paige's. Paige had barely survived her encounter. She didn't want to contemplate what might happen if Gram ran into this man. Even worse, Paige wouldn't recognize her attacker if she passed him on the street. How could Gram protect herself if Paige wasn't able to identify the man?

Sasha set the latte on the counter. "What about a breakfast sandwich or a scone with that? I'm trying a new recipe and I'd love your opinion."

"The blueberry cream cheese scone last week was a winner."

Her friend grinned. "This week it's cranberry orange."

"Oh, man. I'm in." She glanced around to be sure no one was close, then leaned toward Sasha. "Don't tell Gram, but I am tired of apples and apple-flavored desserts."

"Hmm. Blackmail material for the next occasion when I need cheap labor at a town-sponsored event."

Paige scowled. "See if I spill secrets at this counter again."

Sasha laughed. Her gaze shifted to the two men sitting at the corner table, talking earnestly. Her smile faded. "How is Mr. Wilder?"

"Devastated."

"Van could be a little wild, but he was a good kid. He had his whole life ahead of him and now he's just gone."

Paige blinked back the tears stinging her eyes. Her tears would distress Marcus, and he had enough on his shoulders at the moment. "You knew him?"

A shrug. "He came here with his dad every Saturday since I opened the shop. He loved the power sandwiches and the blueberry muffins." She gave a quick smile. "I never could interest him in coffee. He always went for the chocolate milk."

"Did he seem troubled about anything when you saw him Saturday?"

"Can't say he did. The shop was pretty busy, though. Why do you ask?"

"Curious. He and Dalton had a falling out and both boys seemed devastated. Just didn't know if you heard him talking about the fight."

"Sorry. When I brought their order to the table, Van clammed up. Maybe he talked to one of his friends."

"I'll talk to Dalton again, see if he'll tell me what happened."

Sasha dropped her voice a notch. "What's this I hear about you and the hunky pastor?" She slid a plate with the scone in front of Paige. "More important, why didn't I hear the news from you instead of the Otter Creek grapevine?"

She bit into the scone, sighed. "Oh, goodness, this is perfect. You definitely need to add this to the standard menu."

"The balance of cranberry and orange is right?"

"Don't change a thing."

Sasha beamed at her. "Good to know. Now, spill, Ms. Jensen. What's going on with you and Marcus?"

Paige darted a quick glance at the man in question. As if he felt her gaze, he looked up and caught her watching him. He winked at her. That simple action made her heart melt.

She smiled at the man who was slowly capturing her heart, then returned her attention to the coffee maven. "We're dating, but we haven't told many people."

"When did this happen?"

"The night I was attacked. Marcus stayed with me at the hospital and held my hand the whole night."

Sasha sighed. "That's so sweet. Does he have a brother? I haven't had much luck since I moved to town."

"Are you kidding? PSI is full of single men. Trent St. Claire's teammates just moved here and none of them are married."

Her friend wrinkled her nose. "They come in here to purchase big vats of the hardiest coffee I brew and race off to the bodyguard school. None of them have exchanged more than a few polite words with me since they hit town. I'm starting to think I've lost my touch with men."

"They've been busy at PSI. Has one of them caught your eye?"

Sasha turned aside to grab a clean rag and a bottle of cleaner she favored, and started wiping the counter. "Maybe."

"Ooh. Details, please." Paige chewed another bite.

"Doesn't matter if he's caught my interest. He hasn't acknowledged me beyond a head bob to thank me for the coffee."

She racked her brain to come up with a name. Which one of Trent St. Claire's teammates was oblivious to Sasha's charms? "Description."

"Why? We're not in elementary school. You can't nudge him to ask me out. I'm afraid any encouragement from an outside source might scare him off." She slid a pointed glance to Paige. "I don't want him going to my coffee competition to buy his morning brew. At least I see him every day even if he doesn't talk to me."

"I would never sabotage a potential love interest, especially given my long history of wishing Marcus would notice me. I told you about my interest in Marcus. Now it's your turn. Who is this mysterious silent man?"

Sasha seemed skeptical, but eventually nodded. "His name is Cade Ramsey."

Oh, yes. A very good match for her friend. "I've met him. He's a nice guy."

"Wait. He actually talked to you?"

"Sure. He's an interesting man." And now that she knew of Sasha's interest in him, she'd be sure to include her in the invitation list the next time she invited Trent and Grace to dinner along with Trent's teammates. Hopefully, Sasha wouldn't be aggravated with her if dinner was a group event. In fact, now that she thought about it, the gathering would be more fun if she and Gram invited the Durango team and their wives to dinner as well. Gram loved a good party, and she had a soft spot for Josh Cahill.

She would talk to her grandmother before she made definite plans. Paige glanced at the corner table and noticed Marcus had closed the notepad he brought with him. "Could you pour Marcus a coffee to go?"

"Sure. What about one of the power sandwiches? He likes those."

Paige checked her watch. Marcus may not have enough time to stop at a restaurant for lunch. "Do you still have one of those insulated bags to keep his food warm?"

She nodded. "I'll bring him a bottle of water, too."

By the time Sasha placed to-go order on the counter in front of Paige, Marcus laid his hand on Paige's shoulder.

"You ready?"

She nodded, then smiled at her friend. "Thanks, Sasha."

On the sidewalk, Marcus said, "Looked like you had fun with Sasha."

"I did. I plan to talk to Gram about a cookout with Sasha, Durango and their wives as well as Trent, Grace, and his teammates. Does that sound like something you would like to attend?"

He chuckled as they walked across the square to the police station. "If it involves food cooked on the grill, I'm there. Let me know when and what I can bring to help out."

Excellent. Now all she had to do was get Gram on board, then extend the other invitations. Maybe in a neutral place with his teammates surrounding him, Cade would be more inclined to strike up a conversation with Sasha. Playing Cupid for Cade and Sasha might be fun.

As Marcus laced his fingers with hers, Paige noticed people watching them. Did they not have anything better to do than stare at a man and woman holding hands? In all fairness, she wasn't that surprised. She and Marcus hadn't dated other people in years. Wonder if their friends and neighbors were taking side bets on how long this relationship would last?

"What did you find out from Sasha?"

Her head whipped his direction. Had Marcus overheard her conversation? Oh, man. She hoped not. She didn't want Sasha's fascination with a certain Fortress operative to get around town. "Please tell me our voices didn't carry to your table."

His eyes lit with amusement. "Sounds like I missed an interesting conversation. I didn't hear anything, but her shop is a gossip hub. I thought she might have noticed something out of the ordinary or heard rumors that might help us figure out who hurt you and why."

She wished. Finding out that information would mean a swift end to the danger. Then she and Marcus could enjoy their time together without watching over their shoulders. "The most fascinating thing Sasha talked about was her interest in a member of Trent's team."

Marcus's eyebrows shot up. "Explains the sudden interest in grilling for a crowd. You're bringing Sasha and Trent's teammate together in a neutral setting. I like the plan, but why do you need to intervene on their behalf?"

"He's shy around her. Although he goes in every morning for coffee, he hasn't said a word. I thought he might talk if he was surrounded by his teammates."

"Regardless of the reason for the cookout, it sounds like fun." He opened the station door and approached the bulky police man sitting behind the desk. "Chief Blackhawk is expecting us."

The buzz-cut brown-haired desk sergeant inclined his head toward the row of plastic seats against the wall. "Have a seat."

Five minutes later, the police chief pushed open the double doors and motioned them inside the bullpen. He led them through the maze of desks manned by cops and into his office. He motioned to the chairs in front of his desk. "Would you like coffee? It's Serena's signature Home Runs blend."

When they both declined the offer, Ethan sat behind his desk and pulled a yellow legal pad closer to him along with a pen. "Let's get started." He turned to Marcus. "You ready to talk now?"

"As long as I have your promise that whatever we discuss stays in here."

Ethan was silent a moment. "I can't guarantee I'll never be forced to share the information. I give you my word I won't share it lightly and only if I have no other option."

Paige gripped Marcus's arm. "What about your safety? Marcus, if the wrong people find out, you'll be in danger again."

He pressed her fingers. "My priority is your safety."

"Not good enough. I don't want anything to happen to you."

"I don't have a choice. I can't hamper Ethan and Nick's investigation. We don't know if this is about me, Paige. We do know you are at risk and so is Jo."

"Care to let me in on your secrets, Marcus?" Ethan asked, his tone wry.

A snort from the handsome preacher. "You already know, don't you?"

"Humor me."

Marcus recounted his tale, then sat back and waited.

"So, Maddox was the SEAL you saved." Ethan rubbed his jaw. "Didn't see that coming. I knew everything else."

"I haven't told anyone my birth name since I was released from the hospital."

"I still have good connections in the black ops and Special Forces community. Your bravery is legendary in those circles."

"Not brave. In the wrong place at the right time to help Brent. You've been keeping an eye on me since you stepped into the police chief's role, haven't you?"

Ethan's lips curved. "You weren't only what you appeared to be. You were too aware of your surroundings and moved like you were trained. You avoided social media and stayed out of the limelight. I'm a cop, Marcus. Anomalies capture my attention."

"Good thing I'm buried in a backwater town."

"The world's a small place these days. One slip or one picture posted on someone else's social media account, and Otter Creek could have unwanted visitors targeting my favorite preacher."

Marcus stilled. "Should I leave town?" he asked softly.

"Not yet."

Paige's breath caught. Oh, please, no. If he left, she couldn't watch his back. What if O'Reilly or his henchmen caught up with him? Marcus needed someone to protect him. In Otter Creek, many people with black ops training could keep an eye out for trouble. He wouldn't have that support system anywhere else. Losing Marcus would shatter her heart.

CHAPTER SEVENTEEN

Marcus spoke to Nancy Kirkland, hugged her, and left her home with Paige at his side. Nancy's family surrounded her and the last of the mourners left behind a kitchen filled with casseroles, sandwiches, and desserts.

He felt the tension slowly melt away. Handling crowds in an enclosed space was his least favorite part of the job. Paige, on the other hand, had appeared comfortable sharing close confines with the crowd. Because she was a natural, Paige had freed him to concentrate on Nancy and her family instead of multitasking.

"Are you okay?"

He glanced at the woman walking beside him, surprised she was concerned about his welfare. The last time someone worried about him was seven years earlier, another lifetime. He'd forgotten the comfort of someone caring about him as he ministered to his church and community.

"Tired, but not exhausted as usual after a funeral. Those who are grieving have a great need, and my ability to comfort is limited to words, hugs, and a shoulder to cry on. I always feel inadequate."

"You help more than you know, Marcus. I've heard church members say they wouldn't have weathered a crisis without your presence. You have a gift for speaking the truth in love and soothing those who grieve. There's no doubt in my mind that you are called by God to be a pastor."

Not knowing what to say, he changed the subject. "Are you hungry?"

Paige wrinkled her nose. "Not really. You need to eat, though. Let's go back to the B & B. Gram always has food available. Maybe we can go for a walk after we eat."

Great idea. He'd skipped jogging the past three mornings. "Sounds good." Marcus opened the vehicle door for Paige. "How is your headache?"

"Much better. As soon as the bruises on my throat fade, I'll be back to normal."

Couldn't happen soon enough for him. Every time he saw the marks marring her soft skin, he remembered how close he came to losing her, and longed for a face-to-face meeting with the man who hurt Paige. "After the walk, do you want to pick up your car?"

She nodded. "I love your company, but I don't want to tie you down. I know you curtailed your activities to chauffeur me around town."

Not so much curtailing his activities as keeping an eye on her. Convinced the man who tried to kill her would return, Marcus intended to be available to stop him. "Dr. Anderson caught me after the funeral and said he felt comfortable with you driving again."

By the time Marcus parked in the driveway of the B & B, he was more than ready to exchange his black suit for jeans and a long-sleeved t-shirt. After changing clothes, he and Paige found Mason, Nicole, and Jo in the kitchen setting out plates, cutlery, and glasses on the breakfast bar.

"Perfect timing." Jo kissed Paige's cheek, then Marcus's. "We're ready to eat."

"Smells fabulous," Marcus said. "What are we having?"

"Baked spaghetti, one of Paige's favorite meals. Nicole put together a beautiful salad to accompany the main course. That should provide the balanced meal you need, Marcus."

"Thanks, Jo."

She patted his arm. "We all should eat healthier." An hour later, Jo nudged Marcus and Paige out the door for their walk.

"Mase, Nicole, do you want to go?" he asked. Mason had been quieter than usual during the meal. His friend's reticence to talk made him suspicious.

Nicole shook her head. "Because we've been on our feet all day, Mason and I planned to watch a movie with Jo anyway."

"I'll walk you out," Mason said.

Guess his hunch was correct. On the porch, Marcus pulled the door closed behind them. "What's going on?"

"I didn't want to say anything to Jo, but I noticed new scratches on one window at the back of the house."

"Is that how the intruder broke in yesterday?" Paige asked.

"I called Nick before Jo came home. He and Stella checked outside the house earlier today. No scratches. Sometime between noon and five this afternoon, someone tried to break into the house. I didn't say anything to Jo although maybe I should have. I didn't want to worry her."

"You're forgoing the walk to protect Gram."

Even in the dim light of the porch, the stain of color in Mason's cheeks was easy to spot.

Paige stood on tiptoe and kissed his cheek. "Thank you."

Marcus clapped him on the shoulder. "Appreciate it, Mase."

With a short nod, he returned to the house.

Mason Kincaid was a good man. Marcus glanced at Paige as they ambled down the driveway. "Are you worried?"

"Aren't you?"

"Want me to have Zane send an operative to stay at the house?"

She was silent as they walked along the road in front of the inn. Finally, she said, "I don't want to ask an operative who might be needed elsewhere to babysit our house. The idea that someone needing help could die because of us makes my stomach twist into a knot."

"The operative would watch over Jo. Securing the house would be a bonus."

"Ask Josh Cahill to recommend one of the bodyguard trainees. Zane and Brent wouldn't be forced to shuffle Fortress resources and it gives the bodyguard a chance to use the skills PSI is teaching."

"I don't want a trainee protecting you or Jo. I'll set up a meeting with Durango. Maybe they have a suggestion acceptable to both of us."

"I've been thinking about Dalton."

"What about him?"

"We should talk to him again."

He'd planned to, but was curious about her reasoning. "Why?"

"He's a good kid who knows more than he's telling."

"The police questioned him and, if Ethan's interrogation was anything to go by, the questions were detailed."

"They focused on his appearance near a suspicious fire. Ethan and Nick weren't questioning a tiff between two teenagers. But we know the fight was unusual."

Marcus frowned, realized she was right. "You think the fight between Van and Dalton is connected to Van's death?"

"The timing is interesting. No one is considering a connection."

Thin possibility in his opinion. "We'll talk to him together. I don't feel good about you looking into this by yourself. You're a target. If your attacker finds out you're investigating on your own, he might hurt anyone you talk to."

She spun around, her expression a mask of horror. "Sasha! We have to warn her. I shouldn't have asked questions. What if he attacks her? I'll never forgive myself if I endangered a friend through carelessness."

Marcus cupped her shoulders. "You go to Perk all the time, Paige. This man won't zero in on something routine. Going to see Dalton by yourself is not normal for you. I'll mention your concerns about Sasha to Josh. He'll pass the word to PSI and his fellow cops. She'll have a whole host of observers keeping an eye on her plus an influx of new business."

Relief flooded her features. "That's a great idea."

He opened his mouth to reply, closed it again, on alert. What was that? He listened to the noises around him, positive he'd heard something in the woods across the road. He frowned. Nothing. Was his heightened awareness playing tricks on him?

"What is it?" Paige murmured.

Marcus wrapped his arms around her and pulled her close. "I'm not sure. I thought I heard something." And now the skin at the nape of his neck prickled. Not good. He'd learned to trust that instinct. "Let's go back."

The walk hadn't been long enough. He still felt sluggish. Perhaps Jo had exercise equipment. If not, he'd go with his old standby of doing push-ups until he collapsed from exhaustion.

He didn't want to stay in the open with a threat nearby. If he was correct, they were being stalked in the darkness.

He probably shouldn't have walked with her, but he'd wanted a few minutes alone with Paige.

He encouraged her to move faster, expecting to feel hot breath on the nape of his neck soon or, worse, the gaze of someone peering through a rifle scope.

Wood snapped across the road on his left. An animal? He clenched his jaw. Probably a two-legged hunter. He needed to grab his Sig when he returned to the parsonage for clean clothes. He would never forgive himself if he lost Paige because of his own stubbornness. He was licensed to carry and trained. If Paige's life was in danger, he would do what was necessary to protect her.

Marcus tucked Paige close to his side. Wouldn't help if a shooter drew a bead on them from behind, but he believed the man kept pace with them, maybe twenty feet behind them, just inside the tree line.

The sound of someone running through the trees reached his ears. His gut tightened. "Can you run?"

"Watch me." Paige's tone was grim.

"When I tell you to run, race for the house as though you're running the hundred-yard dash. Don't look back."

"You'll run too, right?"

"I'll be right behind you." Using his body to block a shot to her back. The person in the trees would have to stop and aim unless he was military trained. Even then, hitting a target on the run in the dark in unfamiliar terrain was difficult.

When they had almost reached a bend in the road, he released Paige. "Go!"

She took off like a gazelle racing to outrun a leopard. If the circumstances were different, Marcus would have enjoyed seeing her run. Paige was a skilled athlete. Marcus, on the other hand, ran out of necessity although he hated that activity. He preferred his rowing machine. Because most days he was in a hurry, he usually ran three miles, then went on with his day.

Male laughter drifted from the tree line, and a minute later Marcus saw a red dot on Paige's shoulder. "Faster," he snapped as he sprinted to catch up and cover her better.

A shot rang out.

CHAPTER EIGHTEEN

Bark flew off the tree to Paige's right. Her cheek stung and hot liquid trickled down her skin. Paige's heart leapt into her throat. "Marcus!"

"Run, baby."

Breath singing in her lungs, she lengthened her stride. Marcus had dropped back to protect her, but no one was safeguarding him.

Unable to help herself, she glanced over her shoulder to see Marcus racing at her heels. They were a still a quarter mile from the B & B.

She racked her brain for anything to use as shelter from the man shooting at them. She couldn't miss the heaviness of the pounding steps on the other side of the road.

The night was dark and cloudy. How could he see to shoot? Maybe he had a special scope.

She caught a glimpse of something through the trees to her right. The old stone wall. Her great-grandfather had built the wall to keep the neighbors' cattle from trampling through the grounds and destroying his apple trees. If they could shake the shooter long enough, they could hide on the other side of the wall. A dense growth of trees stood about a hundred yards to the right. The tree cover would hide their dive over the wall. Once there, more trees with low hanging branches would make their hiding place difficult to locate.

Paige didn't dare ask Marcus if her idea was good. She whispered a prayer as she darted off the road into the tree line.

She ran between trees, making a beeline for the only shelter until they reached the house. Twenty feet to go. Paige ignored the stitch in her side and pushed herself faster. Ten feet. Five.

Angling for the thickest part of the tree cover, she vaulted over the stone wall and dove to the ground. Paige rolled until her back pressed against the cool rock. Two seconds later, Marcus scaled the wall and dropped, rolling his body to cover hers. He wrapped his arms around her.

Willing herself to breath quietly, Paige buried her face in Marcus's neck. They had to survive. She wanted another date and to share more kisses with this amazing man.

He tightened his hold. "Here he comes," he whispered. "Don't move no matter what you hear."

Running feet drew near. Heavy breathing reached her ears. Soft curses, then, "I see you," came the harsh, sing-song tone. "Did you think you could escape me?"

Although he didn't move, Paige felt Marcus's muscles tense at the shooter's taunt.

"Come to me, and I'll make this quick and clean. I'm not a heartless monster."

Right. She wanted to laugh. Did he think they were stupid?

Headlights swept over the trees, and a vehicle drove toward the B& B.

The shooter muttered a vile curse, then, "Next time you won't be so lucky."

Twigs broke and fabric brushed against trees and bushes, the noises moving farther away with each of the shooter's steps. When she subtly moved away from Marcus, he stilled her movements.

"Wait."

She froze. Cold chills surged up her spine. Would the shooter fake leaving, then double back and kill them when they came out of hiding?

Paige shuddered. Why was this happening? She hadn't done or seen anything that merited death by strangulation or gunshot.

"Cold?"

"Scared."

"Me, too."

Why wasn't he shaking? Still they waited. Paige heard only the wind stirring bushes and tree branches. A bird fluttered nearby. Somewhere close a cat yowled and a dog barked.

Finally, Marcus eased back to look her into the eyes. "I think we're clear. You okay?"

"Walk in the park," she lied with a fake smile on her lips. He wouldn't believe that fabrication, not with her body trembling now the danger had passed.

"The stone wall was the perfect place to hide. The shooter had a night-vision scope on his rifle."

"What does that mean?"

"He could see us through his scope even though we couldn't see him. Something impermeable like rock or stone would hide us from his view. You saved our lives."

"If it's all the same to you, I'd rather avoid running for my life again."

He chuckled. "I needed a run, but I'd prefer different circumstances." Marcus helped Paige stand. "You were amazing." He captured her mouth for a brief, hard kiss. "We should go. The shooter might decide to try his luck again."

He didn't have to tell her twice. Paige set off for the B & B, cutting across the uneven terrain until they reached the driveway. They walked quickly until they spotted a police cruiser in the driveway.

An invisible band tightened around Paige's heart. "Gram!"

Marcus clasped her hand, his grip tight. "The cruiser didn't come with sirens or flashing lights. It also wasn't accompanied by an ambulance. Besides, we have our cell phones. No one called us."

He was right. She needed to get a grip on her emotions. The last thing she wanted to do was alarm her grandmother even more than she would be when she learned of their brush with death. "Sorry. I'm spooked."

"You have a right to be. Let's find out which policeman is here."

They hurried into the house. A low hum of voices led them to the kitchen. Nick Santana sat at the table with a mug of coffee in his hands and a slice of apple pie on a plate in front of him.

Nick's eyes narrowed. "What happened to your face, Paige?"

She pressed a hand to her cheek. Rats! She'd forgotten about the scratch.

Marcus turned her face toward the light, frowned. "You said you weren't hurt."

Jo walked toward her, a scowl on her beloved face. "Did you fall?"

"Not exactly."

Hands propped on her hips, her grandmother pressed her lips into a thin line, waiting for an explanation.

Paige sighed. Gram knew how to wield silence better than anyone Paige had met. The woman was relentless when she wanted something. "The scratch is from flying tree bark."

"Who shot at you?" Nick demanded to know.

"Oh, my goodness." Jo threw her arms around Paige. "Are you sure you're all right?"

"I'm fine, Gram. I don't have other injuries."

"Marcus, you're, all right?" Jo's gaze swept over him.

Yes, ma'am, thanks to your granddaughter."

Nicole stood. "We should clean the wound. Where are your first aid supplies?"

Jo waved her off. "I'll bring what we need. Paige, talk to Nick. Don't hold anything back."

"Start talking," Nick said. "What happened?"

Paige sat across from the detective. "Marcus and I went for a walk. Marcus must have heard something because he insisted we return to the B & B."

Nick's gaze shifted to Marcus. "What did you hear?"

"Maybe a twig breaking or something brushing against a bush. I felt someone watching us."

Nick's lips curved. "Spiders?"

"Yeah."

"Good thing you listened. Then what happened?"

"I didn't hear anything for a while, then I heard a branch break. I told Paige to run when we reached a bend in the road."

Jo returned with first aid supplies and started cleaning Paige's cut.

"He was right behind me, Nick." Paige's voice grew husky. "He put himself at my back to protect me. That's when the man following us pulled the trigger. He missed us, thank God, but he hit the tree beside me. The bark splintered, scratching my cheek."

"Close call. Lucky shot, Marcus?"

"I don't think so. The weapon was a rifle with a night-vision scope."

"How do you know?"

Paige stilled. He couldn't tell Nick everything, not without compromising his own safety. Under the table, she clamped her hand over his.

"I'm curious by nature. I've also spent many hours at firing ranges."

"How did you escape?"

Marcus chuckled. "Paige's fast feet and razor-sharp brain. She took us into the woods and ran for a stone wall behind heavy tree cover. We hopped the wall, dove to the ground, and hid. You drove up the driveway and scared him off."

Mason whistled softly. "Good job, Paige."

"We did it together. Marcus sensed the danger. If he knew Jensen land like I did, he would have known exactly where to hide."

Nick pushed away his empty plate. "Show me where this happened."

Marcus laid a hand on Paige's shoulder. "I can take care of this. Stay here and get warm. I won't be long."

"Be careful," she murmured, her gaze clinging to his for a moment.

He winked. "I don't want to miss my date with a beautiful woman Friday night." Marcus cupped the nape of her neck and kissed her briefly before turning to follow Nick from the house.

Her heart turned over in her chest. Good grief. How had she managed to capture Marcus Lang's attention? Any woman would be blessed to have his interest.

After Marcus and Nick left, her grandmother finished cleaning her wound. "Do you want a bandage on that, dear?"

And call attention to her injury even more than a red streak across her cheek? "I don't think so. Thanks, Gram."

Jo slid her a troubled look. "Maybe you should go on a vacation, Paige. You haven't had one in several years. No one would fault you for taking some time for yourself."

"I have a date Friday night with Marcus. I'm not missing that." The way things were escalating, Paige hoped she lived long enough to go on that date.

CHAPTER NINETEEN

Marcus walked at the side of the road with Nick. Had to admit he felt more comfortable making the trek with someone armed. "Why were you at the B & B?"

"To tell Paige she can open the community center tomorrow morning. I finished processing the locker room and hallway. I also sent in the crime scene cleaners to handle the cleanup in the locker room."

Relief flooded Marcus. He'd made tentative plans to gain access to the center before Paige so she wouldn't have to face the gruesome task herself. "Paige will be happy to return to work."

"Might be good for you to be on hand when she opens tomorrow as well as in the afternoon when the kids arrive."

"I already planned to be there, especially for the children and teenagers. No one handles death well, but those age groups are particularly vulnerable." He also wanted to be there for Paige. The memories of the assault in the hallway would hit her hard. Unfortunately, he couldn't stay all day. Van Wilder's funeral was at 11:00 at the church.

"You and Paige, huh?"

"Yes."

"I'm happy for you, Marcus."

"Thanks. When are you off duty?"

"I stopped by the B & B on my way home."

"And now we've added hours to your work day. I'm sorry, man."

"You and Paige talked to Ethan today while I was out."

"He told you what happened last night?"

"You can trust me to be discreet."

Oh, man. Nick was his friend, but Marcus had followed Maddox's orders to protect his new identity. Now, however, the secrecy might bite him like a snake hiding in the grass. What if the attacks on Paige weren't about her, but about Marcus? What if he was to blame? "I know, Nick."

"Is there something you need to tell me?"

Although the need for secrecy still existed, the more people watched over Paige when he couldn't, the better. For her sake, he couldn't keep everyone out of the loop. If word leaked to the O'Reillys, Marcus would ask Fortress to place active protection around his family. "I'm in private witness protection, and I'm not sure if the attacks on Paige are about her or me, maybe both."

"Fortress?"

Marcus told him about the attack in the restaurant parking lot, the loss of Chelsea, and the need for a new identity. He stopped walking. "No one can know, Nick. Paige's life is on the line if the wrong people learn my location and that she's important to me. I don't want to lose her."

"I'm sorry about losing Chelsea and your family. I know how painful that is."

Yes, he did. Nick's family was murdered his first year in college. Marcus scanned the area. "This is where I heard the man in the woods."

"Show me." Nick turned on a flashlight.

Marcus walked into the tree line with Nick. Ten feet in, he noticed a branch on the ground, broken in the middle. Maybe that's what he heard.

Nick took a picture with his cell phone, noted the location in his notebook, and, pulling a piece of yellow plastic from his jacket pocket, placed an evidence marker near the branch. "If anyone can track this guy's movements, it will be Ethan."

They returned to the road and Marcus turned toward the B & B. "We turned around here."

They walked in silence until they reached the bend in the road. "This is where we started running."

Nick scanned the area. "Perfect place for an ambush."

"The bend in the road blocked us from the shooter's view." He motioned toward the spot where Paige veered off the road. "We ran into the trees here."

"The shooter followed you?"

He nodded.

Nick set another yellow marker on the ground. "Move over ten feet and take me on a parallel path to the stone wall."

Marcus showed the detective where they scaled the wall and hid from the shooter.

"Stay here." Nick studied the ground carefully, placed another marker. "Did he scale the wall?"

"No. He taunted us, claimed he saw us and we wouldn't escape. He said if we gave ourselves up, he'd make our deaths quick."

"Did you recognize him?"

"Never saw him and I can't ID Paige's attacker by voice."

A nod. "Since he didn't climb the wall, we can walk the path you took to the B & B. I'll call Ethan on the way home, let him know what happened."

Nick slid a pointed glance toward Marcus. "Think about relocating temporarily or having extra eyes on you and Paige."

Marcus shoved his hands into his pockets. "I'm not leaving. If O'Reilly comes after me here, he'll face more trouble than he can handle. I won't take out an ad in the *Gazette*, but I'm finished running. This is my home now."

"Even if O'Reilly targets Paige?" the detective asked softly.

He flinched. "I have a plan."

Silence, then, "Josh?"

"Durango and St. Claire's team. They can protect Paige from O'Reilly's henchmen."

"They're the best," Nick agreed. "Stella will know about your situation because Nate will tell her. They don't keep secrets from each other. You know she's a vault when it comes to secrets."

Stella Armstrong, the wife of Durango's EOD man, had been a US Marshal.

"I want your permission to bring Rod into the loop. My brother-in-law may be on scene first if there's another attack on you or Paige. He needs to know what he's up against."

"Rod is married to the newspaper editor."

"They have an agreement. He doesn't tell her anything that can't be published. When it can, she gets an exclusive. You can trust him."

He weighed the risks of broadening his circle. Again, what choice did he have? The last thing he wanted was to endanger the spitfire detective with a heart of gold. "Tell him." If the information protected Rod and encouraged the detective to watch over Paige, Marcus would take the risk.

The B & B's porch light shined like a beacon as they neared the inn. "How serious are you about Paige?" Nick asked.

How did Marcus explain the storm of emotions flooding him when he was with her? "I've never felt like this about anyone, including Chelsea. This is different. More."

"I can't say I understand from experience, but my wife would. Madison told me the love she felt for Luke was different than what we have."

Madison Santana had been married to Nick's partner when they worked for the Knoxville PD. Two years after she lost Luke in a car accident, she fell in love with Nick.

"Does she...?" He stopped. He wanted to ask how a person who had been through loss handled loving someone else, but the question might hurt Nick.

He froze in his tracks. Love? No. It was too soon. Wasn't it?

"Ask, Marcus."

"Does she still love him?"

"Of course. She will always love Luke."

"Doesn't it bother you?"

Nick shook his head. "I loved him like a brother. Luke wouldn't have wanted Madison to be alone the rest of her life."

"Paige asked if I still loved Chelsea."

"Do you?"

"Part of me always will, but what I feel for Paige isn't the same."

"Madison's relationship with Luke was different than what we have. Their communication was easy, their relationship gentle and comfortable." Nick grinned. "She tells me I'm a thousand times more intense than he was, and she has to pry information out of me with a crow bar. Despite the difference, we're an excellent team and I adore my wife."

"It shows."

"If the circumstances were different, I'd recommend you talk to her." A hard glint came into the detective's eyes. "Don't. I don't want Madison at risk for any reason, and your secrets, my friend, are a risk to my wife's safety."

"I understand." But wasn't he risking Paige?

Marcus pushed aside the guilt, whispered a silent prayer for her protection, and vowed to call Josh Cahill before the night was over. "Thanks, Nick," he said as they reached the porch.

"Best of luck, Marcus. I think Paige would be a great pastor's wife."

They returned to the kitchen where the others waited.

"Did you find anything?" Jo asked.

"Too dark for an extensive search," Nick said. "I left evidence markers. Please don't disturb them or the surrounding area."

"They're not in the orchard?"

"No, ma'am."

"No problem, then. The workers will be doing damage control tomorrow, and keeping them away from certain areas would be difficult."

Nick turned. "You can reopen the community center tomorrow, Paige. I don't want you alone in the center for any reason. If your part-time help can't stay, lock the doors, and lock yourself in your office until someone you trust arrives to escort you from the building."

"You sure this is necessary?"

"This guy isn't playing, Paige. From Marcus's description of tonight's incident, your shooter has experience with weapons and stalking prey. Let's not give him another opportunity to target you. Next time, you might not survive."

CHAPTER TWENTY

Marcus saw Nick out, promising to be vigilant. When he turned, Paige stood in the archway to the living room. He spread his arms, inviting her into his embrace.

She crossed the expanse and wrapped her arms around his waist. "What did you find in the woods?"

"A branch broken in the middle as though someone stepped on it. It's what made me suspect we were being followed. Nick will go out there with Ethan tomorrow, see if he can find something significant."

"I doubt Ethan will see anything. I'm afraid this guy didn't leave any trace of himself behind."

"If anyone can find traces of the shooter, it will be Ethan. The members of Durango talk about the police chief's tracking ability."

He lifted his hand and trailed the back of his fingers down her cheek, his touch gentle. Such soft skin. Color bloomed under the living porcelain, making him smile. "Have I mentioned how amazing you were today?"

She shook her head, the color deepening.

"You made a difficult day easier for me and the Kirklands. Thank you, Paige."

"I just loved on them and tried to support you."

He slid one hand to cup the nape of her neck while the other rested against her side. "How is Jo?"

"Worried."

"Aren't you?"

"I keep expecting a bullet or knife in the back. I feel eyes watching me all the time. I'm afraid for myself, Gram, and you."

He bent his head and kissed her. "Don't worry about me."

"What if the shooter works for O'Reilly? He's already hurt you, Marcus. I can't help but be worried about your safety."

"Fear is normal in this situation. I'm afraid, too." A mild description for the terror he felt at the probability that Paige was a target because of him. "We can't let fear paralyze us or we'll be ineffective."

"How do we prevent that?"

"Make proactive plans for our safety."

"Such as?"

Did Paige think he would force her to leave town or insist she stay inside the inn? He respected her too much to do that. If the time came for drastic action, his girlfriend would listen to reason and, if she didn't like the choices, come up with another option. "Talk to Josh Cahill and Trent St. Claire. Like Nick said, you need someone with you at the community center. Caleb isn't a bodyguard, and he can't be with you all the time."

"What about you? You need protection."

"I wasn't a SEAL, but I have training, courtesy of the US government and Fortress."

She looked skeptical although she didn't argue.

"When does Caleb arrive tomorrow?"

"Three o'clock. Why?"

"I want to talk to Dalton and Seth. Would you like to go with me?" Marcus didn't want Paige to ask questions without him.

"I'd love to. Caleb is scheduled to close tomorrow."

"What about dinner at Burger Heaven afterward? Because of the Wednesday night service, we won't have time for a more elaborate meal."

Her eyes narrowed. "This better not be a substitute for Friday's out-of-town date."

He smiled. "No, ma'am. I'm looking forward to dinner away from town scrutiny."

"In that case, I would love to have dinner with you. Burger Heaven is one of my favorite restaurants."

"What time do you need to be at the center tomorrow?"

"Six."

"We'll leave at 5:45."

"Will you go home after you drop me off?"

"I planned to be available in case people need to talk." He wouldn't leave Paige in the center by herself. "Because Van's funeral is at 11:00, I have to leave before 10:00. I'll return as soon as I can. I wanted to be on hand for the teens and kids in the afternoon."

"Thank you, Marcus. I know the kids will appreciate your presence."

He tilted his head. "What about you?"

She brushed his lips with hers. "Especially me. I didn't miss how you're taking care of me, too."

"You matter to me." More than she knew. More than he could admit.

"Paige?" Jo called from the kitchen.

Marcus released her. "I'll be on the porch a few minutes while I talk to Josh." He couldn't afford to be overheard. Bad enough that he had to admit the truth to Josh and Trent. They would have to inform their teammates. Otter Creek had the most efficient grapevine he'd ever seen, far surpassing the bases he'd been assigned to in the military. If word spread through town about his past, O'Reilly's men wouldn't be far behind.

He scanned the yard before sitting in the shadowed portion of the swing. A moment later, Josh answered his phone.

"Cahill."

"It's Marcus."

"What do you need?"

"No questions, Josh?"

"You'll tell me what you can. I'd prefer more information to less. I know you or Paige, maybe both, are in trouble. That's enough for me to offer assistance without strings."

Stunned, he remained silent a few seconds. How could Josh offer help without enough knowledge to protect himself or his teammates? "I need protection for Paige."

"What about you?"

"I'm more concerned about her."

"Fortress or PSI?"

"Paige doesn't want Fortress. She's worried about taking necessary assets away from a mission."

"Durango and St. Claire's team are on site for the next two weeks. We'll rotate bodyguards unless I locate one who's trained but not on a team ready for deployment. That work?"

The tension knotting his gut eased. "Thanks, Josh."

"Can you tell me details?"

"Talking on the phone isn't wise. I can't meet tomorrow. Van Wilder's funeral is at 11:00 and I need to be on hand tomorrow at the community center in case someone needs to talk."

"What about tonight?"

He blinked. "I don't want to take you and the others away from your families."

Vendetta

"Marcus, our wives understand the secrecy necessary when we take on a mission. Where are you?"

"The B & B. We can't talk here."

Silence, then, "Paige knows the details?"

"Yes, but Jo, Nicole, and Mason don't. Safer if it stays that way."

"I'll contact the others. We'll meet in PSI's conference room in 45 minutes." Josh ended the call.

Marcus slid his phone into a pocket. Incredible. Josh wanted details, but if Marcus couldn't share them, the Special Forces soldier would have proceeded with the protection detail anyway, risking himself. Now, instead of speaking to Josh and Trent, their teammates would also be there.

He found Paige in the kitchen alone. The noises overhead indicated the others had gone upstairs to ready themselves for bed.

"Did you talk to Josh?"

"He wants to meet at PSI in a few minutes."

"I'll come with you." She held up her hand before he could protest. "Don't bother. I want to be involved. The more I know, the better prepared I'll be to cooperate with the guards assigned to me and Gram."

No use arguing. In his experience, knowing more was better. "We have a few minutes. Do you want to change clothes?"

Paige frowned. "Why?"

"You don't normally wear dirt and leaves on your clothing."

She looked down at herself and laughed softly. "I guess I should change."

"I'll let Mase know we'll be out for a while."

Fifteen minutes later, they headed toward the opposite side of Otter Creek to the PSI campus. During the drive, Marcus called Zane and reported the latest incident.

"I'll inform Maddox."

"Anything on your end?"

A sigh. "Yeah. Rumors are spreading through the O'Reilly network that an HVT has been located."

A high value target. Was it him or another target of O'Reilly's rage? Based on Zane's grim voice, there was more. "What else, Z?"

"The reward for your capture or death has been doubled."

CHAPTER TWENTY-ONE

Paige gripped Marcus's hand, her stomach twisting into a knot. No. She prayed for his safety and those who would watch over him. After this news, she planned to insist someone be assigned to protect him. If O'Reilly or his men came after Marcus, Paige might lose him. "Zane?"

"Yes, Paige?"

"I want Marcus protected."

"As do we. Marcus, tell Josh to set up a videoconference with me and Maddox. I'm sending a photo of the hit men O'Reilly uses to do his dirty work to your email. I'll also copy Blackhawk, Santana, Cahill, and St. Claire. If you aren't armed, borrow a weapon from PSI before you leave the campus."

"Copy that." He ended the call, glanced at Paige. "You okay?"

"Not even close. I'm afraid for you."

He was silent a moment. "We should wait before pursuing a relationship."

She scowled. "No. I waited more than six years for this opportunity. I'm not allowing a thug from back east to taint what we have together."

"Paige, you're not safe in my company."

"I'm not safe away from you," she corrected. "Remember Strong Man at the center? You weren't around when Strong Man attacked me, but you stopped him from killing me."

"Your attack might be connected to me."

"It also might be connected to something else entirely."

"What's the probability of you being in the middle of two dangerous situations?"

"Almost nil. We still can't rule it out."

"I'm not buying it."

"Tough. I'm not walking away from you. Strap on the weapons you want to carry, and we'll do what we have to do to keep those we care about safe. But I'm not leaving you to deal with this alone. We're in this together, Marcus. I'm already at risk as we saw earlier. I'm safer with you by my side."

"Do you have to be so stubborn?"

She smiled. "Didn't you know? Stubborn is my middle name."

He gave a huff of laughter. "Now you tell me."

"You could walk away."

He slid her a sidelong glance. "Not a chance. It's too late for that."

What did that mean? "Care to elaborate?"

Marcus shook his head as he negotiated the turn into PSI's driveway. At the front entrance to the main building, two tall, muscular men waited. Dressed in black, Josh Cahill and Rio Kincaid met them as they exited the truck.

"Any trouble?" Josh asked, his gaze scanning the area.

"No." Marcus reached for Paige's hand.

Vendetta

"Inside. No need to present a tempting target." Rio motioned them toward the front doors, then he and Josh fell into step behind them.

Paige hated this. She didn't want her friends or Marcus in the line of fire. Inside the entrance, she tried to rush Marcus away from the windows. How could these security conscious men have this much glass where they worked? Weren't they worried about a bullet shattering the glass and striking one of them?

"Paige, you and Marcus are safe." Josh inclined his head to the windows. "Bullet-resistant glass."

She skidded to a stop, shuddered. Bullet-resistant was good. She'd prefer bulletproof although nothing was impermeable with the right weapons.

"Hey." Marcus cupped her face between his palms. "We'll be fine."

Paige pressed her cheek against his hand. How would she survive if something happened to him? The breath froze in her lungs as the depth of her feelings swelled. Not possible. She couldn't be in love with him. They'd only been on one date.

"Paige?"

She glanced at Rio.

"Are you all right?"

"I will be." She and Marcus must survive. She wanted to find out what was ahead for them.

"Conference room's this way." Josh led them across the lobby and down a hallway. Light streamed from an open doorway at the end of the corridor. A rumble of male voices stopped when Josh walked inside the room.

To her surprise, Marcus eased Paige behind him and entered the room first. To walk in front of her was out of character for him. Then she realized he'd placed his body in front of hers as a shield.

She had no chance of protecting her heart from this man. She was in so deep she couldn't save herself from searing pain if Marcus didn't feel the same way. Was she in this deep alone? Goodness, she hoped not. This was a scary place without a life partner to share the roller coaster ride.

Josh's and St. Claire's teammates were seated around the table. The operatives stood when she crossed the threshold.

Marcus interlaced their fingers and led her to two chairs.

Once they were seated, the operatives greeted her and Marcus. All of them frequented the community center to play with the kids. From what she'd seen, the operatives and the kids enjoyed themselves. The afternoons and nights the soldiers were on site, she hadn't been called upon to referee the teens or kids.

Nate Armstrong established the videoconference with Maddox and Zane. Both men seemed to be at their homes.

Regret filled Paige. She hated to interrupt time with their families.

"Talk to me," Maddox said. "I'm reading a bedtime story to Alexa soon. Marcus, start at the beginning so the operatives know what's happening and why."

"Some of this is fact, some is supposition," Marcus began. He summarized the events of the last few days. When he talked about her attack at the center, the operatives scowled.

What had taken days to live took minutes to relate in a succinct manner.

"You have personal enemies, Paige?" Alex Morgan, a teammate of Josh's, asked.

She shook her head.

"Problems at the community center?"

"Only the battle with Mayor Parks."

Nate snorted. "He has his own agenda with every decision the council makes. What he wants isn't always in the best interests of the town."

"What's his problem with the community center?" Quinn Gallagher wanted to know.

"Money, what else?" Paige said to Josh's teammate. "He's holding the town's purse strings tight on every project or budget but his own. He says there's no money for what I need. Of course, he complains if the center isn't open when he wants it to be."

"Paige needs money to hire a full-time employee," Marcus said, his fingers tightening on hers. "She's working 60 to 70 hours per week."

Trent St. Claire whistled. "Way too much."

"You've worked far more than that in a week," she pointed out.

"People's lives depend on us doing our jobs. Although the community might gripe if you don't open the center, they won't die from the inconvenience. We aren't always deployed. Fortress teams rotate, and between missions we spend time with our families and friends. When was the last time you went on vacation?"

She remained silent. Wouldn't help to complain. None of these men had the power to bring about a change.

"That's what I thought." Trent turned to the large television screen where Zane and Maddox watched and listened to the discussion. "Are we sure Marcus's past is connected to Paige's trouble?"

"Given the uptick in communications and activity in the O'Reilly organization plus the sudden hike in the bounty, I think it's a good bet," Maddox said, frowning. "I'm not positive O'Reilly will hand this to one of his usual corral of cleanup men."

"I'll check into it," Zane said.

"Do you think part of this is about Paige?" Josh asked.

"I'm not seeing how the teenager's death fits into the whole. Cahill and St. Claire, come up with a plan. Whatever you need is yours."

"Yes, sir."

"Any progress on the orchard fire?"

"Arson. Gasoline was the accelerant. No surveillance cameras or close neighbors means no witnesses."

"In other words, Santana doesn't have much."

"Not much to go on."

A grunt from the buzz-cut blond. "Keep me up to date. Paige, Marcus, follow the plan the teams come up with to the letter. As soon as we know who's behind the attacks, we'll go after the source. I want to know if Marcus's past is surfacing. If it is, we'll take care of it. Permanently."

Did she really want to know what that meant? Probably not. Paige glanced at Marcus, noted his pallor. Yeah, that was a good indication the solution would be painful for O'Reilly and his henchmen.

A high-pitched voice had Maddox turning aside for a moment. He murmured something soft, then faced the screen again. "I need to go. Anything else?"

"We'll hash things out and get back to you and Zane." Josh ended the video feed. "Let's talk."

CHAPTER TWENTY-TWO

Marcus walked inside the community center with Paige, his gaze searching the darkened corners and corridors. Everything looked normal which made it hard to believe someone had almost killed the woman gripping his hand. He would never forget the gut-wrenching fear and fury he'd experienced a few days earlier. "Glad to be back?"

"Yes and no. I can't help remembering the feel of Strong Man's hands around my throat."

"He's not waiting for you, and you're not alone. I'll be around as much as possible today, and Fortress operatives will be here throughout the day." Marcus locked the door behind them.

He turned on lights, and a florescent glare lit the cavernous room. The air was still, the atmosphere peaceful. Wouldn't last long, he knew. As soon as the public arrived, chaos would ensue, hopefully the good kind.

Paige looked toward the boy's locker room. "I should check the room." Her expression and body language showcased her reluctance.

"The locker room is clean. Nick called crime scene cleaners that work with the police department. They also clean up industrial accidents so they know what they're doing."

"Thank goodness. I wasn't looking forward to the task."

He hadn't been, either. However, to keep Paige from facing the task, he'd planned to don a pair of rubber gloves and disinfect the locker room and the hallway. "Do you want to walk through the center?"

She nodded. "I need to make sure everything is ready. I didn't have a chance to do that the night I was attacked. I'd planned to come early the next morning to take care of the details for the next day's activities, then hit the paperwork that multiplies like rabbits overnight."

Marcus squeezed her hand. "I'll take the grand tour with you."

Together, they walked the facility. The locker rooms had a towel strewn here and there, a pair of flip flops, two shirts, and a hairbrush.

Back in the gym, Marcus glanced at his watch. "People will arrive soon. You ready?"

"Ready to return to normal." Her lips curved. "Unfortunately, our situation can't be classified as normal even if the center's facility is shipshape."

"You still want to visit Dalton and Seth with me?"

"Absolutely. I hope the boys will talk about Van. They know something."

"Agreed." He didn't think they would be any more forthcoming.

Marcus frowned. Something about that whole Croft scenario bugged him. Aside from the fact it would have been difficult to study geometry on a poorly lit porch even with a flashlight, he had a hard time seeing Seth sneaking around to do homework or study for a test at midnight.

Vendetta

Didn't seem like the place Dalton would recommend meeting, either.

"Did you charge your cell phone?" he asked.

"Overnight. Before you ask, it's in my pocket."

He kissed her, slow and easy as though they had hours instead of minutes. This might be his only chance to focus on her without constant interruptions. Once the circus started today, it wouldn't stop until he slipped into bed.

Marcus eased back, reluctant to break their kiss. The woman in his arms looked dazed. He released his hold when someone banged on the center's front door. "Go to your office until I'm sure it's safe."

He walked across the gym to the door. Alex Morgan stood on the other side of the glass, gym bag in hand. He nodded a greeting and surveyed the square coming to life as residents of Otter Creek began the day.

Marcus disengaged the lock for Durango's sniper. "Hope Ivy wasn't upset with your late night at PSI."

At the mention of his wife's name, Alex's face lit up. "She understood. Fortunately, she doesn't have a class until 11:00 today so she was able to sleep in this morning."

His eyebrows shot up. "She waited up for you?"

"If I'm not deployed, Ivy won't go to sleep until I'm home."

"She's feeling okay?" The soldier and his wife were expecting their first child.

A grin. "Never better. Doc Anderson says Ivy and the baby are doing great. We have three months to go."

Marcus squeezed the other man's shoulder. "Glad to hear they're doing well, Alex. Where do you want to set up?"

His friend tilted his chin at the basketball goal. "Right here. I'll be able to see everything going on and keep an eye on Paige."

He scanned the Special Forces soldier, frowned. "Are you armed?"

A snort from Alex.

Right. What was he thinking? None of the Fortress operatives went anywhere without multiple weapons on them. Marcus held up his hand. "Sorry. I know better. I appreciate you protecting Paige."

Alex stared at him a moment, then said softly, "Does she know you love her?"

"That obvious?"

"To me."

"I'm afraid it's too soon to tell her, Alex."

The sniper's lips curved. "I don't think you have anything to worry about."

His heart skipped a beat. Did Paige love him? Is that what Alex had seen? Man, he hoped so. Nothing would make him happier except placing a wedding ring on her finger. He wanted to laugh at himself. Planning to marry a woman he'd dated once? If Paige knew that, she might run from him.

"Marcus?" Paige called from her office.

He turned. "Alex is here."

A moment later, Paige hugged Alex. "Thanks for babysitting me this morning. How's Ivy?"

"Terrific."

A steady stream of people began arriving. Some headed for the workout equipment, unaware or uncaring of the drama surrounding the community center and Paige. Others congregated around Marcus, expressions anxious. A group of women huddled around Paige. In the middle of the chaos, Mayor Parks arrived for his session in the weight room.

The mayor's expression hardened as he made his way across the gym floor to stand toe-to-toe with Marcus. "A word, Pastor Lang."

Marcus shook hands with the few men still hovering near him, encouraging them to go on with their workouts or to play basketball with Alex.

When he broke away from the remnants, he found Parks standing near the stage, bag at his feet. The mayor leaned against the wooden platform, arms folded across his chest. "What did you want to talk about, Mr. Mayor?"

"Fifteen thousand dollars for plumbing."

"Elliott Construction's estimate is a fair one. I asked a plumber from another company for another estimate. His was higher than Elliott's."

"This is an unnecessary expense."

A flash of irritation rolled over Marcus. "Are you getting up twice a night to empty an extra-large bucket filled with water?"

"Of course not."

"I am. Every time I run the dishwasher or washing machine, the leak is worse. If I don't empty the bucket, water will flood the bathroom floor and the church would have an even larger expense to replace flooring. You wouldn't tolerate this in your home. I shouldn't have to, either. Look, I'm not asking for a remodeling job. I'm asking to replace corroding pipes before we have a larger bill."

"You can't do a simple plumbing job?" A sneer settled on the mayor's face.

"All the pipes in the house need to be replaced, and I'm not a plumber. If you force me to become one, I won't have time to take care of my pastoral responsibilities."

"You don't seem to be taking care of them as it is. What's the difference?"

Marcus stared, stunned. "What are you talking about? What responsibility have I neglected?"

"You can't be doing your job. Every time I've seen you around town lately, you're in the company of Paige Jensen."

He stepped closer, dropped his voice. "I have a right to a private life, Mayor Parks. I'm capable of fulfilling my obligations and dating Paige."

"You've moved beyond dating, Lang," the portly man snapped out.

"What do you mean?"

"I'm filing a complaint with Cornerstone's deacon board concerning your behavior. No preacher should ever conduct himself as you have."

Marcus waited until his temper and voice were under control. "Are you accusing me of immoral behavior?"

"You're living with her."

"I'm staying with her and her grandmother. So are Nicole Copeland and Mason Kincaid. We're worried about Paige and Jo's safety. No one else from the church has questioned the arrangement, including the deacons. And before you ask, yes, I informed them of the arrangements. If you still want to go to the deacon board, that is your right. You better have proof before you level that kind of accusation. You want to throw barbs at me? Fine. But I won't tolerate anyone dragging Paige's reputation through the mud."

"Are you threatening me?" Parks hissed, fury filling his gaze.

"Not a threat. A promise."

The mayor stalked off toward the weight room.

Marcus blew out a breath, frustrated beyond belief. How did Parks live with himself? When a basketball sailed his direction, he snagged the ball in mid-air.

Alex jogged over. "Nice job with the mayor," he murmured. "Don't take it personally. Parks is out to get everyone."

"How can I not take it personally? His accusations could cause the church to vote me out as pastor."

"Give our congregation some credit, Marcus." The soldier clapped him on the shoulder and trotted back to the basketball goal.

Marcus trusted his people. But how many would look at him and wonder if he was telling the truth? His ministry at Cornerstone Church may be coming to an end.

CHAPTER TWENTY-THREE

When Marcus left to meet James Wilder at the church, Paige knew something was wrong. His mood had grown more somber as the morning progressed. He still ministered to those who needed it, visited with those who didn't. He'd stayed near her. More than once, she felt his hand on her back in silent support as she answered the same questions. So attentive despite the inner battle Marcus fought.

Did his mood have anything to do with his heated discussion with the mayor? Parks had been in a foul mood when he stomped by on his way to work thirty minutes sooner than normal. He'd glared at Paige as he moved past her to the front door. And when she'd questioned Marcus, he kissed her even though they were in the center of the gym and refused to explain.

The people in the gym had stared at them, most smiling or giving a thumbs up. Very few looked surprised. Not the way she planned to announce their relationship to the town. Marcus, however, hadn't seemed to mind the attention or speculation.

"You okay?"

She turned to the operative watching her. "I'm concerned about Marcus."

Nate Armstrong tapped her nose gently. "Things will work themselves out."

"I hope you're right. I don't know what Mayor Parks said to Marcus, but it upset him."

"He'll tell you if he can."

She mentally took a step back, considering the implication of Nate's words. Marcus was bound by his calling to keep confidences. Paige loved him. She might as well accept he wouldn't always be able to confide in her when he was troubled. All she could do was be there for him and have a sympathetic ear if he needed one. "Thanks, Nate. I needed that reminder."

"Marcus mentioned you were planning a cookout at the inn. Want help?"

She grinned. "Absolutely. I didn't plan an elaborate menu. Hamburgers and hot dogs, baked beans, potato salad. Typical picnic food."

"Let me know when you choose a date. If Durango's in town, I'll lend a hand." His smile faded. "You going to Van's funeral?"

"Caleb is in class and there isn't anyone else to cover for me."

"We'll work it out. Do you need to change clothes before you leave?"

Paige looked down at herself. Her black pants and shoes were fine. Her shirt, however, was a neon blue. The little kids liked it when she wore bright colors, but she didn't think the color appropriate for a funeral. She had a forest green shirt in her office that would work. Keeping clothes on hand to change into had become a habit. She worked with children, after all. Mysterious stains and streaks often appeared on her clothes by the end of the day. It saved time to have an outfit to change into when she had a function to attend after work. "I have another shirt in my office. I'll change before I leave."

"I'm going with you. Another operative will stay on site to keep the center open."

Right. She couldn't be without protection. She'd promised Marcus, and Paige wouldn't go back on her word. Lightening his load meant not adding to his worry for her even if having a bodyguard rankled. "I'll be ready to leave by 11:30."

A nod. Nate snagged a basketball in mid-air and tossed it back to the six businessmen playing three-on-three.

Someone hailed Paige from across the room. She answered another round of questions about her attack and the fire in the orchard. She noticed James Parks, the mayor's son, walk into the gym. He nodded and continued to the weight room for his usual lunchtime workout.

Fifteen minutes before she planned to leave for the funeral, James found Paige in her office. He walked inside without knocking and closed the door.

"Open the door, please." She smiled to take the sting out of her words.

"Why?"

"Safety precaution."

He scowled and, ignoring her directive, dumped his duffel bag on her desk. "Is your grandmother going to sell her property?"

"I already answered that question during the town council meeting. I'm surprised your father and the rumor mill haven't spread the word by now. The land and house are Gram's inheritance from her great-grandfather and the legacy she plans to leave me when she passes away." Hopefully not for many more years.

"The developer will give her a fair price. She can build a newer inn and plant more apple trees."

Seriously? He wouldn't be so willing to sell out himself if he was in Gram's place. "Not the same thing, James."

"Talk to her, Paige. Your stick-in-the-mud grandmother is holding up progress and costing your friends and neighbors a ton of money. They aren't happy about it, either."

Paige's stomach churned. Were Gram's neighbors angry enough to set a fire? "That inn is Gram's home and her livelihood. I'm not pressuring her to sell out when she doesn't want to move."

A scowl. "The developer needs her property. If he doesn't get it, the whole deal is in jeopardy."

"That's not my problem. Tell him to look at other sites around the county."

"There isn't another suitable site. He wants more than 100 acres and there aren't 100-acre tracts of land available somewhere else. The developer worked hard to get this far. The town needs this deal, Paige. The tax benefits will pay for improvements in infrastructure and draw more business to the area. Dad says you want a bigger budget for the center. This is the way you make that happen. You'll benefit as much as anyone if this deal closes."

"I'm not breaking my grandmother's heart to broaden the center's bottom line."

James placed his hands on the desk and leaned toward her. "You might want to rethink your stance. Things might become very uncomfortable for you and your grandmother if you don't reconsider."

"That sounds like a threat."

"Take it however you want as long as you pay attention to the facts and the consequences of any decision you and your grandmother make."

"What are you doing back here, Parks?" Nate strode into the office, stone faced. "This area is off limits to the general public."

"Yeah? So, what are you doing in here?"

"Taking Paige to Van's funeral. You need to leave."

"Our conversation isn't finished."

"Yeah, it is. Go or I'll escort you to the front door myself."

A snort. "You wouldn't dare."

"Try me." Nate glided a step closer, his soft voice eliciting a flinch from James.

The mayor's son turned, glared at Paige. "Be smart." He slung his duffel onto his shoulder and stalked from the room after a last hard stare at Nate.

"Did he hurt you?" Nate demanded.

"No."

"Why are you shaking?"

She dropped her gaze to her hands, realized the operative was right. Her hands were trembling and that ticked her off. James was bully, sure. He'd always been pushy, but he had never hurt her. "He didn't lay a hand on me."

"But he scared you."

Paige had never seen him that intense, that determined. Maybe he'd taken his stance because of his father. Otherwise, he had no reason to get in her face about the development deal. Still, she was grateful Nate interrupted. "I'll get over it. I'm sure he didn't mean to frighten me."

"I'm not. You ready?"

"As soon as I shut down my laptop." A minute later, she stood, and Nate walked with her to his SUV.

"We could take my car," she offered.

"That little tin can? I'll pass." He unlocked the vehicle and helped her inside. "Besides, my SUV is reinforced with armor plating and bullet-resistant glass."

She stared at him as he settled behind the wheel. "Are you serious?"

"Fortress operatives have enemies, Paige. If they discover our identities and where we live, our families are at risk so we don't take our security lightly. Marcus's truck has the same security upgrades. Maddox arranged it for him before he came to Otter Creek."

The ball of ice in her stomach melted to the size of a marble. At least she didn't have to be concerned about a bullet striking Marcus while he was behind the wheel.

"That doesn't bother you?" Nate asked.

"I'm happy he has extra protection when he's driving around town. If someone shoots at him, he'll be safe."

Satisfaction filled the operative's face. "My wife says the same thing."

"Have you needed the protection?"

"More than once. Our safety measures worked. The vehicle Stella drives is also reinforced. We take care of our families, too."

Paige was pleased to see the inside of the church packed with people to support Van's father. Since the service was beginning when she and Nate walked inside the sanctuary, they sat in the last pew.

A teacher and the football coach spoke as well as Van's uncle. When Marcus rose to speak, Paige paid more attention to his body language than the words he shared. He looked tired and disheartened.

An invisible chord tightened around her heart. She wanted to help, but what could she do? He may not be able to share what was troubling him.

When the service was over, Paige walked with Nate to the cemetery behind the church. The graveside service was simple and short. At the end, Marcus prayed for Van's father, extended family, and his friends. He also prayed for the community's healing and for justice to prevail. To Paige, that prayer was more powerful than the words of the sermon Marcus had shared.

Afterward, a few of the teenagers huddled together while several adults spoke with Marcus and Van's father.

One girl separated from the group and mopped at the tears flowing down her cheeks as she hurried to Paige.

"I'm so sorry, Darla," Paige murmured to Van's girlfriend. The teenager dove into her open arms and sobbed on Paige's shoulder. She stroked Darla's back and held her while she cried. Tears trickled down her own cheeks as she grieved with the girl. Such a senseless tragedy that affected so many people and shattered the innocence of their community.

When the storm of weeping passed, the teenager drew in a shuddering breath. "I miss him so much," she whispered.

"I know you do." She'd missed her parents after their deaths. Though young when she lost them, Paige still remembered the pain and sadness she felt when she realized they weren't coming back. Gram and Gramps had held her for hours that night, reminding her frequently that they loved her and she wasn't alone. They had been her rock.

"It's not fair. Van never hurt anybody. Why would anyone kill him?"

That was the question, wasn't it? "I don't know, sweetheart. The police are doing everything they can to find his killer."

"It still won't bring him back to me. We made plans for after high school. We were going to marry and attend college together, then we were headed to med school. Now he's just gone. How can I do this without him?"

Paige's heart ached for her. She was so young. Hard to imagine them having long-term plans in place when they were only fourteen. She certainly didn't craft such detailed plans at that age. "Van wouldn't want you to stop living because he's gone. If being a doctor is your calling, go to med school like you planned. Fulfill your dream. That's the best way to honor his memory. Is your mom or dad with you?" She didn't want Darla by herself this afternoon.

A head shake. "They had to work. I came with a friend."

"Are you going home from here?"

"Jeanine invited me to her house until my mom gets off work. I didn't want to be alone."

Can't say that she blamed her. "That's a smart decision. If you want to talk, call me or Marcus if you can't find your parents."

"I will. Thanks, Paige."

She squeezed the teen's hand. "Any time." She watched Darla walk to her friends. At least she had support there as well as from her parents. They were a tight-knit family. In the aftermath of this tragedy, they would be closer than ever.

A hand touched her lower back. "How is Darla?"

Paige swiveled to face Marcus. "About like you'd expect. She's hurting. She and Van were talking marriage and med school after graduating from high school."

His eyebrows winged upward. "Marriage? They were young to be talking weddings. I'll check on her tomorrow, make sure she's handling things all right."

"Are you coming back to the center now?"

"In a few minutes." His gaze searched hers. "What's wrong, Paige?"

She frowned. "Do I have a neon sign on my forehead or something?"

He waited her out.

"I had a little run in with James Parks at the community center," she said, her voice soft. "I'll tell you about it later." She didn't want to talk about the confrontation in public. If they talked here, someone would overhear the conversation and the incident would be the latest topic on the Otter Creek grapevine.

Marcus reached for her hand. "You're all right?"

"I'm fine. I would tell you if I wasn't."

He slid his gaze to Nate who stood a few feet away.

"I sent him on his way," the operative said to the unspoken query. "He didn't hurt her, Marcus."

"Did he put his hands on you?" Marcus murmured, a fierce light burning in his eyes.

She laid her free hand over his heart. "He didn't touch me."

A relative of Van's called Marcus's name.

Paige squeezed his hand and stepped back. "I'll see you in a few minutes."

With a last solemn look, the man she loved with every fiber of her being walked to the group waiting for him.

Nate escorted her to his SUV and handed her the seatbelt. "Back to the center?"

She nodded. "Thanks for coming with me, Nate."

"It was no trouble." He drove from the church parking lot and turned toward the community center. "Need to stop for lunch?"

Paige started to refuse, but stopped. Marcus needed to eat and so should she. Even though the thought of eating didn't appeal at the moment, they both needed fuel to keep functioning. "Let's stop by That's A Wrap."

"Stellar idea. Darcy always has something good in there, and I'm starving."

"Who is cooking for PSI trainees today?"

He grinned. "Got a recruit who trained as a professional chef. She's covering lunch today in exchange for a pass on PT tomorrow morning."

Sweet deal in Paige's estimation. Why would a trained chef want to be a bodyguard? Thinking about it, she considered the advantages. Who would think a threat came from the cook?

Nate parked in front of Darcy's deli and met Paige on the sidewalk. "Let's see what the special is today."

Turned out the special was a spectacular chicken salad wrap. Perfect for Marcus and light enough for Paige's stomach to handle. She ordered three chicken wraps and two bottles of unsweetened tea along with an apple for Marcus and a banana for her.

At the community center, Nate handed his bodyguard duties over to Cade Ramsey. He nodded when she motioned going to her office, then turned back to the man he'd been talking to.

Thirty minutes later, Marcus tapped on the door frame. Paige rose. "I picked up lunch for us."

"That's great. Thanks." He shrugged out of his suit coat and draped it on the back of a chair.

When he turned, she wrapped her arms around him. She didn't say word, just held on until the rigid tension in his body eased.

Marcus lifted her chin with a finger and indulged in a series of soft kisses with her. "I can't tell you how much I needed that."

"We should eat. Caleb will be here soon, then we can go see Dalton and Seth."

After Marcus swallowed his first bite of the chicken wrap, he asked, "What happened with James Parks?"

CHAPTER TWENTY-FOUR

The longer Paige spoke, the more furious Marcus became. He forced himself to keep eating as she gave him the details of her encounter with James Parks. "I can't believe he threatened you and tried to intimidate you."

"Surprised me as well."

"He doesn't have a stake in this. What's the purpose in using thug tactics?"

"Maybe he's backing his father's agenda. The mayor isn't shy about telling anyone who will listen that Otter Creek needs the shopping center."

"Still doesn't make what James did to you acceptable." A point he would be making the next time he saw the man. Paige was his to protect. "I wish I had been here with you." Yet another instance when he wasn't available to protect the woman he loved. What if the next time something like that happened, no one was around to intervene? His blood ran cold.

"You were needed elsewhere."

"You sure he didn't touch you?"

She covered his hand with hers. "I will never lie to you, Marcus. James didn't lay a finger on me."

But what would have happened if Nate hadn't arrived? The thought that she might have been in danger again without him by her side made Marcus feel sick inside. But the truth was he couldn't stay with her twenty-four hours a day. He had a job to do, at least for now, and so did she.

After their meal, he returned to his truck and retrieved his duffel bag containing a change of clothes. Dressed in jeans, a black long-sleeved t-shirt, and tennis shoes, he hung his suit on a hook in his truck, then headed for the basketball court where he took turns with Cade shooting free throws.

Soon, the high schoolers began arriving at the center. Several of the boys Van's age lingered on the sidelines. After a final basket, he snatched the orange ball and passed it to Cade. "Time for me to go to work."

A nod from the operative. He pointed a finger at one of the older boys and motioned for the teen to join him on the court. The expression of pleasure on the boy's face clued Marcus in to how much Cade's attention mattered to him. To all of them. The Fortress operatives had deliberately interacted with the teens since the day PSI opened. Josh viewed it as a recruiting tool for Fortress and a deterrent to teen delinquency.

Marcus spent the next half hour with the teenagers who hovered on the sidelines, drawing them into conversation, and making sure they knew he was available any time they wanted to talk.

"Won't Paige be mad if we take you away from her?" one asked. "My girlfriend would be ticked off if someone took my attention from her."

"She understands." Marcus inclined his head toward the woman talking with a group of teenage girls. "Call me if you want to talk."

Within minutes, the elementary-age children arrived and, rather than making them look up at him, he chose to sit in the center of the stage. Immediately, kids ranging from six to 12 years of age surrounded him, all anxious and seeking reassurance.

"Pastor Marcus?"

He turned to the first grader. "What is it, Amy?"

"Why did somebody hurt Van?"

"I don't know. The police will figure that out when they find the person who did it."

"What if they don't catch him?"

Marcus prayed for wisdom. He didn't want to give the kids a false sense of security. On the other hand, it wasn't a good idea to scare them more than they already were, either. "The Otter Creek police won't give up until that person is behind bars."

"But what if he comes after us?" a fourth-grader asked.

"He doesn't have any reason to hurt you or your friends."

"What if he tries to take me away when I'm playing outside?" a second-grade boy asked, frowning. "How will my parents find me?"

"Let's talk about some safety rules." Marcus spent a few minutes going over some basic things the kids could do to keep themselves safe. Then they discussed what to do if they were in danger.

By the time Caleb arrived, his elementary audience had dispersed to the study room or game room, more settled now that they had a plan of action to follow if they were afraid. He prayed that the plan would never have to be enacted.

Cade clapped him on the shoulder. "Tough session. You did a great job with them, Marcus."

"I hope it was enough. They're afraid, and I don't blame them."

"I can't imagine these kids know any information worth a repeat of what happened to Van. Somewhere along the line, Van either saw something or someone he wasn't supposed to see. You've done all you can to protect the little ones. The rest is up to the cops."

But would it be enough, soon enough? Marcus wasn't convinced. He worried over their safety.

His gaze sought Paige. More than anyone, she was a target and no one knew why. Was it connected to his past or something else? Marcus longed to spirit her out of town to keep her safe and knew she wouldn't go. Forcing the issue would leave her grandmother alone and vulnerable. He wouldn't do that to Jo or Paige. "Who is shadowing us this afternoon?" he asked Cade.

A quick smile. "You're looking at the shadow."

"Paige and I are going to see Seth Parks and Dalton Reagan, then heading to Burger Heaven before church."

The operative's eyes lit. "I love their burgers."

He chuckled. "Me, too." He reached Paige's side as the last of the teen girls left to join her friends. "Ready to go?"

"As soon as I get my laptop and purse."

Cade met them at Marcus's truck. He was walking around the vehicle with a small, plastic device in his hand.

"What's that?" Paige asked.

"Checks for tracking devices and bugs." Cade turned the gadget around so Paige could see the display screen and demonstrated how it worked.

"The lights are green."

"Green is good. Means the truck is clean."

She turned, looked at Marcus. "You need one of those."

Hadn't been necessary before now, but she was right. With the price on his head doubling, he couldn't afford to take chances any more. "I'll talk to Zane about it."

Minutes later, he parked in front of the Parks home. The flashy red Camaro the teenager usually drove sat in the driveway. "Looks like he's home. I hope he'll talk to us."

Marcus rounded the front of the truck and opened Paige's door. On the porch of the Georgian house, he rang the doorbell.

Seth's eyes widened when he saw them. "Pastor Marcus, Paige. What are you doing here?"

"May we come in for a few minutes?" Marcus asked.

The teenager hesitated. "What's this about?"

"We won't take long," Paige said. "I'm sure you have homework to finish."

"More than I want," he muttered as he opened the door wider.

Marcus and Paige sat on the brown leather loveseat while Seth took the recliner. "What happened to your hand?" Marcus asked, indicating the large white bandage covering his skin.

The kid swallowed hard, dropped his gaze. "Scratched it."

"Big bandage for a scratch." He wondered what Nick made of the injury because Marcus wasn't buying Seth's explanation.

"What do you want? I have to finish my homework before church."

"Geometry?"

A grimace. "Among other things including English."

"You don't like English?" Paige asked.

"I hate to read."

"Go see Del at Otter Creek Books. She'll find you something fun to read." Marcus had asked her help in finding books to entice a youngster struggling to read. The right book made a huge difference.

Seth shrugged. "Maybe."

"Seth, did you hear what happened to Dalton?"

Fear lit his gaze. "Yeah. Is he okay?"

"We know you were with him that night."

"I didn't hurt him."

"No one blames you. Did you see anything?"

"Like what?"

"A person hanging around the area."

Seth started shaking his head before Marcus finished his statement. "I don't know anything. You need to go. I got stuff to do."

"The man who beat up Dalton is probably the same one who attacked Paige at the community center. He's dangerous, Seth. You don't want to mess with him."

The teenager's gaze darted to the finger marks on Paige's throat. "Maybe he didn't mean to hurt her."

Odd thing to say. Marcus narrowed his eyes. "He tried to shoot her last night. He missed." Not for lack of effort.

"What happened?"

"We went for a walk. Someone shot at us, then chased us to finish the job."

"It might be an accident." Seth sounded panicked.

"His shot barely missed us. I don't think this was an accident. You need to tell us what's going on."

"How should I know?"

"Every time we ask you a direct question about these incidents, you lie."

"I can't. My dad will be home soon."

"Are you worried your father will find out about the tutoring or that you're involved with the attacks?" A shot in the dark, but maybe the kid knew more than he admitted.

Seth covered the bandage with his other hand.

Ah. Marcus leaned toward the teenager. "What's really wrong with your hand?"

Silence.

"If Detective Santana looks under your bandage, he'll find a burn, won't he?"

"What's going on?" James Parks strode into the living room, his expression dark. "Why are you in my house, Lang?"

"We buried Seth's friend today."

"As you can see, he's fine. Why single him out?"

"We're talking to the kids who frequent the center. Van's death hit everyone hard."

"If you say so. The kid was nothing but trouble."

"Dad!" Seth protested. "He wasn't like that."

"Go to your room. We'll talk later."

The teen flinched, glanced at Marcus.

"If you want to talk, call me," he said. What more could he do? He didn't want to cause Seth trouble with his father.

He nodded, slid a quick glance at his glowering father, and hurried from the room.

"Next time you want to talk to my son, you go through me first."

"Do his teachers have to talk to you first?" Marcus asked, his tone mild.

"What's that supposed to mean?"

"He's sixteen. He knows how to speak up when he doesn't want to talk." He'd delayed answering questions for several minutes.

"He's a stupid kid who doesn't know better than to open his mouth when someone wants to pin something on him."

Marcus frowned. "I didn't accuse him of anything. What happened to his hand, Parks?"

A snort. "The kid's accident prone. Time for you to go, Lang. Some of us actually work for a living."

Cheeks burning, he helped Paige to her feet. On the porch, he released her hand and nudged her toward the truck. When she was out of ear shot, Marcus turned back to Parks. "Don't corner or scare Paige again," he warned softly.

A sneer from Parks. "Or what?"

"You'll deal with me."

"I'm not afraid of you."

"That's your second mistake. The first was bullying the woman I care about. Stay away from her, Parks."

"We have more influence in this town than you can possibly imagine. That means your job isn't secure, Preacher. All it takes is a few words in the right ear, and your days at Cornerstone are over." He jabbed a finger in Marcus's chest.

He grabbed Parks' hand and twisted. When the man gasped, his face losing all color, Marcus said, "Paige means more than my job." With a final twist, he released Parks and stepped back, ready for retaliation. Instead, Parks spun around and slammed the door.

Marcus slid behind the wheel and cranked the engine, feeling sorry for the man's family. From watching the interaction between Seth and his father, it appeared Parks bullied them as well as everyone else.

"What was that about?" Paige asked.

"I warned him not to corner you again."

Her jaw dropped. "Marcus."

"I care about you, Paige. I won't allow him or anyone else to hurt you."

"He'll cause trouble. I don't want rumors about you floating around town."

"The grapevine is already buzzing." About more than she knew.

"What about?"

"Rumor says we're living together."

"That's ridiculous." Her head whipped his direction. "Wait. That's what Mayor Parks confronted you with, didn't he? Marcus, you should go back to the parsonage. The mayor will stir up trouble at church. Gram and I will be fine with Mason at the house."

"I'm not leaving you and Jo."

"But he'll go to the deacon board and make accusations." She sounded close to tears. "They might ask you to resign."

He kissed the back of her hand. "I told the deacons before I moved into the B & B. They understood I was concerned about your safety and gave their approval as long as Mase and Nicole stayed, too."

"What about the congregation? Some will believe the worst."

"Most won't."

"I don't want to hurt your ministry."

"Baby, everything will be fine."

"And if it's not?"

"I'll handle it. The one thing I can't handle is leaving you and your grandmother to fend for yourselves."

"Promise you'll tell me if staying with us becomes a serious problem. We'll work out a different arrangement."

"You have my word."

By the time he parked in front of the Reagan house, Paige was no longer teetering on the edge of tears. A moment after he rang the bell, Jacob and Matt, Dalton's younger brothers, opened the door.

"Pastor Marcus." Jacob grinned, relief in his eyes.

"Hi, Jacob, Matt. We need to see Dalton."

The boys looked at each other, then back to Marcus and Paige. "We don't know where he is," Matt said.

Marcus stilled. "When does he usually get home from school?"

"Before us. We called his cell phone, but he doesn't answer."

CHAPTER TWENTY-FIVE

An invisible band tightened around Marcus's chest. "If you give me his number, I can talk to him later."

"Sure." Jacob rattled off the number.

"When will your mom finish work?" Paige asked.

"After 10:00," Matt said. "She's working a double plus cleaning tonight."

Marcus grimaced. Too long for these boys to be by themselves. Someone needed to stay with the kids. He also didn't want to alarm their mother in case Dalton was in a dead cell zone. The explanation rang hollow. None of his calls had dropped in Otter Creek. "Is it all right if Paige goes inside with you for a few minutes? I need to call a friend."

Matt tugged her inside. "We have a new video game. Want to see?"

"Have you had a snack since you've been home from school?"

Head shakes. "We were waiting for Dalton. We always eat a snack together."

"Are you hungry?"

"Yeah!"

"Let's take care of that first. Then we'll talk about your homework." As Paige pushed the door almost closed, she motioned for Marcus to go on.

He left the porch so he wouldn't be overheard by the boys, and grabbed his cell phone. When his call was answered, he said, "Dalton Reagan is missing. He was supposed to be home two hours ago. His brothers have been calling his cell, and he's not picking up."

"I'll be there in ten minutes," Nick Santana said, voice grim.

Rather than wait for the detective to set the wheels in motion through legal channels, Marcus called Zane.

"What do you need?" was the tech guru's greeting.

"To ping a cell phone. A fourteen-year-old boy hasn't been heard from in two hours. His brothers called, but he's not picking up."

"Is he avoiding his siblings?"

"He's a responsible kid, Z. The father's not in the picture, and the boys pitch in to help their mom who works two, sometimes three jobs to make ends meet. Dalton's brothers are too young to be alone for so long. He was in the community center minutes before Paige's attack, and he's the one we rescued in the woods."

"Give me the number." When Marcus recited the number, Zane said, "Hold."

While he waited, he scanned the neighborhood. It looked like a great place to raise kids. He'd like to live in an area like this one day, raise a family of his own.

He frowned. Did Paige want a family? Although she hadn't mentioned having kids, she was great with them. If he and Paige could stop dodging bullets or running for their lives, he would ask.

"I'm sending the location of the cell to your email," Zane said. "Take someone who doesn't mind pulling a trigger. Don't go on your own."

"Nick Santana should be here soon."

"He's good. Blackhawk is better. Just because I pinpointed Dalton's cell signal doesn't mean the kid is with his phone. You might need a tracker."

"Thanks, Z. I owe you."

"Not even close, Marcus. You have a lot more favor cards to redeem. Let me know if you need anything else."

As Marcus ended the call, Nick parked in the Reagan driveway.

"Anything new?" Nick asked as he climbed the porch stairs.

"I asked Zane to ping Dalton's cell. He sent the coordinates to my email."

"Pull it up."

The email showed the coordinates and a map with the cell phone's location marked by a red dot.

"What's Dalton doing there?" Nick snapped. "I told him not to go back."

Good question. "Let's find out. Zane suggested we take Ethan."

Nick called Ethan and asked the police chief to meet them at the entrance to the Croft driveway.

"Let me tell Paige where we're going." Marcus looked for Cade, saw him parked two houses down. He motioned to him.

Seconds later, the operative jogged up to the porch. "What's up?"

"Dalton's missing. I asked Zane to ping his phone. I'm going with Nick and Ethan to check it out. I need you to watch over Paige and the Reagan boys."

"I'll take care of them. Be careful, man."

He nodded and walked into the house with Cade on his heels. He found Paige in the kitchen, sitting with the boys as they inhaled peanut butter and jelly sandwiches and milk. She glanced up, unspoken questions in her eyes.

"I need to leave. Cade's going to stay with you."

"Hi, Cade," Matt said.

"What's going on, buddy?"

"We're eating a snack before we have to work on dumb old homework."

The operative grinned. "I'm not fond of homework, either. I like peanut butter sandwiches, though."

Jacob scrambled to his feet. "Want a sandwich? I make good ones."

"Sounds great. Thanks, Jacob."

Paige walked to Marcus's side as the boys worked together to make Cade's snack. "What did you find out?" she asked, voice soft.

"Zane gave me the location of Dalton's phone. Nick and I will check it out with Ethan."

"Come back to me unharmed, love."

He brushed her lips with his, hoped she meant the sweet name she'd called him. "If there's a problem, do exactly as Cade tells you to."

"I will. Please, don't worry about me. Just be careful."

He wanted to be the one by her side, but he needed to help Dalton. He looked up to find Cade's gaze on him. Without saying a word, the other man gave a short nod, conveying a silent promise to protect Paige no matter what it took.

Another soft kiss, and he returned to the porch and Nick. "I'm ready."

"Ride with me."

He hesitated. "I have to watch the time, Nick. Church night."

"I'll either bring you back or have another officer take you."

With a nod, he climbed into the passenger seat of the SUV, buckling in as Nick sped away from the Reagan house. "Am I raising an alarm for nothing?"

Nick flicked him a glance and turned on his blue-and-white lights without the siren. "He's a minor who was attacked by a man we suspect attempted to murder your woman. You're not overreacting."

"I hoped you'd tell me I was wrong."

"I'd rather waste my time hunting for a kid who left his phone on silent than assume he was fine and be wrong."

Minutes later, Nick turned into the long drive of the Croft place. He parked beside Ethan's vehicle.

"Coordinates?" Ethan said.

Marcus showed him the email from Zane along the with map.

The police chief keyed the coordinates into his cell phone, studied the map he'd pulled up a moment. He grabbed a heavy-duty flashlight from his vehicle and walked toward the woods. "Stay behind Nick, Marcus. Walk in my steps. Do not veer off on your own. I don't want to waste time rescuing my pastor."

"Yes, sir." He'd never live it down if Ethan had to extract him from the woods because of his own stupidity. Not only that, the police chief would tear strips off his hide, not something he ever wanted to experience. Marcus had listened sympathetically as several officers in his congregation talked about the verbal reprimands from their commander-in-chief.

Ethan's powerful flashlight swept the ground in front of him. When they'd traveled a quarter mile from the driveway, he held up his fist. "Wait." The police chief walked ahead with silent steps further. A moment later, he called out. "Nick, Marcus."

Marcus and the detective pushed through shrubs into a small clearing. Ethan knelt on the ground next to the prone form of Dalton Reagan.

CHAPTER TWENTY-SIX

Paige glanced at her watch. Again. Eight times in an hour must be a new record for her. Shouldn't Marcus be back by now? She lifted her gaze to Cade whose grim expression mirrored her feelings. Something was very wrong.

"Finished," Jacob sang out.

"No fair," Matt complained. "I always have more homework than you."

"That's how it is when you're in the upper grades, buddy." Cade clapped him on the shoulder. "You're almost finished, too. Won't take long, and you'll be free to play."

"Yeah, but I have English left. I hate English." His tone conveyed his horror.

Paige covered her mouth with her hand, trying hard not to laugh.

"That's too bad, bro. English was my favorite subject in school," Cade said.

The boy's mouth gaped. "Really? Why?"

"I love to read."

"Nuh uh."

"Afraid so, Matt. I spend a lot of money at Otter Creek Books. If you want, I'll take you with me next time I go, and we'll find some books you might like."

His face lit up, then the excitement dimmed. "I better not," he muttered.

"Why not?"

"Mom says we have to watch every penny, that we have to use the library."

Cade nodded. "Libraries are good. I use the one in town, too."

"You do?"

"Sure. Did you know Del has used books in her store that kids and adults read and swap for free?"

Matt shook his head, his eyes wide.

"I'll talk to your mom, see if I can take you with me the next time. We'll find out what Del has for both of us."

"Me, too!" chimed in Jacob. "I want to go to Del's store."

"As long as your mom says it's all right. The more people we have, the more fun it is."

In the midst of the boys' cheers at the prospect of an outing with Cade, Nick and Marcus returned. Paige looked at their faces and her heart sank.

Marcus laid a hand on each boy's shoulder. "Matt, Jacob, pack the schoolwork you haven't finished, some books, and quiet games you can play for a few hours."

"Where are we going?" Jacob asked.

"To the hospital. Dalton is hurt, and your mom asked me to bring you to her. She's at the hospital with your brother."

"Is Dalton going to die?" Matt asked.

A question Paige wanted answered herself. She grabbed their backpacks and laid them on the table where the boys could easily reach them.

"The doctor is looking at him now, buddy. Do you have homework to finish?"

"Yeah. English."

"Let's pack that plus some fun things for you to do."

When Matt finished sliding his English textbook and notebook inside, Cade picked up the backpacks. "Let's see what else we should take." The three of them left the room.

"What happened?" Paige asked.

"We found Dalton in the Croft woods," Nick replied. "Someone beat him and left him unconscious."

Faith would be devastated if she lost Dalton. "Is he going to survive?"

Marcus drew Paige into his strong embrace. "The doctor wouldn't say. We picked up Mrs. Reagan and took her to the hospital, then came here for the boys. When we left, they were preparing Dalton for surgery."

"One of our officers is with him," Nick added. "Ethan would have protected the boy, but he's tracking the perp's footprints through the forest. Paige, the prints match those of the man who fired the shots at you and Marcus."

She buried her face in Marcus's neck. Had she brought danger to Dalton? The same man attacking her and Dalton couldn't be a coincidence. What worried her more was the possibility her presence at the center endangered the other teens and kids. Maybe she should take a leave of absence until this guy was behind bars. If the police caught him. If they didn't, she would be out of a job.

Marcus tightened his hold. "Don't lose hope. We'll find him."

Easy to say. Hard to accomplish. They needed a break.

Cade returned to the kitchen with Matt and Jacob, the packs strapped to their backs. "The boys are riding with me."

Paige stared, thought about his statement. The reinforced SUV. Cade was making sure the Reagan boys were well protected. And maybe it was better for them to be separated from her and Marcus. They had targets on their backs, after all. Only by God's grace had the attempts on their lives had failed. "Matt, do you and Jacob know where Memorial Hospital is located?"

"Sure. It's a block down from Mom's cleaning job."

"Perfect. You can make sure Cade doesn't get lost on the way. He's new in town, you know."

"I'll be in good hands with these guys." Cade ruffled the boys' hair. "We'll lead the way. Can't have you getting lost." He escorted Matt and Jacob to his vehicle.

While Nick locked the front door, Paige walked with Marcus to his truck. Within minutes, Paige was embracing Dalton's mother. "I'm so sorry to hear about Dalton."

"It's such a shock. Who would hurt my baby like that?"

"Any news?" Marcus asked.

"The doctor promised to send someone with an update by six."

Paige led the trembling woman to an empty chair in the waiting room.

"Mom, can we see Dalton?" Jacob asked.

"The doctor is with him. We'll see him later."

"Will he be okay?" Matt asked, his face somber.

"I think so, but Dalton will be grumpy for a while." Her lips curved into a trembling smile. "You know how he is when he feels bad."

Jacob scowled. "Does that mean he gets to pick the movies for a long time?"

That turned Faith Reagan's fake smile into a genuine one. "Let's give him a week after he comes home, okay? After that, you three will take turns again."

Matt sighed. "We'll be watching the Star Wars movies the whole time. I'm tired of Yoda and Chewbacca." His morose tone had all of them chuckling.

Cade sat with the boys a few seats away and began helping Matt with his homework while Jacob pulled out a hand-held video game.

Marcus crouched in front of Faith. "What can I do to help?"

"I need someone to watch the boys overnight and take them to school in the morning. I don't want to leave Dalton here alone."

The Fortress operative glanced over. "I call dibbs on that assignment."

Faith's eyes widened. "You want to stay with them?"

"Oh, yeah. These guys challenged me to a video game match. They're going down."

Both boys protested.

"Are you sure?" Faith asked.

"I have six nephews about their age. I'll be glad to get in some practice before Christmas. Unless I'm working, I'll spend time with my nephews playing the same game. It's their current obsession. I don't mind, Faith. Let me help."

"But what about your job at PSI? Won't they be upset with you taking time off?"

"Let me worry about that."

"Looks like Cade has that covered. What else can we help you with?" Marcus asked.

She gave a soft laugh. "If you hear of a job with better pay and benefits, let me know." A tear trickled down her cheek. "This work schedule takes me away from the boys too much. Maybe if I'd been home, this wouldn't have happened."

"Don't dwell on the 'what-ifs'. There's no way to know if that would have made a difference. I'll ask around about jobs for you." He reached for Paige's hand and Faith's. "Let me pray with you, then I'm afraid I have to leave. Wednesday night service starts in less than an hour." After the prayer, he said, "I'll swing by after church. If you need anything, Faith, call me. The ladies from the benevolence committee will start delivering meals tomorrow night. Wanda Francis will call to ask about food preferences."

"It's not necessary to feed us," she protested.

"You need to focus your energy on Dalton, not worry over what to feed your boys."

"I'll be lucky if I have a job by the time Dalton is released from the hospital."

CHAPTER TWENTY-SEVEN

After the service, Marcus drove with Paige to Burger Heaven. "Drive-thru or dine in?"

"Let's eat here." Paige's gaze locked with his. "You need a break, even if it's only for a few minutes."

His lips curved. "I look that bad, huh?"

"You look as though you're carrying the weight of the world on your shoulders. Set it aside for a few minutes, Marcus. Just be with me."

He enjoyed being with her. A word or a look from Paige often lessened his stress, almost as refreshing as a walk on the beach in the moonlight. And listen to him wax poetic.

At the counter, Marcus ordered their meals, then carried the loaded tray to an unoccupied table in the corner. The noise level in the restaurant dropped until they were seated. He looked forward to their date out of town on Friday. At least they could eat without a rapt audience watching every bite. Over the years in Otter Creek, he hadn't minded the attention of his friends and neighbors.

Now, however, the intrusive attention mattered. He didn't want Paige to be uncomfortable.

Halfway through their meal, a man dressed in a dark suit, white shirt, and flashy tie stopped by their table. Great. The sleazy land developer, Franklin Davidson.

"Ms. Jensen." The developer smiled. "I apologize for interrupting."

Right. The man's smile was as insincere as his apology.

Paige laid her hamburger aside. "Mr. Davidson."

Her cautious tone snagged Marcus's attention.

"Have you talked my proposal over with your grandmother?"

"I told you when we talked before the decision to sell is up to Gram. It's her home, her property. I won't pressure her one way or the other. I told everyone who pestered me the same thing. If she doesn't want to sell, I'll stand behind her decision."

"That would be a serious mistake."

Paige stiffened. "Is that a threat?"

"Of course not. Threats are illegal. I'm merely pointing out the inadvisability of that stance. Jo is a sharp, business-savvy woman. She shouldn't hold on to a house and land for sentimental reasons. She's impeding progress and hurting the town."

The noise level in Burger Heaven dropped again as customers became aware of the conversation in the corner. Marcus's cheeks burned. Davidson had some nerve confronting Paige in public.

"Talk to her," the developer pressed. "Reason with her. I'll make it worth her while. Yours, too. Without her signature on the dotted line, the rest of those who agreed to the deal will lose the money to buy or build somewhere else in the area, and the town will be out millions of dollars in tax revenues."

"That's not my problem, Mr. Davidson. We're finished with this conversation. I won't change my mind."

Marcus covered Paige's hand with his. "You've said your piece, Davidson. More than once. Let Paige finish her meal because we need to stop by the hospital in a few minutes."

The developer's gaze shifted from Marcus to Paige. "Think about what I said, Ms. Jensen. Tension in town is high and emotions are volatile. One wrong word, and the ugly brew will explode. Many people could be hurt, including Jo. You should rethink your stance."

"That's enough, Davidson," Marcus snapped.

The man lifted his hands in mock surrender. "I'll talk to you soon, Ms. Jensen."

"Not if I see you coming first," she murmured after the man had walked away.

"I'm sorry, Paige. Guess I should have chosen the drive-thru option."

"I'm the one who wanted to give you a few minutes without stress. I'd say my plan backfired." She picked up her hamburger. "Davidson was determined to speak to me again. If he hadn't pitched his cause tonight, he would have tracked me down at the center tomorrow or the day after."

"How many times has he approached you about the B & B?"

"This makes four. I'm not doing what he wants. Gram has the right to keep her family heritage. If she decides on her own to sell, I'll back her, but I'm not going to influence her either way."

Marcus watched the developer as he talked and laughed with a group of people surrounding his table. The same people, he noted, who wanted to sell their homes for a tidy profit, the same people casting hot glances toward Paige.

Vendetta

When she finished her meal, he held out a hand to her. "Interested in a milkshake? I hear the flavor offerings don't include apple." Her laughter coaxed a smile from him.

"I'd better not. I'll take a rain check, though."

"Deal." He leaned close. "Besides, the restaurant we going to Friday has better dessert than a shake."

She shot him a curious glance. "Where are we going?"

"That's my secret."

Minutes later, he parked in the hospital parking lot and walked inside with Paige. In the waiting room, Cade sat with the boys, watching them play their hand-held games. Faith was nowhere to be seen.

Cade glanced up. "Recovery."

A place Marcus had been many times over the past seven years. The hospital staff knew him well so he didn't need to check in with the desk nurse. He merely waved at her and kept walking.

"Should I wait with Cade?"

He glanced at Paige. "I doubt the nurses will stop you since you're with me."

An elevator ride later, he walked into surgical recovery. At the far end of the room, Faith stood by Dalton's bedside, her hand resting on his. An Otter Creek police officer stood nearby, watching everyone who came and went from the room.

As they walked closer, Paige drew in a sharp breath. "Oh, Marcus. Look what he did to Dalton."

He squeezed her hand gently. "That he's made it this far is a good sign."

Faith turned, smiled at them. "The doctor says it will take a few weeks, but Dalton going to recover."

The knot of worry in his stomach eased. "That's great news. What were his injuries?"

"Broken arm, broken nose, fractured jaw, fractured ribs. The doctor had to remove his spleen and stop internal bleeding. He was lucky."

"When will Dalton go home?" Paige asked.

"Early next week."

"Has he talked to you?"

Faith grinned. "He told me he wanted a milkshake."

"If he still wants one when he's released, we'll bring shakes for all of you," Marcus promised. "In fact, we'll bring two apiece. That way you can freeze one for later."

"Chocolate," Dalton mumbled. His eyes opened a crack.

"Great choice," Paige said. "I hear you're going to be out of school for a while."

"Mmm." He slipped back under.

"Are you set for tonight?" Marcus asked Faith. "Can we bring you anything?"

"I'm fine. Cade and the boys took good care of me. They made me eat a sandwich from the cafeteria, and Cade brought me the largest to-go cup of coffee I've ever seen."

"Have the boys seen their brother?"

She shook her head. "I wanted to wait until he was in a room first. Makes it easier to help them when they see their brother for the first time. They're going to be so upset." Her gaze swept over Dalton. "They won't understand why anyone would do this to him."

"Nick told me officers will be on guard duty around the clock until Dalton goes home. PSI will keep a bodyguard with him as well. I'll check with Josh Cahill later tonight to confirm."

"Do you think all of this is necessary? Wouldn't the lowlife who did this be gone by now?"

"If I were in your place, I'd accept any protection offered to my wife and child."

"I hope all this precaution won't be necessary for long."

Marcus and Paige lingered a few minutes, hoping Dalton would wake enough to ask why he'd been in the woods. He slept on, however.

Back at the B & B, Marcus filled in Mason, Nicole, and Jo.

"That poor kid." Nicole handed him and Paige glasses of iced tea. "Does Nick or Ethan know who beat him?"

"Ethan says it's the same man who shot at us and attacked Paige at the center."

Mason frowned. "How does he know?"

"Shoe prints matched."

"Do you think Dalton saw something that night he wasn't supposed to see?" Paige asked. "That would explain why he targeted Dalton twice."

"Once he's able to talk, I'm sure the police will ask him that question." Jo set a bowl of fruit in the center of the table. "Now, what else is wrong, sweetheart?"

"Are you sure you don't read minds, Gram?" She sighed when her grandmother's eyebrow arched. "We ran into Franklin Davidson at Burger Heaven after church."

"That blowhard?" Jo shook her head. "Same song and dance, dear?"

"Yes, ma'am."

"He's persistent. I'll give him that."

"I told him he was wasting his time."

"Has he been pressuring you, Jo?" Marcus asked.

A soft snort. "He calls at least three times a day, leaves messages on the answering machine. In the past week, he's upped his offer by $50,000. I don't dare go into town because he shows up wherever I happen to be. My friends and I have been going into Cherry Hill to do our business. I'd rather get my supplies in Otter Creek, but I don't want to deal with Davidson."

Sounded like an ambush. The fact that Davidson kept showing up alarmed Marcus. How did the developer know Jo's location? Maybe people in town tipped him off. Hated to think their friends and neighbors were conspiring with the land developer. He frowned. Maybe the explanation was more straight forward. Was it possible Jo's car had a tracker? "Have you seen him in Cherry Hill?"

"He was there when we went to the movies. We saw him before he saw us and ducked into the movie theater early. By the time the movie was finished, Davidson was gone."

"Do you have a flashlight I can borrow?"

"Of course, dear." Jo rummaged in a kitchen drawer and returned with a yellow flashlight.

"Do you mind if I check your car?"

"Of course not." She dug her keys from her pocket. "Just in case you need to move my car. The key for the side door of the garage has a green cover on it."

"Thanks." He glanced at Mason who gave a short nod. Marcus squeezed Paige's shoulder and walked out the back door. Inside the garage, he turned on the overhead light, blinked at the brightness.

He turned on the flashlight and ran the beam over the exterior of Jo's car. While he was examining the nooks and crannies, his cell phone rang.

Marcus glanced at the screen, frowned. "Lang."

"Where are you?"

He straightened at sharp edge in Josh Cahill's voice. "In Jo's garage. Why?"

"I'll be there in two minutes. Is anyone with Paige and Jo?"

"Mason and Nicole. What's wrong, Josh?"

"Information from Zane. Why are you in the garage?"

"Checking Jo's car for a tracker."

"I'm turning into Jo's driveway." The call ended.

Marcus clicked off the flashlight and walked to the side door, his gut burning. Whatever news Josh had would be bad. Was the news about him or Paige?

Josh's black SUV rolled into view. His friend parked next to the side door. When he stepped into the light from

Vendetta

the garage, Marcus saw the small black bug and tracker detector in his hand.

"Get inside," Josh said curtly.

Marcus moved deeper into the structure, out of the doorway, careful to stay away from the window. Josh closed and locked the door behind himself. "Bad news?"

"The worst. O'Reilly hired a hit man to track you down." He turned on the detector and walked slowly around Jo's car.

"Tell me something I don't know."

"The hit man he contracted with is not one of his normal pack of favored assassins."

"Zane identified the man from the description I gave the sketch artist?"

A nod. "His name is Vincent Bianchi."

So, the attack on Paige was about him, not her. Would she forgive him for putting her life in danger? "I don't recognize the name."

"You wouldn't." Josh flicked him a glance before continuing to scan. "He's experienced and doesn't work alone. He works with a team, two or three other guys. Bianchi's services are very expensive. He doesn't miss, Marcus."

"He already has. Twice." Not for lack of trying.

"Pure luck. Bianchi and his team will keep coming after you and Paige."

"How did O'Reilly figure out where I was? I haven't broken any of Maddox's rules."

As Josh rounded the back driver's panel of the car, the light on the detector flashed red. He held out his hand for the flashlight, then dropped to the ground and rolled under Jo's vehicle. A moment later, he got to his feet with a small black object on his palm.

"The land developer tagged her car?" Marcus shook his head. "He must be desperate."

"Davidson may not be the one responsible for this."

His hand fisted. "Bianchi?"

"It's possible." Josh did a final sweep of Jo's car and handed back the flashlight. "Let's go inside the inn. I need to talk to you and Paige."

Marcus turned off the interior light. When he reached for the door, Josh signaled for him to wait and walked outside. He returned a moment later. "Clear. Move fast. Straight to the back door."

He ran the 100 yards with his friend on his heels.

"Josh!" Jo stood, a delighted smile on her face. "It's so good to see you. What a nice surprise."

"How are you, Jo?" He leaned down and kissed her cheek.

"Not bad considering many of my friends are angry with me these days. Please, sit down. Would you like some iced tea?"

"No, thanks. I need to talk to you and Paige."

"Do Nicole and I need to leave?" Mason asked.

A head shake. "Stay."

Jo sat again. Paige cast a worried glance at Marcus.

How did he explain that he was probably to blame for the attempts on her life? He wouldn't blame her for walking away from him. Marcus sat beside Paige and intertwined their fingers, praying she would give him a chance to make it up to her.

"What's wrong, Josh?" Paige asked.

"Zane identified the man who tried to kill you. His name is Vincent Bianchi, a hired gun, and he's not here alone."

"What does that mean?" Nicole demanded.

"He works with a team of two or three men."

"I have a team of men after me?" Paige blew out a breath. "Why would anyone want to kill me? Wait. Is this about me or someone else?"

Marcus fell a little further in love with her at that moment. Even though she was afraid, Paige still protected his secret from Jo, Mason, and Nicole. Not that it would do much good. The way things were going, the whole town would know the truth before long.

"We're still looking into the details. Bianchi was hired to take out a different target. You may be collateral damage or a means to an end."

"I feel like we're missing pieces of information," Nicole complained.

"You are."

"What can we do to keep my granddaughter safe?" Jo asked.

"We've prepared a safe house. The B & B isn't secure enough. This hit team will keep coming until we stop them, Jo. We want to do it on our turf."

Paige frowned. "What about my job? I can't leave, Josh."

"You will if you want to keep your boyfriend and grandmother safe."

CHAPTER TWENTY-EIGHT

"I can't leave Gram unprotected." Paige wrapped her hands around her glass of tea. Josh Cahill was a cop as well as a Fortress operative. She supposed he could take her into protective custody if she refused to go voluntarily. Man, she hoped that didn't happen. If Paige wasn't a visible target, Jo would be the next choice. She didn't want to lose her grandmother. The loss would gut her.

"I made provisions for her as well."

Jo shook her head. "I have guests coming this weekend, a wedding party. I can't cancel on them at this late date."

"We have that covered, Jo. Trent St. Claire and his wife will stay here as hosts for the weekend. Everything will be fine."

Her eyebrows shot up. "What will you do with me?"

"You and your two best friends are going on a cruise with my parents, courtesy of Fortress Security."

"Really? Where are we going?"

"The Bahamas. Go pack what you need. My teammates will arrive in a few minutes. Two of them will take you to the Knoxville airport. One of the Fortress jets will fly all of you to Florida where you will board the cruise ship tomorrow afternoon. You'll be gone for a week. If Durango hasn't resolved the problem by that time, you'll stay at a safe house down there."

"Why would Fortress go to all this expense for me?"

He smiled. "Don't ask. Nicole, why don't you and Mason help Jo pack."

"We'd love to. Let's see what we can find, Jo." The three of them left the kitchen.

Josh waited until they were out of earshot before he said, "I know you want to argue with me, Paige. Don't bother. We don't have enough time. I'm under orders from Maddox and Ethan to get you and Marcus out of town immediately. Marcus, you know Maddox doesn't overreact. The threat is real. You're both in grave danger."

"I'll do whatever it takes to protect Paige."

"Even if it costs your job?"

"You already know the answer to that question."

"Marcus, no," Paige protested. "You can't give up your pastorate."

"I'll take a leave of absence, but I may be forced to resign when this is finished."

"Why? You haven't done anything wrong."

He looked at Josh. "You're putting us in the same safe house?"

"It's best."

Marcus nodded, a resigned look on his face. "Paige, people will notice when we're both absent at the same time. They'll come to the right and wrong conclusions. We will be out of town together but not for the purpose they'll assume."

An affair. "With a Fortress team tagging along? Doesn't sound like a romantic interlude to me." She glanced at Josh and saw the regret in his eyes. "No one will know you're with us, will they?"

"We can't tell them. If the hit man and his cronies discover we're with you, all they have to do is wait until you leave our protection and strike when you least expect. The best I can do is float the rumor that Jo, her two friends, and my parents are with you."

"Won't someone notice when Durango is out of town at the same time and come to the obvious conclusion?"

"We're sent on missions frequently. Del and my teammates' wives will spread the word we've been sent on a rescue mission, which is the truth. They can't tell where we're going because we never give them the information until we return. It's for their own safety."

Marcus kissed the back of Paige's hand. "When we return, if the congregation doesn't believe other people have been with us, I won't have a choice, sweetheart. I'll have to turn in my resignation. If they don't trust me, I'll be ineffective. How can I counsel couples if they believe I'm a hypocrite?"

Paige wanted to rage at the unfairness. Instead, she did the only she could under the circumstances. She pressed her hand to Marcus's cheek and laid her lips on his for a soft kiss. When she drew back, she said, "I'll go pack. Do you have someone to keep the center open, Josh?"

"PSI has it covered. You have fifteen minutes, Paige. Make them count."

She rushed upstairs to her room and dragged out her luggage. How did you know what to pack for a safe house? Casual, she decided. Tennis shoes, jeans, long-sleeved t-shirts, a jacket, a few books. She wasn't sure where Josh had arranged for them to stay, but she figured she couldn't go wrong with clothes she could run in if it became necessary.

The doorbell rang. The rest of Durango had arrived. Paige grabbed what she needed from her dresser and closet, threw them into the suitcase, along with a smaller bag of toiletries and figured that was all the time she had.

"I'll get that," Marcus said from her doorway. He lifted the bag, glanced around. "Is there more?"

"No. I chose casual clothes, things I can run in if necessary."

"Smart. I hope it's an unnecessary precaution."

She clasped his hand. "Are you okay?"

"Heartsick. I never wanted my past to touch you."

"This isn't your fault. You saved a good man's life. I know you, Marcus. You wouldn't have been able to live with yourself if you had walked away."

"Steep price to pay for saving a life."

Losing the woman he loved, his identity, and his own family. Yes, a high price. "Every decision creates ripples. Some things we anticipate and can adjust. Others we have no way of knowing. No one could have foreseen the results of that night. Even had you known, you wouldn't have made a different choice. Taken precautions to protect Chelsea, yes, although she might not have stayed in place. But you would have still chosen to save Brent. By making that choice, that sacrifice, Maddox and Fortress Security operatives save hundreds of lives every year. Consider that the next time guilt tears at your heart. I don't regret becoming involved with you, Marcus. I will never regret choosing you."

"Ready to roll?" Quinn Gallagher strode into the room. "The convoy leaves in ten minutes."

Paige nodded at Josh's teammate. "I'm ready. What about a bag for Marcus?"

"Nate used some of his more questionable skills and took care of that. The bag's in the SUV."

Questionable skills? She grinned. "He broke into the parsonage."

A wince. "We prefer to use the term accessed."

"What's the difference?"

"Makes Josh more comfortable." He took the suitcase from Marcus. "Escort your girl downstairs while I take this to the vehicle."

When they reached the first floor, her grandmother was waiting for Paige near the front door. Jo smiled and spread her arms. Paige hugged the woman who meant the world to her. "I'll miss you, Gram. I have a feeling you won't miss me, though. Hope you and your friends enjoy the cruise."

"I would enjoy it more if you and Marcus were coming along."

"Sounds like fun." Marcus kissed her cheek. "We'll make plans for a cruise together later."

"I'll hold you to that."

"Ready, Jo?" Rio wrapped his arm around her shoulders. "We have to pick up your friends and head to the airport."

"Who's riding with you?" Paige asked. She didn't want him to be alone in case he ran into trouble.

"Nate. Alex and Quinn are driving you and Marcus out of town. Josh will follow you in another SUV."

"Have him follow you. I want Gram safe."

"Sorry, sugar. Josh is the boss. Besides, you're the one at risk. This late at night, we don't think we'll have a problem with anyone coming after Jo. If they do, we'll handle it. We're trained for this, Paige. Trust us to do our jobs. We'll keep her safe just like we'll take care of you and Marcus."

"What about Josh's parents? How will they get to the airport?"

"Trent St. Claire. Come on, Jo. Time to leave."

After a last hug, Jo left with the operatives.

"Your turn," Quinn said.

After parking Marcus's truck in the garage next to Gram's car and saying goodbye to Mason and Nicole, Paige and Marcus climbed into the backseat of Quinn's SUV. "Where are we going?" she asked.

"To a cabin outside of Murfreesboro," Alex said.

She did a quick calculation. The middle Tennessee area was more than four hours from home. Murfreesboro was also near Nashville, the home of Fortress Security's headquarters. "Does Fortress own the cabin?"

"Rod Kelter does. We've used it before for protection details. I think you'll like it. Meg hates roughing it and she loves the place."

Paige relaxed. Good. She didn't enjoy rustic living much herself. "Will Ivy be all right while you're gone?"

Alex glanced over his shoulder. "Durango's wives are staying together at Rio and Darcy's place. The Victorian house has plenty of bedrooms available, and it will be easier for Adam Walker and his teammates to protect them if they're in one place. If you're worried about the baby, don't be. One of Adam's unit is a medic. Ivy and Del have three months to go. If something happens, the medic will call. We also have a Fortress team on standby to take over the protection detail for you and Marcus if there's a problem in Otter Creek."

Of course, they did. Paige laid her head on Marcus's shoulder. This was what they did for a living, and their expertise showed in their extensive planning.

After they were on I-40, Quinn glanced in the rearview mirror. "We're clear. No tails from town."

"You're sure?" Marcus asked.

"I haven't seen anything and neither has Josh. We'll be on the road for a few hours. Get some rest while you can."

She fell asleep to the quiet conversation between the three men. Sometime later, Marcus stroked her cheek with his fingers.

"We're at the cabin, baby."

Paige opened her eyes to see his beloved face. He looked tired. "Did you sleep any?"

"I'm fine."

In other words, no. She glanced at the front seats, saw they were alone. "Where are Quinn and Alex?"

"Talking to one of their friends. He's been guarding the cabin to make sure we don't have any nasty surprises."

She looked out the window to see the men from Otter Creek in deep conversation with a heavily-muscled dark-haired man. They all looked relaxed so there must not have been any problems. "Can we get out? I need to stretch my legs."

"So do I. Wait until I come around before you open the door."

Still protecting her. How could she help but love this man? Marcus opened the door and held out his hand. They walked to the men who turned at their approach.

"Paige, come meet a friend," Josh said. "This is Eli Wolfe. He and his teammate, Jon, have been on several missions with Durango."

Eli shook hands with them. "Good to see you again, Marcus."

Paige frowned. "You two know each other?"

"He and Jon protected me when I was recovering from O'Reilly's bullet."

"Thank you for keeping him safe."

"We owed him big for saving Brent. We've been keeping watch over him ever since."

"Anything we should know about, Eli?" Alex asked.

"Security measures are in place. The cameras and motion sensors are up and active. Same set up as before. Sensors are set starting at the half mile mark. Marcus, Paige, stay close to the house. There's a trail in the back through the woods that will take you to a creek. You can walk the trail. Don't veer off into the woods. The trail is clearly marked."

Good grief. What kind of security measures were in place around the cabin? She decided she probably didn't want to know the details. If she and Marcus had to run through the woods off the trail, hopefully one of Durango would be with them to steer them around hazards.

"Where's Jon?" Alex asked.

"Inside checking the software to be sure the computer is operating properly."

He glanced at Josh who gave him a hand signal. Alex jogged to the porch and walked inside the cabin.

"Do you need us to stay tonight, Josh?" Eli asked. "Brenna and Dana are together so we can keep watch while you and the rest of Durango sleep."

Josh was silent a moment, then nodded. "Might be best if you're sure Dana's okay for tonight."

"Jon wouldn't be here otherwise. I'll call Brenna, let her know. The rooms are ready. Paige, you take the master bedroom. The men can handle sharing one bathroom."

"Fine with me."

"Let's get you inside," Quinn said. "We don't think the hit team knows where you are, but it's better not to take chances. They'll be here soon enough."

She froze. "They'll be here? I thought the point of coming to Murfreesboro was to get away from them."

"We're drawing them away from town." Josh laid a hand on her shoulder and squeezed gently. "You and Marcus are the bait."

CHAPTER TWENTY-NINE

"No." Marcus spun around to face Durango and the SEALs gathered in the kitchen. "Find another way to deal with Vincent Bianchi and his friends. I don't want Paige used as bait. You want to use me? Fine. Leave her out of it."

"She won't go for that, Marcus." Jon Smith sipped coffee from his mug.

"Why not?" he demanded. The thought of Paige in the crosshairs of a pack of killers made his gut clench. Losing her would kill him because Marcus didn't know if he could fight his way through the grief again if Bianchi succeeded. What he had felt for Chelsea was a mere shadow of what he felt for Paige.

The SEAL sniper watched him a moment. "She's in love with you, Marcus."

He stilled. "What?" he choked out.

An amused smile curved Jon's lips. "Paige loves you. How could you miss it?"

Easy. He was just getting used to the fact he was head-over-heels in love with Paige Jensen. Was Jon right?

Nate clapped him on the shoulder. "Stella thinks Paige is perfect for you."

Marcus dropped onto the nearest barstool, suddenly light headed. From Jon's revelation or fatigue?

"Marcus." Rio walked closer, gaze locked on his face. "You okay?"

Man, he felt weak and his thoughts were sluggish. All he wanted to do was sleep.

"When was the last time he ate?" the medic asked Quinn.

"Must have been before we left Jo's. We didn't stop on the way down here."

"Did he sleep?"

"Nope," Alex said. "He wanted to be awake in case anything happened so he could protect Paige. If it was Ivy with a target on her back, I would have done the same."

"You aren't diabetic. Check the refrigerator for orange juice. I'll be back in minute."

A moment later, Nate pressed a small glass in his hand. "Drink."

It took everything he had to lift the glass to his mouth. By the time Rio returned, Marcus had finished the juice and was feeling a little better.

"What's going on?" Paige walked into the kitchen, her gaze zeroing in on him. "What's wrong, Marcus? You're pale."

"I'll be all right in a few minutes." Still took too much effort to speak those words.

Rio pressed another protein bar in his hand. "Eat this."

"Talk to me, Rio." Paige sat beside Marcus and gripped his free hand with hers.

The medic grabbed a bottle of water from the refrigerator and broke the seal before placing it in front of Marcus. "His glucose level dropped. He's exhausted, stressed, and didn't eat on the way here. My guess is he's also a little dehydrated. He'll be fine."

Marcus fumed as he consumed the protein bar while Paige carried on conversations with the other men in the room about their wives. He knew better, but he'd been so focused on taking care of Paige that he'd neglected himself. Couldn't happen again. He didn't want to be a liability for Durango or the SEALs. Their focus should be on his girlfriend, not him.

By the time he finished the bar and drank the water, he felt almost normal. He glanced at Rio, gave him a nod of thanks.

"It's two o'clock," Eli said. "Time for all of you to turn in for a few hours. Paige has the master bedroom. The rest of you figure out where you want to bunk. Jon and I have the watch."

"I promised to call Darcy." Rio pulled out his phone. "I'll be in the living room for a while. Marcus, you're bunking with me."

"Is it safe for Paige and me to sit on the porch for a few minutes?"

"I'll make sure it is," Jon said. "Eli will be in the security room while I walk the perimeter. When you go inside, I'll sleep for two hours, then spell Eli."

"We won't be there long." Marcus slid from the stool and extended his hand to Paige. Although questions were in her eyes, she went without comment.

Ticked him off that his legs were still shaky. A few more minutes and he'd be back to normal. He snagged a blanket from the couch.

Jon opened the door and scanned the area, then nodded at Marcus.

Once Marcus and Paige were seated on the swing, Jon started his perimeter patrol. Based on the rumors Marcus had heard over the years, they wouldn't see the sniper on his rounds unless he wanted to be seen.

Marcus shook out the blanket and draped it over their legs, then wrapped his arm around her shoulders.

"How do you feel?"

"Almost normal." He pressed a kissed to the top of her head. "Are you too tired to talk for a few minutes?"

"I'm the one who took a nap on the way here. You should be going to bed. What did you want to talk about?"

"Are you sure you want to go through with this plan? Durango and the SEALs are using us, you especially, as bait for Bianchi and his buddies. If you prefer a separate safe house, totally off the grid, Jon and Eli can go with you while I stay with Durango."

"They're SEALs?" Awe filled her voice.

Marcus grinned. "Naval special operators are the best of the best."

"I don't think Durango would agree. I have the impression they are something different although no less powerful and skilled."

Smart lady. "Josh and his teammates are Delta Force, the Army's elite Special Forces soldiers. No matter the mission, they'll get the job done."

"You know some interesting people."

"It's the only reason I trust your safety to them. Do you want to go to a safe house far away from here?"

"I don't want to be separated from you. Talk to me." Her hand tightened around his. "You can tell me anything."

His gaze scanned her beloved face, hoping she could handle the truth. "Are you sure you want our relationship to move forward?"

"Positive." No hesitation.

"Even knowing this crisis may not be the last?"

"I want you in my life and I want to be in yours."

Now or never. "We've been in each other's lives from the beginning of my time in Otter Creek. I've admired the way you care for Jo, the positive attitude and enthusiasm with which you approach life, and your loyalty to friends. I stand in awe of the way you open your heart and love

215

people who use the community center, especially the teens and children."

Marcus cupped her cheeks and kissed her. He eased back to look into her eyes. "We've been friends for seven years, Paige. Now, though, I see you as more than a friend or a girlfriend." Man, why was this so hard?

"How do you see me?"

"As the beat of my heart, the woman I love and want to spend the rest of my life with. I want to love you, care for you, rejoice with you, and raise a family with you. I'm in love with you, Paige. Please tell me I have a chance to win your heart."

Paige pressed her lips to his in a long, heated kiss. "My heart already belongs to you. I love you, Marcus. I think I've loved you for a long time. Nothing would make me happier than to spend the rest of my life by your side."

"I may not always be at Cornerstone." A wry laugh escaped. "If the mayor has his way and the gossips don't buy the story Josh and the others have spread, I won't have a job when we return home."

"Jo doesn't expect me to remain by her side forever. She raised me to let me go when it was time. If God moves us to another place, she'll be fine as long as we come home to visit her and talk on the phone often." Another long kiss. "She will be so happy, Marcus. Gram loves you."

"The feeling is mutual." He drew her into his arms. "Will you marry me soon?"

"Oh, yes. I wish I could tell Gram. I don't know if I can wait until she's off the cruise ship to tell her our news."

"Maybe Josh can arrange a phone call before Jo boards the ship." Although he wanted to linger and enjoy the knowledge that she was his, Marcus released her. "We'll make plans after we get some sleep. Come on. I want to see where your room is located." Hopefully close to his.

They climbed the stairs and walked down the hall. All the doors were closed but two. The master bedroom was in the corner, the light turned on for Paige to see the layout. The door to the room across the hall was also open. Rio's medical supply bag and his Go bag were on one twin bed, the bag Nate packed for Marcus on the other bed.

He'd be close to Paige if something happened during the night. Didn't matter if Delta Force soldiers and SEALs were close at hand to protect her. They weren't in love with her. She meant everything to him, and he would protect Paige no matter the consequences to himself.

CHAPTER THIRTY

Paige woke to the smell of something yummy. Her stomach growled as she breathed deep. Pancakes? Waffles? Only one way to find out. She hurried through a shower and dressed.

She followed the sound of rumbling male voices to the kitchen.

"There you are." Eli slid from the barstool next to Marcus and motioned for her to take his place. "We thought we might have to send your boyfriend up to wake you with a kiss."

"I'm sorry I missed it." She sat beside the man she'd dreamed about. "Anything happen while I was asleep?"

"Josh arranged for you to talk to Jo in a few minutes."

She smiled. "Thank you, Josh."

"Dad said he was taking the ladies shopping this morning. Seems all of them forgot at least one necessary item. Knowing my mother, she forgot several things."

"I hope your father is a patient man. Jo and her buddies treat shopping like a chess game. They deliberate over every purchase. It's all about strategy and discovering the best bargain for them."

"You forget. My father lived in a house with four women until the triplets left home. All but Meg are champion shoppers. She would prefer to shop online and avoid stores altogether."

"She must be your favorite sister," Quinn said.

He grimaced. "I wish her driving record was better."

"Don't hold your breath," Alex said. "Meg could outrace Danica Patrick."

"You don't have to tell me that. Ethan lectures Meg every time she's issued another ticket. She treats speed limits like suggestions instead of laws." He turned to Paige. "Do you want to eat before you talk to Jo?"

"If I have time. Something smells wonderful."

"Apple strudel muffins, scrambled eggs, and cut fruit." Nate motioned to the coffee pot. "The coffee is fresh. If you prefer hot tea this morning, Meg keeps a stash of herbal teas here for Serena."

"Tea sounds good. Any kind is fine."

As Nate plated her breakfast, Josh and the others discussed the security arrangements using so much military jargon, Paige didn't understand half of their conversation.

"How do you feel this morning?" Marcus asked, his voice low.

She nudged his shoulder with hers. "Like a million bucks. How could I not when the man I adore told me he loves me?"

He leaned in and kissed her lightly. "I feel the same way. If Bianchi and his friends were behind bars, we could make wedding plans."

The room fell silent.

"Wedding plans?" Rio set aside his coffee mug, a smile curving his lips. "You and Paige are getting married?"

"As soon as I convince her to set a date."

Paige accepted hugs from each of the men while Marcus shook hands with them.

"Congratulations." Eli saluted them with his coffee mug, "Brenna will be thrilled. She has a soft spot for her favorite preacher."

"Brenna is your wife?" Paige asked.

"She's the love of my life who also happens to be my wife," he corrected. "She also loves a good romance. This news will make her day."

Quinn snorted. "A good romance is her stock in trade, my friend."

"That sounds like a story." Paige looked from one to the other. "Is it a secret?"

Eli shook his head. "Hard to be a secret when my wife is Brenna Mason, the author."

"Oh, man. I love her books. I've missed her last two signings in Del's store because I was working at the center. I hope I'll have someone available to cover for me next time Brenna is in town."

"We'll give you advance notice on our next visit. For some reason, Maddox thinks the best place for our team to train is at PSI."

Josh slugged him on the shoulder. "Delta training trumps the SEAL version any day."

"You wish." Jon walked into the kitchen for a coffee refill. "You're up, Eli. When Josh and the others are ready, I need to check on Dana."

"Go," Alex said, setting aside his mug. "I'll take over the watch."

"You need us tonight, Josh?" Eli asked as Nate handed his partner a to-go cup.

"Depends on what information Zane unearths today."

"We'll stay available. We can be here in an hour."

"Thanks. We owe you."

"No debt among friends." A quick grin from Eli. "Even if those friends are cowboys."

Vendetta

"Watch it, frog boy," Nate growled.

Within two minutes, the SEALs were gone.

Quinn walked to the back door. "I'm on perimeter."

Josh tapped a series of numbers into his phone, punched the speaker button, and laid the phone on the breakfast bar in front of Paige. When his father answered, he said, "It's me. Everything okay?"

Loud feminine laughter sounded over the speaker. Aaron Cahill chuckled. "Does that answer your question?"

"Paige is anxious to speak to Jo."

"I'll see if I can pry her away from the sales rack."

A moment later, Jo said, "How are you, Paige? Is everything all right?"

"I'm safe, Gram. Sounds like you're having a great time."

"I hate the reason for this trip, but as long as I know you're safe, I'll enjoy the experience. How can I not with my best friends and Liz Cahill along?"

Paige gripped Marcus's hand. "Marcus and I have news, Gram."

"Do I need to sit down?"

"Marcus asked me to marry him."

"Can Marcus hear me?"

"Yes, ma'am. You're on speaker."

"Jo, I wanted to speak to you before I asked Paige to marry me," Marcus said. "Unfortunately, circumstances prevented me from carrying out my plan. Forgive me for not approaching you first. I love your granddaughter, and I will cherish her for the rest of my life."

"You're a good man, Marcus. However, I refuse to call my soon-to-be grandson Pastor Marcus. You'll have to deal with me calling you by your given name. I'm happy for both of you. Do you have a date set for the wedding?"

"Not yet. I've waited a long time for her. Do you mind if the wedding is soon?"

"Of course not. You've been dancing around each other for years. I don't blame you for not wanting to wait to start your life together. However, you better not have matching wedding rings on your fingers when I return from this cruise. I want to be at the wedding. I've waited a long time to see my granddaughter married."

"Yes, ma'am," Paige and Marcus said in unison.

"I'm handing the phone to Aaron now. I love you both. Be safe and I'll see you soon."

Squeals and laughter sounded in the background, then Aaron said, "Congratulations, Paige and Marcus. I think your news gave Jo a big morale boost. Anything else, Josh? I think the ladies are ready to invade another store."

"Is the Fortress operative staying close?"

"There are two of them and they're doing a fine job. They're going on the cruise as well although I don't think that precaution is necessary. But who am I to argue with the experts? Besides, Liz and the others enjoy their company."

"If a problem develops, do whatever they tell you. What are their names?"

"Sam Coleman and Joe Gray. Do you know them?"

Paige noticed the members of Durango relaxed when they heard the names mentioned by Aaron. Their confidence made her feel better. She wanted her grandmother safe.

"Yeah, we do. You're in good hands."

"Watch your back, son. I love you."

"Love you, too."

"The rest of you be careful. I don't want to come home to find any of you injured. I'll talk to you soon, Josh." And Aaron ended the call.

Nate nudged Paige's plate and mug of tea closer. "Eat."

The others left to complete the tasks Josh had assigned, leaving her and Marcus alone in the kitchen. "Do you know what the plan is for today?" Paige asked.

"We're to stay close to the cabin. Zane will leak clues to our location in a few hours. He can't drop hints too fast or Bianchi and his cronies will know they're being set up for a hard fall."

Made sense. Bianchi couldn't be stupid or he wouldn't have survived this long in such a dangerous occupation.

"As soon as Zane knows O'Reilly or Bianchi are moving on the information, he'll tell Josh."

"I'd love to walk to the creek after breakfast. You game?"

"I'd like that."

Though the path to the creek took many twists and turns, she could still see the corner of the cabin. Near the creek edge, a fallen log made a natural place for them to sit.

They remained quiet for a time. Despite her reluctance to shatter the peace of the moment, Paige suspected they wouldn't have time alone the rest of the day. The cabin was a hub of activity with the members of Durango going in and out as they prepared for the battle to come.

"Do you think Mayor Parks will stir up trouble before we return to town?"

His expression grew somber. "If Parks has his way, the congregation will have already voted me out by the time this is over."

"The church would be devastated and so would you."

"I've grown to love them over the past seven years, even the cantankerous mayor. The pastor of my home church has been serving for more than 30 years. My dream is to make a similar long-term commitment to Cornerstone. I may have to try again at a different church. If another church will hire me after this."

Shock stole her breath. The long-term implications of Mayor Parks' campaign hurt Paige's heart. A few ugly comments from the man would ruin any chance of future ministry for Marcus.

"Can you see yourself as the wife of a common laborer?"

"I want to be your wife no matter what you job is. Many well-respected people would be willing to write a reference for you. Would Fortress hire you?"

He turned, eyebrow raised. "You think I could be an operative?"

"I believe you can do any job you feel passionate about. Fortress has the training academy at PSI. Why couldn't they teach you how to be an operative or a bodyguard? If you were interested in working for them, that is."

"Hadn't thought about that side of Fortress. Besides, I already work for them."

Her mouth gaped. "You do?"

"I'm a counselor for their operatives. I imagine Maddox would be willing to hire me full-time if I approached him about it."

"At least you'll have options if Cornerstone is foolish enough to let you go. I'll follow you wherever your job takes you, whether it's in Nashville or somewhere else because I love you, Marcus."

"Could you be happy if we moved?"

"As long as I'm with you, yes."

Marcus wrapped his arms around her and pulled her close. "I'm thankful God brought you into my life." Finally, he eased back. "We should go back before Josh or one of the others looks for us."

In the kitchen, Nate turned as they walked inside. "Josh was looking for you. He's in the security room with Alex. He has news from Otter Creek."

CHAPTER THIRTY-ONE

"You have news from home?" Marcus handed Josh and Alex each a bottle of water.

"Thanks. Nick called."

"Did something else happen?" Paige asked.

Josh gestured to two chairs along the far wall. "You might want to sit down."

That didn't sound good. "He found out something new."

"Nick arrested Seth Parks earlier this morning."

"Why?"

"Arson."

"He set fire to the orchard." Paige dropped into the nearest chair. "Why would he burn our trees?"

"When Nick asked him that, Seth said your grandmother is standing in the way of the shopping center."

Marcus rubbed the back of his neck, frustrated at the sheer stupidity of Seth's actions. "He's sixteen years old. I doubt he cares about a mall. What's his real motive?"

"My guess is it has something to do with either his father or his grandfather. Both of them are rabid supporters of this project. What I can't figure out is why they're both pushing the development. Neither one of them owns property up for purchase. At least, I don't think they do." Josh frowned. "I'll see if I can identify the owners of the properties Davidson has targeted. Maybe that will give us insight into Seth's motive."

Marcus hesitated to say anything because he had no proof of his suspicions. Josh was discreet, though. Had to be with his military background. "Josh, have you noticed the relationship between James Parks and Seth?"

"What do you mean?"

"Paige and I were at the Parks home yesterday before we learned Dalton was missing. While we were there, James arrived. There's something off about their relationship. Seth seems afraid of his father. He acted like a scared mouse instead of the confident young man we see at the center."

"Any evidence of abuse before now, Marcus?"

He shook his head, frowned. "If I had noticed bruising or cuts, I would have told you or one of your brothers-in-law."

Alex glanced over his shoulder. "We know Parks is a bully. Wouldn't be surprised to learn he bullies his family along with anyone else he meets in Otter Creek."

"I can attest to that," Paige said. "He came after me in my office at the center."

Josh scowled. "What did he want?"

"For me to pressure Gram to change her mind about the orchard and B & B. He wasn't happy when I refused."

"Did he hurt you?"

"Nate encouraged him to leave."

A snort from Alex. "A very polite way of saying Nate kicked him out. He must not have touched Parks or the mayor's son would have filed assault charges."

Durango's leader grinned. "Nate can intimidate with a look."

Paige turned to Marcus. "Should you be expecting a visit from the police?"

He shrugged. "I don't I regret what I did."

Josh and Alex stared at him. "What did you do?" Josh asked, eyes narrowed. "And it better not be something I have to arrest you for."

"I told him to stay away from Paige, that if he cornered her again, he'd be dealing with me."

"No bruises on either of you?"

"He jabbed a finger in my chest. I persuaded him not to do that again."

"Maybe that explains the black eye Seth was sporting when Nick arrested him."

"He didn't have a black eye when we saw him. Did he say how he was injured?"

"The classic explanation. He walked into a door. Nick didn't buy the explanation and gathered enough evidence to arrest James for battery."

"I wanted James to leave Paige alone. He scared her. I couldn't let that pass without a warning."

"We do the best we can with the knowledge we have, Marcus. There are always repercussions. By saving Brent, you essentially lost your life. No one has stood up to James. If he'd cornered Del, I would have gone after him myself, cop or not."

"Has he tried to intimidate you?"

A flat look from his friend. "He knows better than to try."

Josh and his teammates would wipe the floor with Parks. At least the man was smart enough to avoid a confrontation with Durango.

"At least now, James will think twice before he pushes your girlfriend around." Josh looked at Paige. "Nick also wants me to show you the picture Zane sent of your attacker."

"Why? I didn't see his face. It was too dark in the hallway."

"Will you look anyway?"

She took Josh's cell phone and examined the picture on the screen. "I have seen him somewhere. Around town maybe. No. Wait. I've seen him with the developer and Mayor Parks."

Josh stared at her. "This guy is a hit man. What dealings do Parks and Davidson have with Bianchi?"

"Can't wait for you to tell Ethan this one," Alex said.

"What a mess this is going to be. Are you sure about this, Paige?"

"Positive. I saw them when I took the trash to the Dumpster behind the community center. This doesn't make sense, though. I thought Bianchi worked for the O'Reillys."

"He's a freelancer and Zane is the best in the business at covering a person's trail. Bianchi probably hasn't had much luck with the hunt and took on another job if Davidson or the mayor did hire him. If that's true, it was pure luck that Bianchi crossed paths with Marcus and reported his location to O'Reilly." He scrubbed his face with his hands. "I'll set up a videoconference with Ethan, run this past him and Nick. We can't afford to sit on this. Bianchi is too dangerous to have around Otter Creek."

"Agreed." He couldn't just sit here. He needed to do something, anything. Marcus stood, turned to Paige. "Sweetheart, do you want more tea? I need water. I'm under Rio's orders to drink plenty of water today."

"Actually, water sounds good. A bottle for me, too, please."

He leaned down and brushed a kiss over her lips, then returned to the kitchen.

Nate turned away from the stove, eyed him. "You okay, Marcus?"

"I suppose."

"Don't sound convincing. Try again, the truth this time."

"The man who attacked Paige might be connected to Mayor Parks and Franklin Davidson. He's also the man being paid to kill me."

"Double dipping. We've done that a time or two."

"Durango only kills when it's necessary. Bianchi makes a living at killing and he enjoys his job. Who does that?"

"People with no conscience. Unfortunately, the world is full of them."

"He could have killed Paige. If I hadn't walked into the community center when I did, he would have. The attack wasn't about me at the time."

"How is that possible?"

"O'Reilly hired him to find me, but Josh thinks he picked up the side job for Parks and Davidson. Bianchi must have thought he'd won the lottery when he saw me with Paige. Talk about an easy job."

"Locating you was a stroke of luck. The good news is you're not an easy man to kill, Marcus."

Small comfort. "Losing Paige would gut me."

"You won't. Know how to handle a weapon?"

He nodded. "Maddox insisted on training me himself."

"You carrying?"

"Ankle holster."

"Good. If a time comes when you need to pull the trigger to protect yourself or Paige, don't hesitate. Second guessing yourself will get both of you killed. We'll do our best to make sure the choice of whether or not to pull the trigger isn't necessary. If he slips past us, do what you have to."

Even their best preparation and skill may not be enough. Bianchi or one of his men might slide through Durango's defenses. Faced with the choice of possibly killing a man or dying, he'd chose to live and protect Paige every time. Resolve replaced the icy knot in his gut. "Thanks. I needed the reminder."

A nod. "Cold drinks are in the fridge, including water." Nate gave him a pointed look.

"Rio has a big mouth."

"Only when he's concerned about the health of someone he cares about. You are among that number. Count yourself lucky."

No point in rebutting Nate's unsubtle reminder. Marcus grabbed two more bottles of water and carried them into the security room, handing one to Paige. "Did you talk to Ethan?"

Josh twisted in his seat. "He's on a conference call. He should be in contact soon." As if on cue, Ethan's face appeared on the computer screen along with Nick's.

"Sit rep."

Josh spelled out what they'd learned and surmised.

The police chief's eyes glittered. "Have you contacted Murphy yet?"

"I wanted to run this past you first."

"Do it. Tell Z I want to know everything yesterday. Do you have enough backup in case the op goes south?"

"Fortress is only an hour away," Alex said.

"You could be dead in seconds and you can't guarantee Bianchi won't bring in more help, especially if he figures out you and your teammates are protecting Marcus and Paige."

"Eli Wolfe and Jon Smith are available."

"Bring them in." He turned, looked at Nick. "You have something to add?"

"James Parks bonded out of jail since he hasn't been arrested before. He'll get a slap on the wrist and told to take anger management counseling."

"In other words, he could go after his family or Paige again." Marcus scowled. "How is this fair?"

"Small town, Marcus. The judge we drew is on friendly terms with the mayor. I have eyes on Parks. He won't be able to sneeze in town without someone knowing and reporting it."

Josh leaned closer to the screen. "Who?"

"Jake Davenport and Remy Doucet will trade off with PSI trainees."

Marcus shook his head. "Not good enough, Nick. That doesn't stop him from hurting his family."

"No, it doesn't. Unless his wife is willing to file a complaint against him, our hands are tied."

"What about Seth and his arrest?"

"His family needs to hire a top-notch attorney. We found his prints on a gas can at the orchard. I obtained a court order to check under his bandage. He lied about having a scratch. No question the injury is from a burn."

"Has he confessed?" Alex asked.

"Not exactly. He keeps saying he was trying to help and never intended for anyone to be hurt."

"How does burning my grandmother's orchard help? The fire could have spread to other parts of the area, including our B & B. Is that what he wanted? To put us out of business?"

"He refused to say."

"The fire must be connected to the shopping center. Both the mayor and his son are pushing hard for the development. What we don't know is why. That's the only thing that makes sense."

"Agreed," Ethan said. "Find me that connection, Josh, something I can use to tie Bianchi to the mayor and the shopping center project."

Paige gripped Marcus's hand. "Can't you arrest Bianchi, Ethan?"

"If we can find him, we'll book him on an attempted murder charge. The problem is he's not been seen around town since you left Otter Creek. Josh, tell Zane to call in every marker he has. I don't want this clown hurting more of my people."

A nod. "I'll call him as soon as we finish."

"Are you going after Mayor Parks?" Paige asked.

"If he's guilty of conspiracy to commit murder, you bet I am."

Alex folded his arms across his chest. "And if he's guilty of only having bad taste in friends?"

A cold smile curved the lips of Otter Creek's police chief. "I'll point out the danger dogging his companions and taint any prospects he has of reelection. It would be my pleasure to leak the news to the media sharks, especially Meg. Keep me posted, Josh, and watch your back."

"Yes, sir. Any rumors making the rounds about Marcus?"

"Some people think he has a family emergency or he's ill and didn't want to worry anyone. The majority bought the idea that he was with Paige, Jo and the others."

"Nothing about Gram going on a cruise?" Paige asked.

"Not so far. I hope we'll have Bianchi under wraps before long and we won't have to worry about their safety. Marcus, focus on yourself and Paige. Trust us to take care of the rest."

"You have a plan?"

Ethan smiled.

CHAPTER THIRTY-TWO

Marcus looked at the operatives around the table. "You sure there's no other way?"

"Do you want to be looking over your shoulder the rest of your life?" Josh countered.

"Of course, I don't. I want my wife to walk down the streets of Otter Creek in safety, for my kids to play without fear." But could he sanction what they were proposing?

"The plan will make sure that happens."

"Will it? You can't guarantee the results. What if O'Reilly digs in and sends more hit men instead of backing off permanently?" He shoved his hands through his hair. "You don't know him, Josh. He's utterly ruthless and doesn't care about the fallout as long as his goal is met. What if he refuses to fall in line?"

Alex set his empty coffee mug on the table surface. "Do you want to know the answer to that question?"

"No, but I think I have to know the truth."

"We eliminate the threat to you and Paige."

Eliminate. The word sunk deep. Nausea swirled in his gut. "You're a cop, Josh. You're sworn to uphold the law."

"You're my principal, Marcus. My job is to protect you and your future wife."

"What about your badge and the oath you took?"

"Ethan and I have an arrangement. If I hand him my badge without an explanation, he knows not to ask questions."

"What if you're caught?"

"I won't be. Besides, I won't be going in alone. I'll have my teammates and Adam Walker's team."

"The Zoo Crew will want in on the op as well as Maddox," Jon said.

Eli snorted. "He'll probably take over the operation, especially since it's his debt to repay."

If only his life was in jeopardy, he'd convince the operatives to come up with a different plan or relocate him. But he was tired of hiding. More important, he was afraid for Paige. At least they knew what Bianchi looked like. If Durango or the OCPD took down Bianchi, O'Reilly would send more hit men, and the next time they might kill the woman he loved more than his own life.

"Trust us, Marcus. This is what we do for a living." He grinned. "No one does intimidation better than Fortress."

Marcus looked at Jon. "Can Dana handle you being gone?"

"She'll be with Brenna. Since we don't know how long the operation will take, Zane and Claire extended an invitation to our wives. Dana is comfortable with Zane and she loves Claire as much as she loves her own sister."

At least that was one worry off his shoulders. Dana wasn't comfortable around most men, but since Zane was wheelchair bound, she thought the Fortress tech guru was harmless. Z was a SEAL. Wheelchair bound or not, the man was one of the most highly trained operatives on the planet. Probably just as well Dana didn't realize that Zane Murphy would kill without hesitation to protect his wife and Eli and Jon's wives.

A phone signaled an incoming text. Josh checked his screen and smiled. "Zane started dropping hints about our location three hours ago. He says O'Reilly got word and passed the information to Bianchi. Looks like he's taking the bait."

"How long do we have?"

"Five-hour drive plus recon. My guess is we'll have visitors between two and four in the morning."

"How many people is Bianchi bringing with him?"

"Doesn't matter. We'll handle them. You know what to do if they slip past us?"

Marcus tapped his head. "We've been through the plan several times. I've got it."

"Good. Get some rest, Marcus. The sensors are operational around the property. We'll wake you when there's a perimeter breach."

Marcus started to refuse, but a narrow-eyed look from Rio had him holding up his hands in surrender. He left the kitchen and noticed the light burning in the living room. He frowned. The room had been dark after he walked Paige to her room and went to talk to the others. He doubted Quinn would have come out of the security room to turn on a lamp. Special Forces teams preferred to work in darkness.

Since Quinn was in the security room, that left Paige. Marcus found her asleep on the couch, a book clutched in her hand. He crouched. "Paige."

She opened her eyes and smiled. "Hi."

"Why are you down here?"

"I wanted to be near you, but the guys wouldn't talk freely if I sat in on your discussion."

"The security arrangements involve you. They wouldn't have minded your presence."

"Are you finished?"

His lips curved. "They booted me out. I have a feeling none of them will be sleeping tonight."

Paige sat up. "Why not? What's going on?"

"Zane dropped hints about our location in the right places and O'Reilly passed the message to Bianchi."

"He's on his way here?"

"Josh estimates six hours, maybe less."

"What should I do?"

"Rest while you can. I'll do the same." Although he figured the attempt would be unsuccessful on his part. He glanced at the book in her hand. "What are you reading?"

"*Mage Code* by Max Irons."

"Any good?"

"The book is a fast read with great dialogue. It's fun."

"Great cover. I might pick up a copy for myself."

"You can read mine. Dalton might like the book, though."

"He'll have plenty of time to read for a while. I'll buy him a copy when we return to Otter Creek." He held out his hand. "Come on. I'll walk upstairs with you."

At the threshold to the master bedroom, Marcus wrapped his hand around the nape of Paige's neck and kissed her. Long minutes later, he broke the kiss and smiled at the sight of her unfocused gaze.

He nudged her into the room. "Sleep in your clothes in case we have to move fast."

Marcus waited until she shut her door before going into his room. He stretched out on the bed in the darkened room and prayed for the safety of Durango and the SEALs as well as Paige and himself.

Sometime later, Rio walked into the room. "Marcus."

He sat up.

"Company. Get your girlfriend up and make sure she's ready to run." And he was gone.

Marcus checked his weapon and shoved two extra magazines in his pocket. He crossed the hall to Paige's room and opened the door. A dim night light lit the room, throwing a soft glow over her face.

Not wanting to startle her awake, he sat on the side of the bed and gently rubbed her arm. "Paige. Wake up, sweetheart."

"What's wrong?"

"The perimeter alarm went off. Where are your shoes?"

She gave him a sleepy smile and shoved aside the quilt. "On my feet. I wanted to be ready to run at a moment's notice. I didn't count on needing a vat of coffee to wake up."

"I don't think we have time to brew a pot. Will a soft drink work?"

"As long as it has caffeine."

He dropped a quick kiss on her lips. "I'll be back. Leave the lights off. We don't want Bianchi or his buddies to know we're awake."

"Got it."

Marcus made his way downstairs to the kitchen. Eli turned from the back door where he was keeping watch.

"Paige awake?"

"Yeah. I'm getting her caffeine to clear the brain fog. Anything yet?"

"The first perimeter alarm is set a half mile away. The sensors at the quarter mile mark haven't tripped yet."

"Marcus."

He swung around with Paige's drink clutched in his hand. "Yes, Josh?"

"Bring Paige to the security room."

"Two minutes."

"No more." Josh melted into the shadows again.

Marcus blew out a soft breath. These guys were seriously good. He returned to Paige's room. Her eyes lit at the sight of the soft drink in his hand. "Josh wants us in the security room," he said as he broke the seal and handed her the bottle.

"I'm ready. What should I do with my bag?"

"Is there anything in there you can't do without?"

"My ID, debit card, keys, and cell phone are in my pockets. Everything else can be replaced easily." She slid him a look as they descended the stairs. "Will I have to leave everything behind?"

"If we have to run, you don't want anything weighing you down. Every second counts and so does every foot of space between you and the pursuer."

"Personal experience?"

He squeezed her hand.

"I'll take that as a yes."

They entered the security room where Alex and Josh manned the bank of computers. The screens were split into four quadrants each.

Josh glanced over his shoulder. "There's an ear piece for each of you. We'll be able to communicate with you no matter where you are. They're small, so no one will know you have a comm device. That gives us an advantage."

"Communication goes both ways," Alex added. "Anything you say the whole team will hear so no whispering sweet nothings in each other's ears."

Marcus picked up an ear piece, relieved to recognize the apparatus. Maddox had made him practice using one when he was still recovering from the gunshot wound.

He slipped the device in his ear, then helped Paige with hers. When Josh demanded an update, each member of the protection detail checked in. Their voices sounded as if they were in the room with them. The only person who didn't report in was Jon.

Josh straightened. "Jon, sit rep."

Nothing.

"Eli, go. Rio, cover the back."

Both men acknowledged the order.

At that moment, a red light began flashing on each computer screen.

CHAPTER THIRTY-THREE

Paige gripped Marcus's hand. "What's happening?"

"Quarter mile perimeter alarm," Alex answered. "Quinn, you have eyes on our visitors?"

"Affirmative," came his whispered response. "Four in sector B."

One by one, each operative aside from Jon and Eli reported in. Paige kept a mental tally in her head. By the time they finished, she'd counted twenty people converging on the cabin. They were slowly being surrounded by men with no conscience.

She exchanged glances with the man she planned to marry soon, noted the same concern in his eyes that she felt. Durango and the SEALs were outnumbered two to one.

Where had Bianchi found so many men to help him? Was their objective to capture or kill? When she edged closer to Marcus, he wrapped his arms around her.

A whisper came over the comm system. "It's Jon. Eli is with me. Permission to start the hunt?"

"Go." Josh glanced at Alex.

His teammate shoved back from the console, and grabbed his pack and the rifle beside it. He nodded at her and Marcus as he passed.

"Quinn, Alex is moving into position."

"Copy."

"Nate, on my mark."

On the screens, groups of men moved through the area. Bianchi and his buddies, she assumed. None of the Special Forces guys were bunched up.

"Come on," Josh muttered. "A little closer."

The seconds ticked away, ratcheting the tension higher and higher. None of the operatives seemed fazed by the pressure. Then again, this was probably normal during their missions.

"Nate, sector F."

"Copy."

A moment later, an explosion ripped through the night, lighting up one of the quadrants on the computer screen.

Paige jerked in the circle of Marcus's arms.

"It's okay," he murmured.

"None of ours were hurt?"

"They know where the charges are set."

"Sector D," Josh snapped.

Another explosion.

A moment later, Eli broke in, his voice urgent. "Josh, incoming."

Josh shoved away from the console. "Marcus, run. Go, go, go."

Marcus grabbed Paige's hand, raced down the hall and out the back door. Rio sprinted to Paige's side as Josh leaped from the deck to the ground. They ran for the cover of the tree line.

Seconds later, Josh said, "Down."

Before she could draw in a breath, Paige was on the ground, Marcus covering her body with his. A massive explosion rocked the world. She glanced back at the cabin, squinting at the fireball turning night into day. Her breath caught. The cabin had been obliterated, the flames slowly destroying what the bomb had left.

Josh leaped to his feet. "Tangos at ten o'clock and two o'clock. Rio, take the right. I'll take the left. Marcus, follow the plan."

Marcus yanked Paige to her feet and broke into a run. He seemed to know where he was going. A good thing since the forest surrounding them was filled with thick brush and foliage along with dense shadows.

She stumbled and would have gone down if Marcus hadn't maintained a strong grip on her hand. Minutes later, he stopped. Marcus looked back, a finger to his lips, indicating the need for silence.

What had he heard? She heard nothing but her heartbeat thundering in her ears. She scanned the area, straining to see in the gloomy forest. The back of her neck prickled, a sure sign of trouble.

She wanted to laugh at herself. Trouble definitely dogged their steps unless Josh and the others captured or killed the men after her and Marcus. How would they find them all? There were so many men hunting them. She didn't know the number Nate stopped with his explosives, but some had survived because someone stalked them in these woods. Paige could feel it.

Suddenly, Marcus thrust Paige behind him. From a holster at his back, he pulled a gun.

Her eyes widened at the sight of the black weapon in his hand. She didn't know Marcus had a gun or knew how to handle one.

Over the ear piece, Paige heard their protection detail engage in battle. Gunfire echoed in the night air all around them.

Marcus reached back and grasped her hand. "There's a ravine five hundred yards ahead on the right. If we get separated, you head for that ravine. I'll find you."

"I don't want to leave you. I can help." Being apart from Marcus was a really bad idea.

"I want you safe, baby." He got them moving again. They walked in silence for a few minutes.

Somewhere ahead, a twig snapped, the noise sounding like a gunshot. Marcus spun, hustled her deeper into the shadows, and pressed her back against a tree. He peered around the trunk.

Minutes passed. Paige stayed still, listening, watching over his shoulder in case Bianchi or one of his men tried to sneak up on them.

Marcus stiffened, raised his weapon. "That's far enough," he said. "Drop your weapon."

A vile curse reached Paige's ears along with the sound of a muffled thud.

"Now your backup piece."

"Don't got no backup," came the growled response.

"On your knees, hands behind your head."

More cursing.

"Paige, are you familiar with weapons?" Marcus murmured.

"Enough to steer clear of them."

"I have to restrain him. I need you to hold the gun on him. Will you do that?"

"To keep you safe, I'll do anything."

"Stay behind me." Marcus eased out from the tree cover. He kept his gun trained on the man kneeling on the ground, glaring at them.

Paige stayed close but made sure Marcus's movements remained unencumbered.

"Face down on the dirt, arms spread to the side."

"You're a dead man, Watson."

"Matt Watson has been dead for seven years."

"Yeah? Well, you ain't the only one we been watching. You should give yourself up. Maybe no one else will get hurt."

Cold chills surged down Paige's back. Was he talking about her or Marcus's family? The thought that they might be under surveillance by O'Reilly's people made her stomach churn. If Marcus had tried to see them under cover of darkness, the surveillance team would have killed him. She owed Brent Maddox big for convincing Marcus to stay away from his family.

"Down on the ground," Marcus snapped.

The man shifted his gaze to Paige.

"Don't look at her." Marcus gave the man a wide berth as he led Paige to the left side of Bianchi's cohort. "If you even twitch a muscle, I will shoot you."

A snort. "You're a preacher. You don't kill people. You're bluffing."

"Want to bet your life on that?" Silence. "I didn't think so." He slipped his left hand into his pocket and pulled out a plastic zip tie. "Take the weapon, sweetheart."

Praying her hands didn't shake and give her fear away to the enemy on the ground, she took the gun from Marcus, doing her best to mimic his grip, and pointed the barrel at their prisoner. Paige hoped he wasn't stupid enough to try something. She'd probably end up shooting herself or Marcus rather than the man glaring daggers at her.

Marcus secured the man's hands behind his back, then used another zip tie to truss his ankles together. He reached into his pocket again and pulled out a small roll of black tape.

"You can't escape all of us."

"The only one I see right now is you. I'll handle the others if they slip past my friends." Marcus smiled. "But I wouldn't count on that if I were you." With that, he slapped a piece tape over the man's mouth.

Marcus took the gun from Paige. They resumed their journey to the ravine Marcus had mentioned. At the edge of a clearing, he paused. "The ravine is fifty feet in front of us."

"How do you know where everything is? If it wasn't for the fire at the cabin, I wouldn't be able to find my way back. I've been turned around since we ran into the woods."

"Josh made me memorize a map of the area. He and the others discussed escape options after I walked you to your room the first time last night." He scanned the open space between them and the ravine. "Stay here. I need to check the ravine. I don't want to send us both headlong into danger if I can help it."

"Be careful."

"Always. I plan to spend many years with you." Marcus picked his way across the terrain to peer over the edge of the ravine.

A footstep sounded behind Paige. Before she could turn, a muscular arm circled her neck and yanked her back against a rock-hard chest.

CHAPTER THIRTY-FOUR

Marcus scanned the ravine. He didn't see anyone lying in wait for them. Relief skittered through him. If he hid Paige behind the rocks on the left, she would be safe until Josh or one of the others escorted them out of the woods.

Paige gasped.

He swung around, weapon raised. A river of ice ran through his veins when he saw Bianchi with his arm around Paige's throat, a gun pressed to the side of her head. His worst nightmare was playing out mere feet in front of him.

"Let her go, Bianchi. I'm the one you want."

Through the ear piece, Josh said, "Marcus, stall. Jon, you or Eli clear?"

"Negative," came the whispered response.

"Rio, go."

"Copy."

"Marcus, Rio will come up behind Bianchi to your left. Don't shoot my medic. Rio, capture him alive if possible. We need information from him."

Bianchi smirked. "You know better than that, Watson. The lady is my ace in the hole. You can't shoot me without risking your woman. Drop the weapon before my hand shakes and I shoot her by accident."

A real funny guy, Bianchi. "Do you know why O'Reilly hired you to find me?"

"Money talks. Don't matter the reason as long as I get paid." Another smirk. "I already have a million in a Cayman account. Another million will be wired to my account when I deliver you to O'Reilly."

"O'Reilly wants me dead because I shot and killed his son." A fact which still haunted him in the deep watches of the night. He hadn't had a choice. Faced with the same situation, he would still pull that trigger. To do otherwise would cost the life of a good man. "Do you think I'm going to lay down my weapon and let you kill Paige?"

An ugly smile spread across Bianchi's face. "Who says I'm going to kill her? I might keep her around a while. O'Reilly don't care what happens to her."

"Keep stalling, Marcus," Rio murmured through the comm device. "I'm almost in position."

"Why did you try to kill Paige? Was it on O'Reilly's orders?"

"What purpose would that serve? Told you, he don't care about your woman."

"You didn't know Paige and I were together, did you?"

The hit man laughed. "Lady Luck sure turned my way. Been hunting for you for months, and you practically fall in my lap when I'm on another job. Easy payday for me."

"You splitting the two million with nineteen other guys?"

A snort. "Don't be stupid. Two are part of my crew and I'll pay them. The others belong to O'Reilly."

Rio emerged from the tree line with a Ka-Bar in his hand.

Knowing one twitch or shift of his gaze would give Rio away, Marcus focused only on Bianchi and Paige.

Vendetta

"What are your orders? Kill me and deliver proof of death?"

"Naw. O'Reilly wants to pop you himself. I'm supposed to transport you to a safe location and wait for him to show up and finish you off."

Rio edged closer, shifted the hold on his knife.

"You think he'll let you live? You know too much and he has a stable of assassins ready to do his bidding for less money. He doesn't need you."

Irritation flickered in the man's gaze. "He's paying me a boatload of money. If his pet assassins were so good, why'd he hire me?"

"You're disposable."

Rio plunged the knife into the killer's left shoulder. Bianchi screamed as his arm dropped away from Paige's neck to grab reflexively at his shoulder. She ran to Marcus as Rio confiscated the assassin's gun.

Marcus wrapped his arms around her, grateful she was alive. "Are you okay?"

"I am now." Her body trembled.

"Marcus, is she all right?" Josh demanded over the comm system.

"She's fine, thanks to Rio."

The medic retrieved his knife, wiped the blade on the assassin's pants before sliding the weapon into his leg sheath. "You did the hard work, Marcus. Josh, Bianchi is down."

One by one, the rest of the protection detail checked in. Twelve casualties and eight injured or bound and gagged including Bianchi.

"Fire department's en route," Alex said. "Cops won't be far behind."

"Josh, take Marcus and Paige to a safe location," Eli said. "Fortress headquarters is the best place for them. Jon and I will deal with the police."

"You can't explain all the bodies."

Eli chuckled. "Want to bet? We're SEALs. People think we're supermen."

"Take Bianchi with you," Jon said. "Have Nate interrogate him."

Josh was silent a moment.

"You need to know who sent him after Paige," the operative reminded Durango's leader.

Marcus palmed the back of Paige's head as though protecting her from further danger. They needed all the information they could get. Otherwise, the danger to her could resurface, and next time she might be alone.

"Alex, Quinn, head for the SUVs. Nate, rendezvous with Rio and make sure our guest doesn't cause problems. Marcus, you and Paige stay with Rio until I meet up with you."

After Josh's orders were acknowledged, Rio hauled Bianchi to his feet. "Nate, quadrant B."

"Watch yourselves. Emergency responders are on scene."

To prevent Bianchi from raising a ruckus, Rio slapped a piece of duct tape over his mouth and shoved the hit man into motion.

"Come on," Marcus murmured as he turned Paige to follow the others. "The sooner we get out of here, the quicker I can get you someplace warm with hot tea."

Five minutes later, Nate emerged from the shadows and clamped a hand on Bianchi's arm. Between him and Rio, the two frog marched the thug in a wide circle around the frantic activity at the cabin. Although the wannabe killer tried to impede their progress, the two operatives forced him to move forward.

Josh joined them and gripped Paige's other arm. "How are you holding up?"

"I'm fine. Marcus, I don't want to spend my honeymoon anywhere near a forest."

"Sun and sand all right?"

"Perfect. The sooner the better."

His head whipped her direction. "Are you serious?"

"Come on, Marcus," Quinn chimed in. "You know she is. Take your woman at her word and get a marriage license."

The other members of the protection detail chuckled.

"Quinn's right." Paige flashed Marcus a grin. "I am serious."

He couldn't believe Paige still wanted to marry him despite the danger she'd been in because of his past. "I'll take care of the license at the first opportunity today."

By the time they reached the SUVs, Paige stumbled every few steps and would have gone down if not for Josh and Marcus keeping her on her feet.

Josh hustled them into the back seat, then climbed behind the steering wheel. "Go," he ordered the other two SUVs and followed them down a side road away from the cabin. He activated his Bluetooth.

Zane answered. "Talk to me."

"It's Josh. Durango is coming into headquarters hot. We have Vincent Bianchi. We need to interrogate him without interference from the local cops."

"We'll be ready for you. Maddox is already on site. Is Paige with you?"

Josh glanced in the rearview mirror. "Say hello, Paige."

"Hi, Zane."

"What do you need?"

"A super tall mug of hot tea, mint or chamomile. I'm freezing and I can't stop shaking."

Marcus tugged her tighter against his side and rubbed her arm. He turned his head to check the cargo area and saw one of those Mylar blankets the Fortress guys all carried. He wrapped Paige in the blanket and tugged her once again into his arms.

"Adrenaline dump and fatigue," Zane said. "I have just the tea you need. I keep it on hand at Fortress headquarters for my wife."

"You're not going to work this early just for me."

Zane laughed. "I'm on site as well. Maddox and I wanted to be on hand in case our operatives needed assistance."

"How can I ever thank you?"

"Not necessary, Paige. I'm looking forward to meeting you in person. Marcus, you unscathed?"

"Not a scratch or bruise."

"Excellent. What do you need?"

"Hot coffee would be nice."

"That we have plenty of. Good and strong. Josh, we'll be waiting. Let me know if you encounter a problem." And he ended the call.

"Settle back and relax. We have at least an hour drive into Nashville, depending on traffic," Josh said as he followed the other two SUVs onto I-24.

In his arms, Paige trembled and her teeth chattered. "The shaking is ticking me off," she muttered.

"When it passes, you won't be able to keep your eyes open."

"Why aren't your teeth chattering out of your head like mine?"

"My body reacts differently than yours to the adrenaline. I won't be able to eat for a couple hours."

"Alex is like Marcus," Josh added. "Rio listens to his wife's piano music. I'll hit the gym at Fortress if we have time. We all handle adrenaline dump in different ways. Close your eyes and rest, Paige. You expended a lot of energy in that run through the woods."

She smiled at Marcus. "May I borrow your shoulder?"

"Any time, baby." He shifted Paige until she leaned on his chest, her head resting over his heart. The trembling slowly eased and her breathing evened out until she went boneless in his arms.

Josh glanced back. "She out?"

"Yeah."

"You did well out there, Marcus. Would have been easy to panic when your woman was in Bianchi's hands but you held it together. Would you have pulled the trigger?"

"In a heartbeat."

A nod. "Rest. This isn't over yet."

CHAPTER THIRTY-FIVE

Paige walked into an office to see a buzz-cut blond behind the desk. The tall, muscular man rose to greet her and Marcus.

"Glad you escaped the woods unscathed, Paige." He held out his hand to Paige. "Brent Maddox. I owe your boyfriend my life."

She smiled. "The PSI teams speak highly of you. Thank you for keeping Marcus safe for the past seven years."

A nod, then, "Great job with Bianchi, Marcus. Those hours drilling you in how to handle a crisis paid off. You and Paige come with me. Zane is waiting in the observation room."

As they followed the Fortress CEO, Paige asked, "Do you know if my grandmother is all right?"

"Jo and the others left port with Sam and her partner. I talked to them before the ship sailed. If you want to confirm, I'll give you Sam's sat phone number and you can talk to your grandmother. According to Sam, the ladies are keeping Aaron Cahill on his toes."

She could just imagine. Josh's father must be a good sport to do this. "I'd love to talk to Gram. Thank you, Brent."

He opened the door to a darkened room where the only light came from a computer screen. The man keying information into a laptop sat in a wheelchair. On a table beside him were two to-go cups.

The computer tech glanced up, smiled. "Marcus, good to see you." He shook Marcus's hand. "Introduce me to your girlfriend."

"Paige, this is Zane Murphy, computer guru for Fortress."

Zane handed her the larger cup. "Chamomile mint tea."

"Exactly what I need. Thanks, Zane."

Marcus glanced toward the large observation window and into the room beyond. "Where's Bianchi?"

"Should be arriving soon. Rio's treating his knife wound. Can't get answers from the man if he's dead." Zane handed him the second cup. "Sit. Might as well be comfortable while you wait."

The tea's scent brought a sense of comfort to Paige. "Where are the others?"

Maddox grabbed a chair and sat. "Quinn is eating. Nate's with Rio. Josh is pounding the heavy bag in the training room. Alex is on the phone with Ivy."

Paige wrapped her hands around the cup, savoring the warmth as the hot liquid slid down her throat. When she'd finished half of her tea, the light flickered on in the room on the other side of the window.

Zane tapped a few keys on his keyboard. "Recording is activated."

"Bianchi won't be able to see you in here," Maddox said to Marcus and Paige. "This is a two-way mirror. If you don't want to see the interrogation, I'll have someone escort you to our breakroom. I'll pass along the information we learn."

Marcus covered her hand with his. "If you don't want to watch, I'll go to the breakroom with you. Zane can send me a copy of the interrogation."

"I want to hear what he has to say. I need to know who wants me dead."

The door to the other room opened and Nate and Rio led Bianchi into the room, and pushed the thug into a seat facing the mirror.

"Why are Nate and Rio questioning him? Shouldn't the others be involved now?" Didn't seem fair. The rest of Durango must have some interrogation skills.

Zane glanced up. "Bianchi has seen their faces. We don't want to introduce him to each member of Durango."

"He already knows where to find them."

"Won't have a chance for revenge."

Paige set her cup down on the table with a soft thud. "They plan to kill him?" Might be necessary on one of their missions in another country, but they couldn't do that on US soil. Could they?

"Law enforcement takes a dim view of murder. However, Bianchi will be out of commission until he's too old to be a threat."

She frowned. Not really an answer. Probably wiser not to know for sure.

In the other room, Rio leaned one shoulder against the wall and Nate circled behind Bianchi. "Let's talk," he said quietly.

A snort. "You can talk all you want, but I ain't saying squat. I want to call my lawyer."

"Do we look like cops?" Rio asked. "You're not talking to anybody but us."

Bianchi frowned. "Who are you?"

"Your worst nightmare, Bianchi." Nate laid a hand on the man's injured shoulder that earned a pained grimace from the man. "You know how the game is played. Answer my questions, the pain stops."

In the next moment, the skin on Paige's nape prickled at the prisoner's scream of pain. "What's Nate doing?"

"Using pressure points, targeting specific nerves to cause excruciating pain without permanent damage." Maddox laid a hand on her shoulder. "Nate is one of the best interrogators I've worked with. We need information, Paige. Your safety depends on it. I'm not going to stop the interrogation until we have what we need. Can you live with that knowledge?"

She thought of her precious grandmother who might become the next casualty of someone like Bianchi. Yeah, she could handle the knowledge of his temporary pain to protect the life of the woman who had raised her. Paige nodded.

When tears streamed down Bianchi's face, Nate leaned close. "Who hired you to find Marcus Lang?"

"I can't tell you. He'll kill me."

"Wrong answer." Nate shifted his hand and the screams began again, this time higher pitched, his wails long and loud. When the noise abated to soft sobs, Nate repeated his question.

"I'm a dead man if I talk."

"You're dead if you don't. You might escape the person who hired you. You have zero chance of escaping us."

"You're bluffing."

"Want to bet?" He moved his hand again.

"No! Please. All right, all right. Sean O'Reilly, okay? It was O'Reilly who hired me."

"Why?"

"He wants Lang dead for killing his son."

"Mick O'Reilly was a leg breaker for his father. He died when Lang shot him to protect himself and another man."

"Don't care why. It was good money."

"Hope the price you'll pay is worth the payoff," Rio said.

Bianchi cast a wary glance his direction. "What do you mean?"

Nate adjusted his hold and Bianchi hissed, perspiration beading on his face. "Who sent you after Paige?"

"It was just business, man. Wasn't personal."

"Attacking Paige was personal to her friends and family." His voice dropped to a growl. "Especially to the man who loves her. You're lucky to be alive right now. He was within a split second of pulling the trigger. Now see, if you had attacked my woman, I wouldn't have ended your life so soon. You would have suffered for days before I killed you. Marcus has a soft heart." He leaned close to Bianchi's ear. "I don't. Last chance. Who sent you after Paige?"

"The land developer, Davidson."

Shock rolled through Paige, then shifted into bone-deep fury. Slimy Davidson, the creep who was pressuring Gram to sell the B & B and orchard, had hired Bianchi to kill her? If he thought Jo would sell everything if Paige was dead, he was a fool. If anything, Jo would dig in her heels and pour herself into the work. She'd done the same when her son and daughter-in-law were killed in an accident when Paige was five, and again when she lost her husband. No, Gram wouldn't sell because of grief or pressure from an outsider.

"Why?" Rio asked. "What purpose would her death serve?"

"He figured the old lady would sell if she had nobody to pass the legacy to."

"Anyone else involved?"

"Only one person is paying me."

"That's not what he asked." Nate hit another pressure point.

Bianchi gasped and the blood drained from his face. "Stop, please."

"Talk."

"No one else is paying me. I swear."

"Who else knew?" Nate pressed.

"Parks. Don't know their first names, man. I don't know those small-town hicks. An old one and a middle-aged man. That help?"

"Did you kill the kid at the center?"

Bianchi tried to jerk away from Nate's hold and yelped when the operative clamped down on his shoulder.

"Answer the question."

"Yeah, I did. You satisfied?"

"Not even close. Why did you kill Van Wilder?"

"He and his buddies saw me with Davidson and Parks. They could identify me and O'Reilly don't like loose ends."

"You tried to kill Dalton Reagan in the Croft woods?"

"Would have succeeded if it hadn't been for the preacher. I tried to finish the job at the hospital, but there were cops and private security everywhere."

Nate glanced up at the window, waited.

Maddox leaned over and pushed the intercom button on the wall. "Black site."

Rio and Nate pulled Bianchi to his feet over his loud protests and curses, and escorted him from the room.

"What does that mean?" Paige asked. "What's a black site?"

"Bianchi will be taken to a site off the grid. No communication with the outside world. He needs to be incommunicado for now. When we have the O'Reilly situation handled, we'll make other arrangements for him." He looked at Zane. "Send a copy of the interview to Blackhawk. Make sure you blur Rio and Nate's faces and voices. He'll know members of Durango did the interrogation, but doesn't need to have proof of it."

A few key strokes, then, "Done."

"Contact Josh and Alex. Have them meet me in my office. We have plans to make."

"Plans?" Marcus looked from Zane to Maddox.

"We have a mob kingpin to take down."

CHAPTER THIRTY-SIX

Marcus stared at Brent Maddox. "This isn't a government-sanctioned mission."

"When has that stopped me from doing what's necessary? I can't let this continue. You gave up everything to save my life. It's time I repaid the favor."

"I don't want you to do this. It's too dangerous for you and your operatives. O'Reilly's men are ruthless. Someone will get hurt."

"Someone will get hurt all right," Zane muttered. "But it won't be us."

"You have two choices, Marcus." Maddox pinned him in place with a hard look. "Go along with my plan or I'll relocate you again with a new name and a new life. I don't want to use the second option. If my plan works, you'll be free to live your life however you choose without wondering when O'Reilly will put a bullet in your head. As evidenced by Bianchi's appearance in Otter Creek, unexpected things happen. You followed my rules and still your safety was compromised by pure accident. It's a matter of time before O'Reilly or one of his pet assassins catches up with you again."

Marcus grimaced. "You're right. If I relocate, I'm still at risk. Worse, Paige and Jo are in danger whether they're with me or not." Did Paige realize if he requested a new identity, she would be forced into hiding with him? No question in his mind that the love of his life would volunteer to go with him into another place of exile. Jo, however, was in her seventies. By the time the mess with Sean O'Reilly was settled or he died, Jo would probably be gone. He couldn't ask that of Paige. Letting go of his own family had devastated him. Jo was the only family Paige had left. If Marcus relocated, he would lose her.

Soft hands cupped his cheek and turned his face toward her. "It's time to end this, Marcus."

His heart stopped, then restarted on a painful lurch. "Paige?" And he'd thought losing Chelsea was painful. He prayed for strength to do what was right for Paige. She deserved better than what he could offer her. Would she wait for him to be free from his past?

Maddox stood. "I'll be in my office awaiting your decision," he murmured and signaled Zane. The two men left the observation room.

After the door closed behind them, Paige leaned forward and kissed Marcus, her touch as light as gossamer wings. She drew back. "I want you to give Brent permission to handle the problem with O'Reilly."

He blinked, hardly daring to breathe. She wasn't cutting him loose. "You want me to fight back?"

"I want you to reclaim your life, my love. O'Reilly has taken seven years of your life. He stole your identity and your family. He has to be stopped. You can't be the only person who suffered at the mobster's hands. With the help of Fortress, we can stop him from hurting anyone else."

"Baby, there's a good chance someone will die. O'Reilly's men won't surrender without a fight."

"I think Fortress can handle O'Reilly and his men. They've survived the worst mankind has to offer on the battlefield. O'Reilly and his men are amateurs compared to the terrorists the operatives have defeated. We have to trust Fortress. We don't have a choice. I love you, Marcus. I want a life with you, one free from fear. I don't want to wonder every time I answer the door if Ethan or Nick or another policeman is there to tell me you've been murdered. If Brent's plan doesn't work, I'll go with you into the private witness protection and try to talk Gram into coming with us. I've waited years for you, Marcus. I'm not giving you up."

"You'll lose everything. You friends, your job, the town you love. As much as I want to, I can't ask that of you."

"We belong together. If you choose relocation, I'm going with you."

He captured her lips in a hard, heated kiss. "I love you, Paige."

"I love you, too. Time to talk to Brent."

The Fortress CEO took one look at their faces and smiled. "You're going for it. Good. Let's go to the conference room." He picked up his phone and punched in a number. "Z, conference room. I need Durango, Eli, and Jon if they've arrived, and the members of the Shadow unit still on US soil. The Zoo Crew as well if we can get them."

He stood. "Follow me." Maddox led them down another corridor and opened a door on the right. In the center of the large conference table sat a vast array of breakfast wraps, cut fruit, soft drinks, and bottles of water. On a side table sat a large coffee urn with mugs waiting to be filled. "Fill your plates and eat." He slid a look at Marcus. "Figured you and Paige needed a meal after your early morning wakeup call. By this time, Durango will be hungry as well."

"We could have eaten later."

"I don't want you wandering around town. We can't be sure O'Reilly doesn't have more people here."

In a city the size of Nashville, the possibility one of O'Reilly's men would see Marcus was slim at best. However, Fortress was one of the top security firms in the world for a reason. Only a fool ignored the advice of an expert.

He nudged Paige toward the plates. "Choose what you want. When the rest arrive, they'll devour everything in sight."

Soon, the conference room was filled with operatives busy devouring their meals.

Paige leaned close to Marcus. "I'd like to talk to Gram. Do you think this is a good time?"

Marcus nodded. "Z, can Paige borrow a sat phone to call Jo?"

The tech guru reached into a side pocket of his chair and handed her a black phone along with a charger. "This one is yours to keep. It's secure so you can talk to Jo without compromising her safety or yours. Sam's phone number is already programmed in. So is Brent's, mine, and the number for Marcus."

She planted a light kiss on his cheek. "Thank you, Zane."

His cheeks flushed. "Glad to help."

Paige smiled at Marcus and hurried to the hallway.

Minutes later, Brent stood. Immediately, the room fell silent. He told them about the original operation in which he'd run afoul of O'Reilly and his son, and the part Marcus had played in saving his life. "O'Reilly sent a hit man, Vincent Bianchi, after Marcus in Otter Creek. The price on his head has been doubled. Nowhere is safe for him or his girlfriend now. I have operatives on Marcus's family in case O'Reilly makes a play for them. Now it's time to end the threat to Marcus and Paige permanently."

Zane flashed a satellite view of an estate on the television screens around the room. "This is O'Reilly's estate in upstate New York. He has sixteen men who serve as security guards. They are heavily armed and have three pairs of German shepherds also patrolling the grounds, one pair per shift."

"Hope you brought your dart gun, Rio," Nate said.

"In my mike bag. Do you know how much the dogs weigh, Z?"

"About 80 pounds each. I've already been in contact with Dr. Sorensen about the proper dosage and sent the information to your email."

"How are we doing this, boss?" Eli asked.

"In order for this plan to work, we need to touch every member of O'Reilly's family, especially those grandchildren he dotes on. We need surveillance on every person. To do this right will take at least 48 hours. I don't care what plans you had for the rest of this week. Cancel them. Nothing takes priority over this operation."

Maddox moved a white board into place at the head of the table and picked up a marker.

Four hours later, he asked, "Anything to add?"

Marcus wrapped his hand around Paige's, hoped she understood what he was about to do. "I'm going with you."

CHAPTER THIRTY-SEVEN

"Last chance to back out, Marcus," Maddox murmured without looking at the man crouched by his side. "No one will think less of you for changing your mind."

"I need to see this through. Paige was right. It's time to finish this."

"Doesn't mean you have to be involved. You were caught in the backwash of a mission gone bad seven years ago. Now you have a choice. You can choose to walk away."

"Mick O'Reilly made this my problem when he shot me. I'm in this until the end."

A nod, then, "Follow orders without hesitation. Stay with me or Eli. Do what you have to, Marcus. Don't second-guess yourself or you will get hurt, possibly die. I don't want to be the one to inform Paige of your demise."

"Yes, sir." His stomach knotted at the prospect of having to pull the trigger to save his own life or the lives of his teammates. He'd do it, just the same. Marcus had the best incentive in the world to survive the coming encounter unscathed. He planned to marry the love of his life as soon as Jo returned from the cruise. He and Paige had called Jo, and the three of them agreed it would be best for Marcus to marry Paige in Nashville before returning to Otter Creek. If he still had a job, the congregation would want to have a reception for them.

Maddox activated his mike. "Two minutes."

The leaders of each team acknowledged his order.

Marcus scanned the area, watching for a change in the rhythm of the guards or for one of the dogs to alert. So far, the night watch pattern remained unchanged. He adjusted his mask, preparing to move on Maddox's order.

At the two-minute mark, Maddox said, "Josh, go."

Somewhere on the other side of the compound, Durango moved to intercept the pair of guards and their four-footed companions. A minute later, Josh's voice came over the comm system. "Dogs and handlers are down."

"Nico, go."

Marcus shifted his gaze to the left side of the estate where five dark-clad figures separated from the inky depths of the tree line and surged across the open expanse of terrain until they reached the darkened wall at the side of the house.

"Nico, guards will be coming around the corner in fifteen seconds."

"Copy."

Fascinated with the tableau playing out in front of him, Marcus almost missed the signal from Maddox to be ready.

"Guards are down," Nico murmured.

"Copy. Zane, any change inside the house?"

"Negative. O'Reilly is still in place. Doesn't look like anyone knows the estate is under attack. So much for state of the art security."

"It's not one of ours. Continue monitoring."

Marcus followed Maddox across the darkened expanse of grass. Back pressed against the wall, he waited for Eli to breach the house as Nico and Josh were doing at their entrance points.

Over the comm system, Zane said, "Nico, Brent, go. Josh, hold. Roaming guard coming your way."

Eli looked at his boss, nodded. Receiving the signal to go, he stood to the side of the door and eased it open. A moment later, he slipped inside, followed by Curt Jackson, then Maddox and Marcus.

The interior of the house was dimly lit. Soft footsteps sounded nearby.

"Boss, company on your six."

Immediately, Brent shifted to stand in front of Marcus, weapon drawn, as the rest of the team hugged the shadows. Eli nudged Marcus even further against the wall.

The door behind Marcus opened and a girl, maybe four years old, stepped into the hallway. The dark-haired waif looked at him, eyes wide.

Marcus pulled his half mask down under his chin and crouched in front of her. He smiled. "Why are you awake this time of night?" he whispered.

"I had a bad dream. I think there's a bad man in my closet."

He glanced at Maddox, got a chin lift in response. "Want me to check the closet? If there is a bad man, I'll chase him out."

The girl nodded.

Marcus wrapped his hand around hers and walked into her room, pulling the door almost shut. At least he could keep the little one from raising an alarm while the rest of the team dealt with O'Reilly's guards.

He glanced around the doll and ruffle paradise until he saw the closet door. "Climb into bed and I'll look in your closet." When she pulled the covers to her lap, Marcus turned on the closet light switch. Girl clothes and shoes, a lot of them, but no bad men. "All clear," he murmured, and turned off the light. "No bad man. You need to stay in your room. Your grandfather will be awake soon and you don't want him upset about you wandering around the house by yourself. Will you promise me to stay here until it's daylight?"

The girl yawned and snuggled into her pillow. "Okay. Thanks for checking the closet."

"Sleep well, little one." Aware of the mission clock ticking, he tugged his mask back place and slipped into the hall.

"Nice job." Maddox inclined his head down the corridor.

Marcus followed in his wake, alert for anyone coming up behind them.

"Z, O'Reilly?"

"End of the corridor, last room on the right. One of his men is in the room to the left. Looks like both are asleep."

Maddox signaled Curt to take care of the guard. Eli, Maddox, and Marcus crept their way along the hall, clearing room after room or incapacitating the occupants when they found them.

Finally, they approached the mobster's door as Curt reappeared in the hall. He gave a hand signal to Maddox. After a nod, he whispered into the comm system, "Going in now."

Marcus held his weapon at his side, ready to aid the others if they needed assistance.

They breached the room in silence. The men spread out with Maddox on one side of the bed, Curt on the other. Eli and Marcus stood at opposite sides of the foot board.

In sleep, Sean O'Reilly looked like a harmless grandfather. From appearance alone, Marcus couldn't believe this man was the cause of so much pain in his life for the past seven years.

Maddox clamped a hand over O'Reilly's mouth as Curt pressed the barrel of his weapon against the man's ear.

The mobster's eyes flew open. He thrashed until Curt clamped a hand across his throat and squeezed in warning.

"I'm going to lift my hand," Maddox said softly. "If you yell or attract attention, my friend will pull that trigger. My men are all over this estate. One word from me, and your family dies. I'd hate to kill your beautiful dark-headed granddaughter sleeping down the hall."

Marcus's muscles tightened at the harsh words. The Fortress CEO had a daughter of his own. He wouldn't hurt an innocent child. If Marcus didn't know him, however, he would have believed Maddox. Ruthlessness and menace filled his voice.

O'Reilly narrowed his eyes.

"I'm here to talk, but I'll be happy to rid the world of your presence and that of your motley crew. Do we understand each other?"

A reluctant nod.

"Excellent." He slowly lifted his hand from the mob boss.

"You're a dead man," O'Reilly spat out.

Maddox flicked a glance at Curt. The operative tightened his grip around the man's throat. After several seconds, the hold eased, allowing O'Reilly to drag in much needed air.

"I want two things from you, O'Reilly. If you want your family to survive, you will call off the hunt and bounty on Matt Watson. You will also leave his family alone. If an unfortunate accident befalls any of them, you and your family will pay in blood."

"Watson killed my boy."

"He shot your hit man to save his own life and that of another man. Unlike Mick, Matt didn't plan to kill anyone."

O'Reilly's fists clenched on top of the blanket. "And if I don't cooperate?"

"You'll die, then we'll sweep through the house and kill the guards, the dogs, and your family members who are here tonight. Once we've finished here, we'll go to the houses on Wilshire, Westcott, Magnolia, and Beaumont, and kill your daughters, their husbands, and children. The cops will look at the Zambini family as their prime suspects because there won't be any trace of our presence."

When O'Reilly remained silent, Maddox pulled out his phone, turned it so the screen faced the man stubbornly refusing to concede he'd been defeated by strangers.

"Pictures taken of your family in the past week, O'Reilly. We know Angelina is sleeping down the hall and attends daycare at Miss Mabel's Academy. Joseph is enrolled there, too. The rest of your grandchildren are attending St. Michael's, a pricey private school. Your daughters are members of the country club and plan to attend a luncheon today given by the gardening society. Your sons-in-law are lieutenants in your organization and are neck-deep in criminal activity. We have proof of their work waiting to be delivered to the feds." As Maddox talked, he scrolled through the pictures his operatives had taken of the O'Reilly clan. "I have people everywhere. I'll know if you break your word. Don't think you can hide them from me. Your communications are being monitored as well as your movements. You and your family won't escape me."

"Say I agree to your terms. How do I know you'll keep your word and leave my family alone?"

"You don't. Take it or leave it. Do you live to see another sunrise or die where you lay?"

Silence for a moment, then, "All right. I'll call off the hunt for Watson and withdraw the bounty."

"Wise decision." Maddox grabbed the man's cell phone and thrust it into his hand. "Take care of it."

After a vicious curse, O'Reilly snatched the phone and placed a call. Within one minute, the task was complete.

Dazed, Marcus drew the first relaxed breath he'd taken in seven long years. Maybe now he could see his family and introduce his wife to them.

"Get out of my house," O'Reilly snapped as soon as he ended the call.

Maddox signaled the others and as one they backed away from the bed.

Marcus kept careful watch on the old man. Maddox had warned him this was the most dangerous point in their operation. Because he was watching so closely, he saw the decision to act in O'Reilly's eyes before the other man moved a muscle.

The mob boss shoved his hand under his pillow and whipped out a gun. Before he could shoot, four suppressed weapons fired. The old man fell back on the bed, unmoving.

"It's finished," Maddox murmured. "Let's go home."

CHAPTER THIRTY-EIGHT

Paige stared at the sky again. Where were they? She had watched planes land over the past hour, none of them the Fortress plane carrying Marcus and the operatives returning from the O'Reilly estate. Who knew the John C. Tune airport was so busy?

"Relax, Paige," Zane said. "They'll be here soon."

Zane's wife, Claire, smiled at her. "Where will you and Marcus go for your honeymoon?"

Her heart gave a little kick at the thought of marrying the man of her dreams. "He promised me sun and sand."

"The beach. Excellent choice. The weather is perfect right now. Do we need to go shopping for your wedding?"

"I have to. I don't even have a wedding dress."

"You're in luck. Nashville has several shops selling wedding attire. We'll have you and Marcus ready to tie the knot in no time."

She hoped so. The plane carrying Gram and her traveling companions was due to stop here within the hour. Gram was staying in Nashville while the others were flying to Knoxville. Durango would drive two SUVs to Otter

Creek after the wedding, and leave the third for Marcus and Paige.

"There it is." Zane pointed at the plane taxiing on the tarmac. "Wait until I'm sure it's safe for you to get out." The Lear jet slowed to a stop. When the door opened, Zane said, "Go."

Paige flung open the door. As men carrying bags of equipment streamed down the stairs, she leaped from the vehicle and ran.

Though all the men were dressed in black, Paige recognized Marcus immediately and raced toward him. He dropped his bag and Paige threw herself into his arms.

"Marcus."

His arms clamped around her and he captured her mouth with his, the kiss long and heated. When he broke the kiss, he laid his forehead against hers. "It's over, baby. You're safe."

"Are you sure?"

He nodded. "O'Reilly's dead."

Paige's heart skipped a beat. "You're okay? The operatives?"

"We're fine."

Maddox clapped Marcus on the shoulder. "Grab your gear. We'll wait for Jo in the private lounge."

Marcus slung the equipment bag over his shoulder and wrapped his hand around Paige's. They crossed the tarmac to the single-story structure where the Fortress CEO led them to a heavy metal door that he unlocked. He checked the room, then motioned for them to go inside.

After stowing his equipment bag against the wall, Marcus dropped into the nearest chair and urged Paige sit in the chair beside his.

She wasn't sure she wanted the details, but from his body language and eyes, he needed to talk. "Tell me."

After receiving a nod from Maddox, he told her everything, including the split second when he made the decision to pull the trigger.

Her heart hurt for him. To face that choice and be forced to pull the trigger must weigh heavy on him. "You had no choice, Marcus." Paige tightened her grip. "He would have killed you or your teammates. Again, you chose to protect."

Maddox handed Marcus and Paige a bottle of water each. "She's right. O'Reilly was aiming at me. Marcus, you didn't make that decision alone. There were four of us in that room. Three of us had Special Forces training and had faced that choice many times over the years. We reached the same decision. There wasn't another alternative. O'Reilly took the choice out of our hands. We reacted the way we were trained, the way I trained you."

"I know," he said, his voice soft. "Doesn't make living with pulling the trigger any easier."

"It's not easy for any of us. If it was, we wouldn't have a conscience."

Marcus might have the training to be a Fortress operative, but he didn't have the heart for the work. Paige cupped his face between her palms. "You fired the gun for me, Marcus. Thank you for protecting me, for protecting the family we'll have some day. Our children will be safe because of what you did."

Some of the pain left his eyes. "I love you."

Her lips curved. "I love you, too."

"You didn't fire the fatal shot."

Marcus turned to stare at Maddox. "I didn't?"

The operative's lips curved. "O'Reilly had three shots center mass, one in the right shoulder. We're trained to take out threats, Marcus. It's second nature. Your bullet hit the shoulder, an incapacitating, but nonlethal wound."

"I still pulled the trigger."

"To protect in a firefight," Paige pointed out.

Maddox's phone chimed. He checked the screen. "Good news. Jo's plane is on final approach. I'll take your equipment bag with me." He tossed a set of keys to Marcus. "Take your almost grandmother to the Garden Hotel in Murfreesboro. You have a suite reserved."

The next day passed in a whirlwind of activity. Claire knew the exact places to go for Paige's wedding dress and shoes. The second half of the day was spent replacing items she lost when the cabin exploded.

At least Rod and Meg Kelter were getting a new cabin, courtesy of Fortress Security. The insurance company had balked at rebuilding a dwelling lost from an RPG.

On Friday morning at 11:00, Paige walked down the aisle of a church on the outskirts of Nashville on Brent Maddox's arm. She smiled at Nicole and Mason who waited at the front of the church with Marcus and the church's pastor.

Brent stopped beside Marcus. The Fortress CEO kissed Paige's cheek before sitting beside his wife. Claire snapped pictures during the short ceremony.

Finally, the minister said, "Marcus, you may kiss your bride."

The audience of operatives and their families applauded and cheered as Marcus lingered over the kiss. When he lifted his head, he escorted her to Jo.

Her grandmother wrapped her in a tight hug. "I'm so happy for you both, Paige."

"Are you sure you don't want to stay in Nashville for another day or two, Gram?"

"I miss the orchard, dear. It's time for me to go home."

"All right. We'll be home Sunday afternoon so we can pack for our trip to Orange Beach."

Jo grinned. "Sunday night will be interesting. I can't wait to see the faces of our church family when you and Marcus walk into the auditorium with matching wedding bands."

Marcus led her to the other side of the aisle to the dark-haired couple wiping tears from their eyes despite the broad smiles on their faces. He bent down and kissed the cheek of the woman. "You okay, Mom?"

"Are you kidding? I'm terrific. I thought I wouldn't see this day in your life. I'm so grateful to have this chance." Francesca Watson hugged her son, then Paige. "I'm so happy Matt has you."

"You don't mind him keeping his new name?"

"It's simpler for your congregation and your town. And truthfully, we almost chose Marcus for his first name when I was pregnant with him."

Neil Watson wrapped his arms around Paige in a gentle hug. "Welcome to the Watson family, Paige. You let me know if my son doesn't treat you like a princess."

"Oh, come on, Dad," Marcus muttered.

Paige smiled. "Yes, sir. You don't have to worry, though. He treats me like you treat Francesca."

Satisfaction gleamed in Neil's eyes.

They continued down the aisle, greeting the operatives and their families as they went. In the church's fellowship hall, tables loaded with food ringed the room.

Nate turned to Paige and Marcus. "Everything is ready. Fill your plates and sit at the head table. I'll take care of Jo as soon as Mason escorts her and Nicole down here. Better start eating. Once people arrive down here, you won't have a chance."

Four hours later, Marcus unlocked the door to the honeymoon suite at Opryland Hotel and drew Paige inside. Her breath caught as she surveyed the lush furnishings and thick carpet. "Marcus, you didn't have to do anything this extravagant."

"I wanted the best for you."

She wrapped her arms around his neck. "Thank you, love."

He kissed her briefly. "Would you like to walk around the atrium?"

"I'd love to."

He brushed a hand down the sleeve of her wedding dress. "Need help with this?"

Paige's cheeks burned. "I can handle it." Why was she so nervous? She adored this man.

"Go change, then. I'll wait for you here."

Within minutes, they were walking hand-in-hand through the plant-filled atrium. After exploring the walkways and visiting the waterfalls, he led her to the Delta section with the boutiques and shops situated along the indoor waterway. By the time Paige and Marcus had eaten a light dinner and returned to their suite, darkness had fallen.

Marcus cupped her face between his palms, his gaze filled with love and understanding. "Still nervous?" he murmured.

Paige shook her head, took his hand in hers, and led him to the bedroom. Her husband smiled, gathered her into his embrace, and shut the door.

CHAPTER THIRTY-NINE

Marcus circled the front of his truck and opened his wife's door. He bent his head and kissed her, lingering against the softness of her lips. When he lifted his head, Paige smiled at him.

"When will we leave tomorrow?"

"Maddox wants us at the airport by two o'clock."

"I can't believe he's sending a Fortress jet for us."

"It's his wedding gift." Marcus glanced around the parking lot, surprised so many people were in attendance on a Sunday night.

He and Paige walked toward the door to the church when Ethan Blackhawk stepped out and approached. "Ethan, what's going on?"

"First, congratulations on your marriage." He shook hands with Marcus and kissed Paige's cheek. "I'm happy for both of you."

"Thanks, Ethan." Marcus wrapped his arm around Paige's waist, felt her trembling.

"Second, Nick arrested Franklin Davidson a few minutes ago. We didn't want to tip our hand to Parks."

Marcus stiffened. "You're arresting the mayor here?"

"I'm escorting the mayor and his son to the station for questioning. They'll be placed under arrest there. You should also know Parks is planning to cause trouble tonight. Since you're supposed to be out of town, the mayor feels this is the perfect time to bring up your questionable moral character and encourage a vote to oust you from Cornerstone." The police chief's mouth curved into a grim smile. "He won't be happy to see you."

"The feeling is mutual. Do you know why the mayor, his son, and Davidson were so desperate to have the development go through?"

"Money. Parks and his son formed a holding company. That company owns two of the parcels slated for the shopping center. Mayor Parks heard about Davidson from a buddy in New York. The developer is from that area, and is well known for large deals. When Jo wouldn't cooperate, Davidson got Bianchi's name from a recently deceased Irish mob boss with his fingers in many real estate deals. Parks and his son stood to gain a ton of money on this deal."

Heartsick, Marcus looked at Paige. "Ready?"

"Let's do this."

Ethan moved aside. "You have a lot of support, Marcus. I think Mayor Parks will be unpleasantly surprised to know how much influence he doesn't have in this church."

He prayed Ethan was correct. Perhaps he should have waited to marry Paige until his future was more secure. The truth was, though, he didn't regret marrying the woman at his side.

If Cornerstone voted him out, Marcus still had the counseling job with Fortress. Maddox had assured him before they left Nashville that Fortress would be thrilled to employ him full-time on the counseling staff. The salary the Fortress CEO quoted had stunned him. Yeah, he could definitely take care of his wife without difficulty on that salary. He still felt called to pastor, though. He'd love to stay at Cornerstone.

Marcus opened the door to the vestibule for Paige. Together, they walked into the auditorium. As the service was already in progress, Marcus opted to sit in the back row, waiting to see how the night would play out.

The associate pastor noticed them and smiled. When it was time for him to speak, he stood behind the pulpit and said, "I have a very special announcement to make. Marcus, Paige, please come forward."

The congregation twisted in their seats to watch as they walked the aisle to stand in front of the stage.

"It's my great honor to introduce to you Marcus and Paige Lang."

Gasps were heard before the congregation applauded.

"We have light finger foods ready in the fellowship hall so we can celebrate with our newlyweds. We'll plan a reception after they return from their honeymoon. Come congratulate Marcus and Paige."

Before the first person stepped into the aisle, Henry Parks stood. "How can you celebrate with this man of questionable character?" he shouted.

All conversation stopped in the auditorium as people stared at the mayor.

The associate pastor held up his hand. "This isn't the time, Mayor Parks. This is a celebration, not a witch hunt."

"On the contrary, this is the perfect time to decide if Marcus Lang should continue as pastor of Cornerstone Church."

Ethan started up the aisle.

Marcus caught his eye, shook his head slightly. He turned his attention to the mayor. "What is it you think I've done, Parks?"

"Why don't you tell everyone when you married that woman?"

"Paige and I were married Friday."

Triumph gleaned in the old man's eyes. "You've been gone a week. Before that, you were living together in the same house. How appropriate is it for the pastor of our church to have an affair in full view of the town?"

"It would be totally inappropriate if it were true. It's not."

"Got any proof of that?"

"I stayed at the Bed and Breakfast with Jo, Paige, Mason Kincaid, and Nicole Copeland to protect my wife from the man who attacked her. This same man broke into the B & B while we were out and left a threatening message on Paige's bathroom mirror. I was never alone with Paige in the house. Jo, Mason, and Nicole will corroborate my statement."

"That doesn't explain the week you spent together before you married her," Parks snapped.

Josh Cahill stood and walked up the aisle. "Marcus and Paige left town on my orders." His cold gaze fixed on the mayor. "A hit man hired by Franklin Davidson had targeted Paige. Marcus went with his wife to protect her."

More gasps echoed in the auditorium.

"You expect us to believe you?"

"Marcus and Paige were with me and the rest of Durango plus two Navy SEALs. If you don't believe me, ask my teammates." He waved at the grim-faced members of his team, now also standing. "The hit man and his buddies tracked us down and tried to kill the Langs." He paused. "But you already know that, don't you?"

"What are you talking about? I don't know any such thing."

"Of course, you do, Mr. Mayor. You and your son were in on a deal with Davidson regarding the shopping center development, and you would lose a great deal of money if the deal didn't go through. When Jo Jensen stood in your way, you three conspired to get rid of Paige in an effort to force Jo into selling her property. I'm happy to say your plan failed, Mr. Mayor."

"This is outrageous. I had nothing to do with that."

"Then you can explain why Davidson is down at the station with Detective Santana, pointing a finger right at you and James."

James leaped to his feet, his face red. "You're the one with a vendetta, Blackhawk. We're going to sue you and your whole department."

Josh stepped forward, handcuffs clutched in his hand. "Let's go, James. You can explain it all to Detective Santana."

"Forget it, Cahill. You're nothing but a two-bit thug."

The muscle-bound policeman smiled. "I'm a thug with a badge, Parks. You either come with me voluntarily, or I'll place you under arrest right here."

With a roar, James swung at Josh who neatly sidestepped the punch and took Parks to the ground. A moment later, he hauled the cursing man to his feet and led him from the auditorium.

Ethan laid a heavy hand on the mayor's shoulder. "Come with me, Mr. Mayor." All the way out of the church, Parks protested his innocence and threatened to take Ethan's badge.

When the door closed behind them, the associate pastor looked at the Cornerstone congregation. "Any further questions for Marcus and Paige?"

Stunned silence in the sanctuary.

"We'll leave justice in the hands of the police. If the mayor and his son are innocent, I'm sure Ethan and Nick will turn them loose and find the guilty party. For now, though, let's celebrate with our pastor and his new wife before they leave tomorrow for two weeks at the beach."

Marcus and Paige accepted the congratulations of their church family. When the evening was over, Marcus escorted Paige to his truck.

"I didn't think to ask where we were staying tonight."

"The B & B. You don't want to stay at the parsonage. I have a leak in the bathroom. Mason will take care of the plumbing problem while we're out of town."

"I don't care where we stay, love. As long as we're together, I'll be happy."

Marcus kissed the back of her hand. She was right. As long as they were together, nothing else mattered. Seven years ago, he lost everything. His future wife, his family, his identity. His life had been filled with pain and despair. Now, he'd regained everything plus more. From darkness to light, from despair to hope. He'd been given his greatest gift, one he'd never take for granted. A life with the woman he loved. Together, they would face whatever challenges lay ahead and enjoy years filled with laughter and love. He couldn't ask for anything more.

Vendetta

ABOUT THE AUTHOR

Rebecca Deel is a preacher's kid with a black belt in karate. She teaches business classes at a private four-year college outside Nashville, Tennessee. She plays the piano at church, writes freelance articles, and runs interference for the family dogs. She's been married to her amazing husband for more than 25 years and is the proud mom of two grown sons. She delivers occasional devotions to the women's group at her church and conducts seminars in personal safety, money management, and writing. Her articles have been published in *ONE Magazine*, *Contact*, and *Co-Laborer*, and she was profiled in the June 2010 Williamson edition of *Nashville Christian Family* magazine. Rebecca completed her Doctor of Arts degree in Economics and wears her favorite Dallas Cowboys sweatshirt when life turns ugly.

For more information on Rebecca . . .
Sign up for Rebecca's newsletter: http://eepurl.com/_B6w9
Visit Rebecca's website: www.rebeccadeelbooks.com

Printed in Great Britain
by Amazon